I0675562

Deeply saddened by the murder of Will Ramsdell, the retired police chief of Wisteria, Virginia, who helped her with her first investigative assignment, Abby Burlew, who suffers from bipolar disorder, heads to Wisteria to make sure Will's killer is brought to justice. Ignoring the likelihood that she will cycle into mania brought on by the strain of her investigation, she partners with Marty Stith—a friend of Will's who lives and works at Pinecroft, the mom-and-pop golf course where Will was murdered. Suspects abound, including Marty Stith himself, who Abby has reason to believe is orchestrating what she learns and when she learns it. Two of the suspects are murdered, and a third person, with no apparent reason for wanting Will dead, claims to be his killer. As Abby struggles to make sense of all this, she comes ever closer to losing her sanity—and her life.

KUDOS for *No Reason to Kill*

Also by John W. Daniel

The Intended Victim

Deadly Assignment

No Reason
to Kill

John W. Daniel

A Black Opal Books Publication

GENRE: MYSTERY-DETECTIVE/WOMEN SLEUTHS/THRILLER

NO REASON TO KILL
Copyright © 2018 by John W. Daniel
Cover Design by Jackson Cover Design
All cover art copyright © 2018
All Rights Reserved
Print ISBN: 978-1-626949-71-3

First Publication: JULY 2018

Published by Black Opal Books **http://www.blackopalbooks.com**

To Sharon for your invaluable help

Prologue

*O*PENING DAY OF DEER SEASON!
When Will Ramsdell saw the headline, he felt a strong urge to break out his twelve-gauge Mossberg and a box of shells and head across the Shenandoah River to a stretch of lowland where a few days earlier he had spotted several white tails grazing. His shotgun was ready—hadn't been fired since he cleaned and oiled it nearly a year earlier.

But then Will thought of his old friend Walter Hux. He could almost hear the veterinarian's voice from the grave. *You're backsliding on me, Will. That's not exactly the way to honor a friend's memory, you know.*

"Just one deer," Will muttered. "I'll make absolutely sure every bit that's edible gets eaten."

You don't even like venison. You'd be taking a creature's life for the sheer pleasure of it—the thrill of the kill.

"That's an oversimplification, Walt, and you know it."

Is it? I suggest you take a close look at exactly what you'd be doing. And while you're at it, try this on for size: Real men don't get their kicks from killing animals.

Will started to object, tell his old friend in no uncertain terms that he was being unreasonable. Then he decided that today, at least, he would let him have the last word. Instead of going deer hunting, Will would stick to his original plan and go golfing. "Don't think you've won, though, Walt. Next time we get on this subject, I won't let you off so easily."

Will finished eating his breakfast while scanning the *Hawthorne Observer* for other items of interest. Then, after washing and drying the dishes, he tossed his golf clubs in the back of his pickup truck and headed for Pinecroft.

ℒℙℒℙ

Twenty minutes later Will climbed the stairs to what doubled as the course's pro shop and the Langs' living room.

"Looks like I beat the crowd," he teased when he saw Jamie Lang standing behind a display case containing an assortment of golf balls, gloves, and tees. Though not as slender as she once was, she still had the ability to quicken his pulse.

"Not a soul on the course, Will. Figured you'd be out chasing Bambi like everybody else."

"I considered it. Decided I needed a real challenge— Pinecroft's back nine."

In the process of paying some bills, Jamie slid a check into an envelope and licked the flap. "The woods are full of hunters today. There's less chance of getting hit by a stray bullet if you play the front."

"I haven't had a decent round on the back all year, Jamie. I'd like to change that before the snow flies. Is Nelson hunting?"

"He was up at the crack of dawn." Jamie affixed a stamp to the envelope and set it on top of two others. "Said he was going over to Herman Williams's farm."

"What about Marty?"

"He's out cutting brush." Jamie tucked a loose strand of

blonde hair behind her left ear and leaned against the case, her right arm resting against the glass top. "You'll probably run into him if the hunters don't get you first."

"I'll be careful. Got any Precepts left?"

"Laddie or Lassie?"

Will chuckled. "I'll leave that up to you." He extracted a score card and a stubby pencil from the small plastic container next to the cash register. "How are things going with you and Nelson?"

"Pretty good."

"You don't sound too sure about that," Will said and reached for his wallet.

Jamie shrugged. She handed him a sleeve of balls with "Laddie" printed on the side and took the twenty-dollar bill he extended in her direction.

"I see you've got a bruise on your arm. Nelson's not responsible for that, is he?"

"No, that was my own damn fault. I slipped on the back steps yesterday when I was bringing in groceries. Not as young as I used to be, Will—or as agile." Jamie's lips formed a smile her eyes didn't fully participate in. "Don't worry about Nelson and me," she said, handing Will his change. "We're doing okay, especially now that Marty is helping out. We're actually starting to make a few improvements to this raggedy-assed golf course."

"If things with Nelson start going south again—"

Jamie touched a finger to Will's lips, stopping him in mid-sentence. "Time to focus on your golf game, Will Ramsdell. The golfing world is waiting to see who's tougher, you or the back nine. My money is on you. I think you've got a good round coming today."

"I hope you're right. When do you expect Nelson back?"

"Not until late this afternoon. Why?"

"There's something I need to discuss with him—and you."

Jamie's brow furrowed. "What's it about, Will?"

"I'd rather not go into it until I've got the two of you together. I'll tell you this much, though—what I've got to say will come as a surprise, maybe even a shock, especially to Nelson." Will tipped the orange hunting cap he was wearing in place of his usual golfing hat and headed for the stairway.

Before Jamie could find the words to say anything else, he was down the stairs and out the door.

ᏬᏬᏬ

Will began his round with a double bogie on the tenth hole, a narrow par five that invariably seemed to give him trouble. He got a stroke back on the par-three eleventh when his chip shot, which he thought for sure he'd hit too hard, clanked against the pin and dropped into the cup.

"Yeah!" he yelled and pumped his fist in his best Tiger Woods impersonation. "All right!"

As though in response, a shotgun boomed, the sound reverberating through the hills. Will extracted his ball, kissed it, and headed for the next tee, hoping his good luck would continue.

Although surprised that Jamie had referred to the course as "raggedy assed," Will knew the term wasn't inappropriate. By conventional standards Pinecroft was not a good golf course, especially the newer holes, which had lumpy greens and rocky, uneven fairways. Few people who took their golf seriously played the course more than once.

Will was a serious golfer, though, and he rarely played anywhere else. The other courses in the area were too crowded for his taste, even on weekdays, but if he arrived at Pinecroft before nine in the morning, chances were his truck would be the only vehicle in the parking lot. No other course let him play at his own pace, regardless of the type of game he brought with him that day.

Pinecroft had another advantage too, particularly this time of year when the hills were still awash with color. Will often found himself stopping in the middle of a round and gazing at his surroundings, soaking up the beauty. The fact that there would be few, if any, golfers in his field of vision made the view all the more special.

In spite of the fact that the twelfth fairway resembled a pockmarked moonscape and the green was riddled with bald spots, Will managed to par the hole. On the thirteenth, a long, down-hill par three, he pulled his tee shot badly. The ball disappeared in the woods well short of the green, not far from where a young man wearing an orange hat similar to Will's was yanking on a vine attached to a birch tree.

"Hope you saw where my ball went, Marty. I've got a decent round going."

"There's good and bad news about your ball, Will. It ended up in that pile of brush I've been adding to all week. No way you'll ever find it. Fortunately, that pile is a temporary, man-made obstacle, so you're entitled to a free drop."

Will headed in the direction Marty was pointing, soon realizing the futility of searching for his ball. The brush pile, full of vines and limbs of all sizes and shapes, including numerous saplings, was large enough to hide a small automobile. Will dropped a ball two club lengths from the obstruction, picked out an area between two pine trees, and chipped back to the fairway.

"Smart play," Marty said. "By the time spring rolls around, I hope to have all these overgrown areas thinned out. Any decision yet on the mayor's offer?"

Will slid the seven iron back in his bag. "I've decided to take him up on it, Marty."

The young man stuck out his hand. "Congratulations, Chief! When do you resume duties?"

"First of the month. Any chance I can lure you back to the force?"

Marty shook his head. "I really enjoy it out here, Will. Not that I didn't like working for you. But what I do for the Langs doesn't seem like work. It's more like therapy."

A shotgun boomed in the distance. Before the echo died, there was a second blast and then a third, the reverberations rumbling like thunder.

"Glad things have worked out for you, Marty. Try not to make this course so player friendly folks will start flocking out here in droves."

A moment later Will pitched onto the green and, thinking his chances for a good round had slipped away, two-putted for another double bogie. After scrambling for pars on the next two holes, however, he revised his opinion. He parred the sixteenth hole as well, and as he headed for the seventeenth tee, he realized he was in position to accomplish something few people had ever achieved: break forty on Pinecroft's back nine.

As he approached the elevated tee, a series of shotgun blasts cascaded from the hills. Will paid no attention to the noise, too absorbed in what he needed on the final holes—two more pars, a bogie and a birdie, or a double bogie and (yeah, right) an eagle. Totaling no more than eight strokes on the next two holes would require his best effort—and a lot more luck than he had a right to expect.

Setting his golf bag on the ground, he took out his driver and removed the club's headcover his wife had knitted for him the summer she died. He set up on the right side of the tee box, hoping to hit his normal shot, a power fade.

As he started his waggle, he detected movement out of the corner of his eye and backed away from the ball. Someone carrying a shotgun and wearing an orange hunting vest and matching hat emerged from the honey-suckle thicket on the right of the teeing area.

"What're you doing up here?" Will asked in surprise.

Without replying, the person took two more steps in Will's direction and then stopped and chambered a round.

"This some kind of sick joke?"

When Will realized the answer, fear surged through him like a cold jolt of electricity. Out of desperation, he flung his driver, hoping to disable his assailant. The club landed harmlessly in the weeds.

The shotgun boomed, the blast knocking Will backward and to the ground. Gasping for breath, his chest heavy with pain, he closed his eyes, hoping the person would think one bullet was enough.

Realization quickly set in. It didn't matter if there was a second shot or not. Will's body was shutting down.

Soon he would be dead, even without another shot being fired.

Will felt a tangle of emotions, fear at first then regret. He thought of Abby Burlew, wishing he hadn't written that ridiculous poem for her and Marty to find. How could he have been such a fool?

He opened his eyes and, with effort, slowly inclined his head toward the honeysuckle vines. His vision was too blurred to make out anything but a vague colorless shape. He tried to speak, say the words of explanation he wanted the shooter to hear. "You…" he muttered, but that was all he managed to say.

Overhead, a dappled sun shone through the branches of a nearby maple tree, its red and yellow leaves ruffling in a gust of wind Will could no longer feel.

Chapter 1

Abby Burlew sat in her cubicle at the *Scarboro Gazette* and stared in stunned disbelief at her friend and co-worker Becky Stroup. "Will is dead? Murdered?"

"Here's a copy of the story. I ran across it in a *Richmond Times-Dispatch* I was checking for something totally unrelated. I'm sorry, Abby. I know how much you thought of him."

Abby read the brief article. Will Ramsdell had been shot to death while playing golf at a family-owned course seven miles east of Wisteria, Virginia. Although his death was being treated as a homicide, the sheriff investigating the case hadn't ruled out the possibility of an accidental shooting by a careless hunter.

"He was like a father to me, Becky. This is just awful."

The young woman gently patted Abby's shoulder. "Is there anything I can do?"

Only if you can turn back time, give me a chance to do for Will what he did for me. "No," she said with a sigh. "Assuming I can pull myself together, I'll try to find out what's happened since that article came out."

"I'll be glad to make some calls for you."

Abby shook her head. "Thanks anyway."

After Becky left, Abby went down the hall to the

women's bathroom and locked herself in a stall. For a long time she wept, the knowledge that Will Ramsdell was dead almost more than she could stand. After splashing cold water on her face, she returned to her desk and gazed out the window, staring toward, but not really seeing, the three-story bank building and the double-decked parking garage next to it that loomed in the middle distance.

Eventually focusing on her computer, Abby looked up the Wisteria Police Department's phone number on the Internet. Her hands trembled as she dialed it, and her voice cracked as she asked to speak to Marty Stith. When told that he no longer worked there, Abby explained that she had been a friend of Will Ramsdell's and asked if any progress had been made in solving his murder.

"You'll have to ask the sheriff about that. The shooting took place outside the town limits, so it's his jurisdiction."

"I'd like to talk to Marty before I do that. Have you got a phone number where he can be reached?"

"Last I heard he was living out at the golf course where Will was killed. Apparently, he sank some money in it a while back. Bad move if you ask me. Hold on, I'll see if it's in the phone book."

A few moments later Abby dialed Pinecroft's number. The man who answered told her Marty was out on the course and asked if he could take a message.

"I need him to call me as soon as possible," Abby said after identifying herself and explaining that she had been a friend of Will's and had just learned of his death. She was about to provide her cell phone number when the man cut in.

"Hang on. I just heard a golf cart drive up. It's probably Marty."

❧❧❧

A half hour later Abby knocked on her boss's partially open door and entered the office. A short, plump woman with a myopic squint, Charlene Greer had just returned from a meeting which, judging from her mood, had not gone well.

Her mood didn't improve when Abby requested time off to investigate a friend's death.

"What friend are you talking about?"

"Will Ramsdell. He helped me with the Sheila Bostrum investigation. He was murdered last week."

Choking back tears, Abby explained what she knew about Will's death. Even before she finished, her boss was shaking her head.

"I don't want you getting involved in that. The *Gazette* needs you right here in Scarboro covering local news."

"The man saved my life, Charlene. I owe it to him to make sure his murder is solved."

"What makes you think it won't be solved without your help?"

"I just got off the phone with an ex-cop who knows all about law enforcement in the Wisteria area. He doubts the sheriff is capable of solving the crime, and he said the acting police chief actually had a motive for killing Will." Abby explained that Will had recently been offered the police chief's job, the same position he resigned two years earlier, after his wife's death. "That wouldn't have been welcome news for the acting chief."

"I hate to be hard-nosed about this, Abby, but the answer is still no. Now if you'll excuse me, I have another meeting to prepare for."

Abby's temper flared. "Damn it, Charlene. You're being unreasonable about this."

The woman locked eyes with Abby. "Apparently, you think it's reasonable to take time off to investigate a murder that has nothing whatsoever to do with your job," she said in a measured tone. "It makes me wonder if you're still taking your meds."

Abby glared at her boss. "I don't appreciate that, Charlene. In fact, I resent the hell out of it."

"And I resent you swearing and raising your voice at me. Do it again and you'll find yourself looking for another job and having less than a glowing recommendation from me."

Her cheeks burning, Abby was the first to break eye contact. "Sorry," she said and took several deep breaths, trying to tamp down her anger. "Will was a wonderful friend."

"I understand that. But it makes no sense to get involved in his murder investigation. I won't allow it."

On the verge of returning to her cubicle, Abby thought of something that might bolster her argument. "What if I went to Wisteria as a reporter and submitted articles about Will's murder and the efforts to find his killer?"

"That wouldn't be remotely interesting to the *Gazette*'s readers. Will wasn't Scarboro's police chief. He probably never even lived in North Carolina."

"But Sheila Bostrum and Rhonda Tolbert did. Our readers lapped up everything we could print about those murders. If they knew Will helped me solve them and saved my life in the process, don't you think they'd be interested in knowing what happened to him and why?"

Charlene's face showed a flicker of interest. "That's an angle I hadn't considered. I'll give it some thought and let you know my decision this afternoon."

⁊⳨⁊

"My guess is she'll agree to it," Becky said as they waited for their orders at Curley's Chicken Shack, their favorite lunchtime spot. "You've already proved you can investigate a murder, and this sounds like a perfect story for the *Gazette*. I know I'll be anxious to read it. Did you ask your mom if she'll take care of Kevin?"

"Not yet. But that shouldn't be a problem."

They were sitting in a booth across from the take-out window. Abby had ordered iced tea and a salad, the news of Will's death having robbed her of her usual hearty appetite.

Becky had selected her old standby, a chicken barbeque sandwich, and a side order of coleslaw.

"Tell me more about this ex-cop who works at the golf course where Will was killed," Becky said. "When did you meet him?"

"Last year when I stopped at Wisteria's police station. Marty gave me directions to Will's house. The next day he provided information that turned out to be crucial to my investigation."

"I remember that—and meeting you in Caledonia later that day with some useful information of my own."

Abby nodded. "If it hadn't been for the two of you, the high point of my journalistic career would have been covering the debutante ball."

Becky chuckled. "Working at a golf course is quite a come down from being a cop, don't you think?"

"Apparently, Marty is part owner. Don't ask how he managed that on a cop's salary."

"Sounds like an interesting guy. Are you taking your golf clubs with you?"

"I don't have any golf clubs, Becky. Besides, I'd be surprised if Charlene lets me go."

"Not me. One thing you can count on with our little Napoleon—she never misses an opportunity to make herself look good."

లుళుల

It was almost five o'clock, Abby's normal departure time, when her phone finally rang and she was summoned to her boss's office.

"Have a seat and tell me the latest about the Wardlaws," Charlene said, looking more relaxed than she had earlier in the day.

Abby told her that Earl and Donna Wardlaw were still staying at the Knight's Inn on Scarboro's west side. "I tried to interview them by phone and in person, but they refused to talk."

"What about their kids?"

"The daughter is out of intensive care, but it sounds like she might have some brain damage. At least, that's what one of the nurses told me off the record."

"Any mention of a lawsuit?"

"Not yet. My guess is the Wardlaws are playing a waiting game. If they really were operating a meth lab, they'll probably wait to see if they get charged for that. I think they're also waiting to see how well their kids recover."

Abby explained that she had contacted the gas company earlier that morning and its position was the same—the explosion wasn't its fault. "The cops are still tight lipped about the whole thing, though my source at the police department did say they sent a segment of cracked pipe found near the Wardlaws' gas meter to a testing lab. The results should take about ten days."

Charlene adjusted her glasses and leaned back in her swivel chair. "Sooner or later this case will break wide open, Abby. When it does, I want you available and ready to run with it. Regardless of what caused that explosion, there's a follow-up story here, probably a whole series of them. Right now I don't see a problem with you leaving for a few days, as long as you're prepared to return at a moment's notice. Call me when you get to Wisteria and let me know where you're staying. And keep your cell phone on. If I need you in a hurry, I don't want to get your voice mail. *Comprenez vous?*"

Abby nodded, stifling the urge to reply *Mais oui, Madame Salope*.

"One other thing. You're going to Wisteria as a reporter for the *Gazette*, not as a private investigator. Have you got a problem with that?"

"No," Abby said, still too overwhelmed by Will's death to savor, even for a moment, this small, rare victory over her bitch of a boss. "No problem at all."

Chapter 2

The eastern sky was flush with color, a blaze of orange and red heralding the rising sun. *Red sky in the morning, sailor take warning*, Abby mused and the adage proved apropos. Long before she reached the Virginia line, all trace of the sun had disappeared, the sky resembling a slate gray dome that pressed close against the earth.

As she drove, Abby thought of her near flare-up in Charlene Greer's office. She had almost lost control of herself, and she wondered if she might be on the verge of a manic episode. Even though she had been taking her lithium and Seroquel as prescribed, she knew that people with bipolar disorder can cycle into mania, depression, or a combination of the two after experiencing a major change in routine, anything from prolonged lack of sleep to a life-altering event. Will's death had hit her hard, the kind of shock that could trigger such an episode.

Soon after she crossed into Virginia, rain began to fall, a cold steady drizzle. By the time she reached Charlottesville, it had become a downpour. Forty minutes later, just before Abby turned south onto a county road a few miles east of Wisteria, she felt as though she were in a carwash. Water pounded the hood of her nine-year-old Toyota Corolla and splattered against the windshield, rendering the wipers all but useless. Visibility was so poor she didn't see the *Pinecroft* sign until too late to make the turn. She had to go another half mile before finding a safe place to turn around.

The access road to the course was slick with mud, as was the small empty parking area. Abby parked as close as she could to a modest split-level house with a balcony overlooking a tiny putting green. Dodging puddles, she hurried up the stone walkway, stopping beneath the overhang just long enough to read the sign on the door: *Winter rates—$5 for all the golf you can stand.*

She knocked and went inside, finding herself in a small entryway between the lower and upper floors. At the top of the stairs, she noticed a smoke-gray cat peering down at her. Deciding she wasn't a threat, he began his descent.

"Anybody home?" Abby called, leaning over to pet the cat, who immediately flung himself down on a step and began purring.

"Just me and Bogie," said the young man who appeared beyond the top step. Wearing jeans and a Georgetown sweatshirt, he reminded Abby more of a college student than an ex-cop turned entrepreneur. He was even better looking than she remembered. "Welcome to Pinecroft, Abby."

"What the hell's going on, Marty?" Carefully stepping over the cat, she climbed to the top of the stairs. "Why would anyone want to kill a sweet man like Will?"

"I wish I knew. Did you have any trouble finding the place?"

"I drove right past it. But that was my fault—and the rain's. This course sure is out in the middle of BFE."

"BFE?"

"Butt fucking Egypt. Excuse my French."

Marty chuckled. "That's what Will liked about it. As far as he was concerned, Pinecroft's greatest asset is its lack of play. The Langs and I hope to change that eventually."

"Are you finished with the criminal justice system or just taking a sabbatical?"

"Haven't decided yet. Guess it depends on how well things go here at Pinecroft. Can I fix you something to eat?"

"No thanks. I had lunch about forty-five minutes ago in a little berg called Fork Union. I could use something to drink, though. Decaffeinated pop if you've got it, but water is fine."

"How about some ginger ale?"

"That'll work. Mind if I use the bathroom first?"

"There's one at the bottom of the stairs. First room on the right."

A few minutes later, as she headed back upstairs, Abby noticed through the front door's window that the rain had slacked off. She crossed the living room to a small kitchen/dining area and joined Marty at a rectangular wooden table where a plate of chocolate-chip cookies and a glass of ginger ale awaited her.

Shortly after she sat down, the cat jumped in her lap.

"You must be a good golfer. Generally Bogie ignores people unless they break ninety on a regular basis."

"I'm a lousy golfer, but I do like cats." Abby petted Bogie for a moment, then gently set him on the floor. "When the rain stops, assuming it does, could you show me where Will was killed?"

"According to the forecast, it should have stopped an hour ago." Marty pushed the plate of cookies in Abby's direction. "Jamie Lang made these last night. She and her husband Nelson own Pinecroft."

"I thought you were part owner," Abby said and drank some of her ginger ale.

"I am, but in the same way someone who owns a few

shares of General Motors stock owns the company."

Nodding, Abby selected a cookie and took a bite. "Mmm—delicious. Tell me about the acting police chief, Marty."

"His name is Mel Taggart. He showed me the ropes after Will hired me. Actually, he's a pretty good cop—or would be if he didn't have different standards for different people. If you've got clout in the community or stand out in some way, he'll give you a break quicker than he would the ordinary Joe. I never thought much about it until one day we pulled over a blond with a drop-dead figure. She was drunk as a skunk, and all Mel did was give her a warning after we escorted her home. And he acted apologetic about that."

Abby reached for another cookie. "Showing favoritism is a long way from being a murderer."

"That's true. And I don't have any evidence that Mel had anything to do with Will's death. I do know he'd really like to have the chief's job. No doubt he was disappointed when Maggie offered it to Will."

"Maggie?"

"Maggie Calahan. Her husband Graham is Wisteria's mayor. He had a heart attack a while back, and Maggie has been helping him out with his duties. She also owns and operates an antique shop in town. And she's Nelson Lang's partner at the YMCA bridge tournament in Hawthorne."

"Sounds like a busy lady."

"She does get around."

The way Marty said it made Abby wonder if there was more going on between Maggie and Nelson than playing bridge. "Yesterday on the phone you said there were other people besides Mel Taggart who might be suspects. Who are they?"

"Will's son Ben is one," Marty said, glancing at the

window to Abby's left. "Another is a local bad ass named Wardell Tharp. I'll tell you about those two later, Abby. The rain seems to have stopped. I'll get a golf cart ready and meet you out front in about five minutes. In the meantime, help yourself to more cookies."

Abby was able to restrain herself after one more cookie, mainly because she doubted she'd be able to keep up her normal exercise routine while in Wisteria. She knew from experience that weight gain was a side effect of taking her meds and that in order to keep any semblance of a decent figure, she had to eat less than she wanted, especially when she wasn't able to get her usual amount of exercise.

By the time Marty brought a golf cart around to the front of the house, the sun had broken through the clouds. It glistened in puddles here and there and on water droplets clinging to the trees.

"Hop in and hold on tight," he said. "Riding in a cart on Pinecroft's back nine is a little like being on a bucking bronco at a rodeo."

The ride was circuitous as well as bumpy—up and down hills, over a plank bridge that crossed a swollen creek, through pine woods that separated fairways. For the most part, Marty stayed off the fairways, taking cart paths when they were available, maneuvering through the rough when they weren't. Twice the cart got stuck, but both times he was able to rock it back and forth until the wheels broke free.

The final few yards proved tricky because of the sloping terrain that led past a nearly leafless maple tree to the seventeenth hole's elevated tee. Marty gunned the cart up the incline and brought it to a skidding stop. "It's soggy up here, so be careful where you step," he said, locking the brake with his foot. He pointed toward two white stakes, one on either side of the tee box. "Will was lying next to the tee marker on the right. His ball was still teed up. I'd just talked to him a couple hours earlier when he was playing the thirteenth hole, which is where I was cutting brush that morning. When I went in for lunch, I noticed his truck was still in the parking lot. I figured something was wrong and went looking for him."

"Did you hear a shot?"

"I heard several. It was the first day of deer season, and hunters were all over the place."

Abby recalled the article in the *Richmond Times-Dispatch*. "Maybe the shooting was an accident," she said. "I mean with so many hunters around, couldn't Will have been hit by a stray bullet?"

"I doubt it. We're pretty much out in the open up here." Marty nodded toward the maze of honeysuckle vines that stretched the length of the teeing area. "The way I figure it, the killer was hiding in those bushes and came out when Will got ready to hit his drive. I found his driver at the edge of that honeysuckle. Looked to me like he must have thrown it at the shooter."

Abby visualized Will throwing his club, imagined the horror he must have felt knowing it might be the last thing he ever did. "How often did he play golf out here?" she asked, struggling to keep back tears.

"Twice a week normally, maybe a little less this time of year. Usually he played the front nine. The back is a tough walk."

"Didn't he take a cart?"

Marty shook his head. "He didn't even use a pull cart to carry his clubs."

"Did he usually play by himself?"

"Almost always. Will was as gregarious as the next guy, but when it came to golf, he liked playing alone."

Careful where she stepped, Abby walked to the front of the teeing area to examine the honeysuckle thicket from a different angle. She had no idea what she was looking for, and when she saw nothing out of the ordinary—just a tangle of vines and bushes with a few pine trees rising up behind—she felt foolish. *What did you expect to find, Sherlock? A written confession tucked away in the bushes?* She wondered why she had thought she could actually help solve Will's murder. Was this trip just another of her grandiose ideas, something a person with bipolar disorder might dream up?

Stop putting yourself down. You're taking your meds. You're not manic. Just do whatever you can to help.

Through a gap in the trees, Abby noticed what looked like the dark surface of asphalt. "Is that a road over there?"

"Same one you drove in on. The part you see is about a thousand yards from Pinecroft's entrance. The killer could have parked there and had easy access to where we're standing. Even if people saw him, they probably thought he was just another deer hunter."

"Whoever killed Will must have known he'd be golfing that morning. He also must have known Will would play the back nine and be alone. Would many people have access to that kind of information, Marty?"

"It was common knowledge Will liked to play by himself. The killer could have followed him to the course and watched to see which nine he started on."

The sound of an approaching vehicle caught Abby's attention. Glancing at the road, she saw a navy blue sedan heading in the direction of Pinecroft's entrance.

"That's Nelson's car," Marty said.

Taking a final look around the teeing area, Abby decided she had seen—or not seen—enough, at least for the time being. "Guess I'm ready to go back. Hope I haven't taken up too much of your time."

"Not a problem. I'm glad to do whatever I can to help out. I still have a lot of work to do before winter sets in, but I can usually get away for an hour or two. Keep in mind

I've got police experience that might come in handy in a pinch. Don't feel like you've got to do all this by yourself."

Marty took the same circuitous route back to the clubhouse, deviating only at the end when he drove around back where the other motorized carts were parked. The sedan Abby had seen a few minutes earlier was parked nearby, not far from a motorcycle covered by a large sheet of clear polyethylene.

"That's my hog," Marty said as they exited the cart. "I sold my car so I'd have more money to invest in the course."

Hearing a door open, Abby looked up and saw a trim middle-aged man with wavy salt-and-pepper hair step onto the deck. "Not exactly golfing weather," he called, a voice Abby recognized as belonging to the person who answered the phone yesterday when she called Pinecroft.

"Abby, meet Nelson Lang, the senior partner in my modest financial venture. Nelson, this is Abby Burlew."

"Pleased to meet you, ma'am." Nelson gave Abby a nod and a perfunctory smile, and then he focused his attention on Marty. "Our finances just took a turn for the better. Guess who your friend left his money to. His estate, by the way, is worth somewhere in the neighborhood of a half million dollars."

Marty's jaw dropped. "You're kidding."

"Nope. Will left it to Pinecroft. Can you believe that, Marty? Will Ramsdell left the lion's share of his estate to this golf course. We're finally out of the woods. If Pinecroft can't compete with other courses now, we're the ones who should be shot."

Chapter 3

A year earlier, when Abby's investigation of Sheila Bostrum's and Rhonda Tolbert's murders had taken her to Wisteria, she had stayed at the Shenandoah Motel. Now it was the Shenandoah Inn, though aside from its rooms costing ten dollars more a night, nothing seemed to have changed. It was the same drab beige structure with a view of the same ugly hill scraped bare by a long-ago strip mining operation.

After unpacking her suitcase, Abby left a message on her mother's cell phone. "Hope Kevin is behaving himself," she said. "I forgot to tell you he's got a history paper due Friday and he hasn't started it. Thanks for letting him stay with you, Mom. I'll talk to you later."

She then dialed Charlene Greer's number at the *Gazette* and left a message saying she had been to the golf course where Will was killed, talked with two of the owners, and learned that Will had left his estate to the course, an angle she intended to pursue in case it had a bearing on his murder. She gave the inn's telephone number and her room number, promised to check in tomorrow with an update, and ended the call.

Almost immediately she got a return call from her mother. Kevin had mentioned the history paper, Lillian said, and asked her to drop him off at the library after supper. "I told him I could do better than that. I've got a coupon for Applebee's that's about to expire, so I told him we'd have supper there, and then we'd both go to the library, which we did. I read magazines while Kev did his research."

"Has he decided on a topic yet?" Abby asked.

"Right now he's leaning toward North Carolina's participation in the Civil War. I suggested he choose something really significant, like Jesse Helms's contribution to the Civil Rights Movement."

"Great idea, Mom. Kevin can submit some blank sheets of paper and cover the subject with complete accuracy."

"We'll come up with something, Abby. You just focus on your investigation. And for God's sake be careful. The last thing Will would have wanted is you putting yourself in danger."

ဢ

Expecting Marty to arrive on his motorcycle, Abby was surprised to see him emerge from a black Chevrolet Spark that had pulled into the parking space next to hers. She grabbed her jacket, turned off the lights in her room, and opened the door just as Marty was about to knock.

"Jamie loaned me her wheels," he said. "She didn't think you should have to ride on the back of a motorcycle, especially this time of year." After helping Abby on with her jacket, Marty asked which she liked the best—seafood, Italian, Chinese, Mexican, or typical American fare.

"All of the above. I'm starved."

"Okay, I'll put it a different way. Would you rather pig out at Red Lobster, the Olive Garden, Ruby Tuesday's, the Golden Dragon, Chi Chi's, or the Mountain Top Inn?"

"I'm surprised a berg this size has all those options."

"It doesn't. Most of those restaurants are in Hawthorne, which is nine miles away."

"I ate at the Mountain Top Inn with Will. It's nice, but I'd rather go somewhere else tonight. I haven't had sweet and sour chicken in a while, so how about we try the Golden Dragon?"

"Excellent choice, madam." With a deferential flourish Marty opened the Spark's passenger-side door and waited for Abby to get in. "As your escort for the evening, I consider it my duty to point out all landmarks of aesthetic and/or historical interest—assuming any are to be found."

On Church Street Marty indicated Bygone Daze, a boutique sandwiched between a barber shop and a store that sold vacuum cleaners and related products. "That's Maggie Calahan's shop," he said. A block later, after turning right on Jefferson Avenue, he nodded at a familiar cinderblock building Abby recognized from her previous visit as being the police station. "Guess I don't have to tell you what that is. I'll show you the sheriff's digs when we get to Hawthorne."

"What's he like, Marty?"

"The sheriff? Not exactly what you'd call a straight shooter. For the right price Quentin Grice can be bought. At least that was Will's impression, which I have no reason to doubt."

"Did Grice question you about Will's murder?"

"He did, but only because I'm the person who found Will's body. He didn't ask my opinion about potential suspects, and I didn't volunteer any."

A hardware store called the Do-It Center caught Abby's eye, as did the clapboard building next door with *Wisteria Veterinary Clinic* printed on a sign in its empty parking lot. A block later Jefferson Avenue merged with Highway 64, and they headed west into the setting sun.

"Tell me about Ben Ramsdell," Abby said, pulling

down the sun visor in front of her. "He has a possible motive?"

Marty waited until he passed a slow-moving pickup truck before replying. "Ben has a serious drug problem," he said as he maneuvered the Spark back into the right lane. "Will did what he could to help the kid, including putting him through various rehabs. He even let him live at home. But when Ben started stealing from him, Will cut him loose, though not before setting up a small trust fund. As Will explained it to me, it was enough to keep Ben from living on the street, but not enough so he wouldn't have to work for a living."

"You think Ben expected to inherit Will's estate and killed him to get the money sooner than later?"

Marty shrugged. "If an addict gets desperate enough, there's no telling what he'll do."

Abby recalled her own drugging days when her mother had to keep her antique collection under lock and key. Even that didn't keep Lillian's collectibles safe. "What about the other suspect you mentioned, Wardell some-body?"

"Wardell Tharp. He's a black guy who has a hand in a lot of the crime around here, most of it drug-related. Will arrested him a few years ago and Tharp spent some time behind bars. He wouldn't have been looking forward to Will becoming police chief again."

୧୬୧୬

After the waitress brought their meals, Abby started in on her sweet and sour chicken, finding it very much to her liking. "Was there bad blood between Nelson Lang and Will?" she asked.

"What makes you think that?"

"The way Nelson referred to Will as *your* friend when

he told you about the inheritance. Plus his comment about Pinecroft's owners needing to be shot if they can't make a go of the course now. That's not the kind of thing someone would say about a recently deceased friend."

"True. And Nelson wasn't exactly fond of Will."

"Why?"

"The short answer is Jamie left Nelson for a while last year, actually moved out of the house. Part of the time she was gone, she stayed with Will."

Abby nodded. "I can understand why Nelson might have bad feelings."

"I'm not sure they're justified, but it's a long story."

"I'd like to hear it."

"Well, first you need to know some of Pinecroft's history," Marty said and began cutting up his egg roll. "About twenty-five years ago Nelson's parents bought the land for the course and put in the original nine holes. They both had regular jobs at the time and saw Pinecroft as a way to surround themselves with some scenic beauty in their later years as well as a way to supplement their retirement income. Nelson was in college at the time, and he helped them design the course. Eventually he inherited it."

Marty put down his knife and fork and focused his attention on Abby. "Nelson had always been a good golfer, so instead of selling the course, he and Jamie tried to make a go of it themselves. They borrowed money to expand the course, thinking that if Pinecroft had eighteen holes it could compete with the established courses in the area. Unfortunately, by the time they were ready to landscape the new holes, the bank had changed hands and refused to lend them any more money. That came as a shock, especially to Nelson. As I understand it, he started drinking and became hard to live with, at times even abusive. Finally Jamie got a room at the Shenandoah. A few days later she moved in with Will."

"How serious was their relationship?"

"I'm not even sure I'd call it a relationship. I think it was more like two troubled souls commiserating with each other. Will hadn't gotten over the death of his wife, and Jamie was suffering from a depressed and abusive husband. To make a long story a little shorter, Nelson finally realized he needed help, got treatment for his depression, and convinced Jamie to return to Pinecroft."

By this time Abby had doused her egg roll with plum sauce and began eating it. "Think Jamie might have known about the inheritance prior to Will's death?"

"No, I don't. Clearly she was shocked when she got home today and Nelson broke the news. Even if Jamie did know about the inheritance, I can't imagine her committing murder. Nelson either, for that matter, if that's what you're thinking."

"The possibility did occur to me."

"The Langs are good people, Abby. If you focus on either of them as a potential suspect in Will's murder, you'll be barking up the wrong tree."

Not sure how much credence she should give Marty's opinion, Abby nodded. "Is there anyone else who might have wanted Will dead?"

"Jamie's father wouldn't have shed any tears, but he didn't kill Will."

"Oh? You know that for a fact, do you?"

"Close enough for government work."

"What's her father's name?"

"Ned Copeland."

"Tell me about him."

Marty looked at Abby's plate and then at his own. "I'm lagging behind here," he said and reached into his shirt pocket. He pulled out a folded sheet of typing paper and handed it to Abby. "Check this out while I catch up. I'll tell you about Ned Copeland later, assuming you're still curious about the guy."

Unfolding the sheet of paper, Abby saw what looked like a hand-written poem with the title "Leaving the Station."

If you were surprised to see me go
And regret my departure wasn't a bit more slow,
Don't worry, think trains, think the mighty C&O.
Its steamers were my favorites, my pride and my joy.
They gave me thrills and not just as a boy.
They lifted my spirit with their power and grace.
One even provided me a hiding place.

But I digress, I ramble, as train buffs tend to do.
My intention here is to provide you a clue.
Be true to yourself, never go on a bender,
If in a quandary, check the yellow belly's tender.
And should you think my advice a bit queer,
Seek out Abby Burlew, its one-time engineer.

Abby didn't know what to make of the poem until the end when she saw her name. "This is really weird, Marty," she said, thinking back to the evening she had spent at Will's house a year earlier. "Where did you get it?"

"This afternoon's mail. Graham Calahan's law office was stamped as the return address. I know Will was into model trains and had a layout in his basement, but I never saw it. Apparently you have first-hand knowledge of that layout."

"I do," Abby said and handed the poem back to Marty. "One of Will's engines was a big Lionel steamer he called a yellow belly. He even let me run it. My guess is he put something in the tender that he wanted you—or maybe the two of us—to find."

Chapter 4

A full moon had just crested the hill across the road, and hundreds of stars sparkled overhead. Normally the Langs didn't sit on their deck this late in the year, but Nelson had brought home two bottles of champagne and didn't want to celebrate in a living room cluttered with golfing paraphernalia.

Jamie didn't care where they drank the champagne. She had told Nelson she didn't feel like celebrating, that the news of Will's inheritance was so shocking that she needed time to adjust. "Never in my wildest dreams," she said as they sat down for a dinner she hardly touched. "I still can't believe it."

"Well, it's true. And I couldn't be happier. Seems like you'd be happy too."

"It's just so…unreal," she muttered, her eyes filling with tears.

Nelson had hoped the champagne would get Jamie into the spirit of things, but it hadn't turned out that way. She drank slowly, less than one glass to his three, and she seemed as dazed and withdrawn as she had been at dinner. After Nelson's third glass of champagne, the fact that Jamie didn't share his joy at their good fortune no longer seemed to concern him.

"How about a refill?" he asked after filling his glass for the fourth time.

"No thanks."

"You don't think the news we got today is worth celebrating?"

"It's not that. It's…"

"What?"

"For one thing I have to work tomorrow."

"You don't need that job anymore, Jamie. We've got enough money now to turn Pinecroft into a course Donald Ross himself would be proud of. And we're going to do it—with or without the help of that goddamn First Citizens Bank. From now on they can kiss our royal asses."

Jamie's expression didn't change. "Maybe I'll have a little more," she said without enthusiasm.

Nelson poured her glass nearly full, set the empty bottle on the deck floor, and leaned back in his chair. A host of stars wheeled overhead, many so bright it seemed he could reach out and touch them. "Look up there, Jamie. Imagine being stuck in a city all your life and never seeing the Milky Way. Or the Big Dipper. Or even a real moon." He raised his glass. "Here's to you, Mr. Moon. You're looking especially handsome tonight. Keep on a'shinin'." He lowered the glass to his lips, drank, then raised it again. "Here's to all you stars, planets, asteroids, comets, and whatever else's up there. You're a sight to behold." He paused, his face suddenly taking on a melancholy look. "Here's to you, Mom and Dad—for having the vision and the good sense to buy this land and turn it into a golf course. Wish you could be here to help us celebrate."

"I miss your folks," Jamie added in a small voice.

"And here's to you, Will Ramsdell. I hope you get a membership in that great country club in the sky. And if you do, I hope you break par each and every round you play."

"I wish you wouldn't talk that way, Nelson. A generous man is dead. He deserves more respect than that."

Nelson raised his glass higher. "And here's to you, Jamie Lang—the belle of Pinecroft. The best-looking woman in all of Augusta County."

"The champagne has obviously gone to your head."

He clinked his glass against hers, then pulled his chair closer and reached for Jamie's hand. "It was true when we met, and it's still true today."

A dog barked in the distance, causing Bogie to stir on Jamie's lap.

"Remember when we lived in Hawthorne and the Sherwoods dropped by with that batch of hashish?" Nelson asked. "We all thought we were acting perfectly normal until our neighbor across the street appeared out of nowhere and asked if everything was all right. We must've been making one hell of a racket."

"I'm sure we were."

"Remember what we did after the Sherwoods went home?"

"Not really."

"Made love on that fluffy old living room rug. That was the best sex I've ever had in my life."

The sound of a train's horn drifted across the night, a long wail followed by two shorts and another long, four mournful notes of a distant saxophone. The dog began to howl. Bogie raised his head.

"Like to see if we can recapture a little of that old magic?"

The rising drone of diesels was followed by the clicking of wheels against the joints of rails.

"I don't think so. Not tonight."

Nelson sighed. "Silly me, thinking tonight would be special enough to make a difference. I should've known better."

"What's that supposed to mean?"

"It means we don't have a sex life, Jamie. That's what it means."

The throbbing of engines and the clatter of wheels grew louder, merged into a cacophonous crescendo, and finally began to recede. The horn sounded its doleful refrain, barely audible in the distance. The dog resumed his periodic barking. A night bird called from near the eighteenth green.

"Do you know how many times we've had sex this past year?" Nelson asked.

"I haven't been keeping count."

"Exactly twice. The last time was on my birthday, and that was three goddamn months ago."

Under the deck a cricket began to chirrup. An owl hooted from along the first fairway.

"I can't help it if I've lost my libido, Nelson. A hysterectomy can do that to a woman."

Nelson took a final swallow of champagne and stood up. "I'm not sure you ever had a libido, Jamie" he said and flung his glass against the side of the house. It exploded in a shower of shards and smaller particles. Bogie sprang from Jamie's lap.

"That was bright," she said. "Now he'll cut his paws."

Glass crunching under his shoes, Nelson picked up the cat and gently deposited him inside the kitchen door. Then he walked to the edge of the deck. After a brief hesitation, he headed down the steps.

Jamie pushed back her chair and stood up. "Where are you going?"

"None of your business," Nelson called over his shoulder. At the bottom of the stairs, he turned toward his car, tripped, and almost fell. "Goddamn fuckin' root!"

"You're in no condition to drive."

"Don't worry about me, Jamie. If I don't make it back,

you shouldn't have any trouble at all finding another eunuch to take my place."

The car door slammed and the engine roared to life. Headlights flashed on, illuminating the row of golf carts and the polyethylene-covered motorcycle. The car lurched backward a few feet, paused, and then surged forward, bouncing over ruts as it headed toward the road. When it reached the dark slab of macadam, it veered left and, with a squealing of tires, sped north toward Route 64.

Long after Jamie could no longer hear the car or see its fading lights, she stood next to the deck railing and quietly wept.

Chapter 5

The noise kept hammering away in Ben Ramsdell's head like a woodpecker attacking a nearby tree. Periodically it would stop and then start again with a vengeance. Groggy from an evening of drugging, Ben covered his head with his pillow, pulling it tightly around his ears. As he drifted toward sleep, there it was again, not as loud as before but just as persistent. "What's a guy gotta do to stack some Z's around here?" he groaned.

Finally Ben realized that the sound was knocking and that it was coming from the front door of his apartment. Raising his head, he squinted at the alarm clock on the chest of drawers across the room. Not even midnight yet. Too early for Mitch Folby to be back with his Richmond goodies, stuff that, according to him, was cheaper than anything available locally, with the added bonus of not having to deal with Wardell Tharp or one of his arrogant toadies. Besides, Mitch had his own key and didn't need to knock.

"I'm trying to sleep," Ben called and turned over in the bed, deciding it must be Shannon Pfeiffer at the door. If she didn't start giving him more space, he'd ditch her sorry ass. Maybe he would anyway. Now that he'd banged her a couple times, she wasn't nearly as interesting.

After another flurry of knocking, Ben heard his name

being called, a deep masculine voice, definitely not Shannon's. Probably a stoner needing to score, he thought. If so, he'd charge the guy extra for disturbing his sleep. Anybody needing weed this time of night was desperate, willing to pay through the nose.

"Hold your water, hoss. I'm coming."

When Ben opened the door and saw who was in the hallway, his heart sank. Once a highly-touted lineman at Ferrum College, Wardell Tharp had been expelled his sophomore year for a string of offenses that included beating up a fellow student and a rape charge that eventually was dropped because the victim decided not to testify.

"We need to talk," the big man growled. "Right here or inside—your choice."

"We can…uh," Ben began, not sure what he feared more, being alone with Tharp or having his neighbors in the apartment complex overhear their conversation. "Why don't you…uh…come in."

Tharp pushed into the living room and plunked himself down on the best piece of furniture in the apartment, a plush leather recliner Ben had purchased a few days earlier using Maltby's buy-now, pay-later plan. It groaned under the big man's weight.

Closing the door, Ben made his way to the room's only other place to sit, a raggedy sofa Mitch had rescued from the dumpster area.

"When were you going to tell me about your big fuck up?" Wardell asked.

"What big fuck up?"

"Don't play dumb with me, dipshit. You know what I'm talking about. What a crock—claiming you were the beneficiary of your old man's estate."

Ben's first impulse was to lie, pretend he hadn't heard the tragic news. "I had every reason to think that inheritance was mine, Wardell," he said, deciding to take his medicine now and get it over with.

"When did you find out who the real beneficiary was?"

"Late this afternoon."

"Before or after you took delivery of that last batch of weed?"

"After," Ben replied a little too quickly. "I didn't hear about it until right before supper."

"You're a lying sack of shit. I know when Calahan read that will. I also know you were in his office when he read it."

Ben sighed and rubbed sleep from his eyes. "Nobody can slip anything past you, can they, big guy?" he said, hoping to score points by massaging Tharp's ego. "You're absolutely right. But just for the record, it damn near broke my heart. There's nothing you can do or say that'll hurt any worse than hearing that god-awful news."

A spasm of laughter erupted in Wardell's throat. "There's plenty I can do that'll hurt a whole lot worse. But we'll skip that part for the time being. Right now I want to know exactly what you intend to do about your debt?"

"I'm gonna pay it, of course," Ben said in the most sincere and contrite voice he could muster. "It'll just take a little longer than I figured. But you'll get your money, Wardell. I promise."

The big man chuckled. "You must think I'm stupid to keep feeding me the same old bullshit."

"It's not bullshit. I'm gonna pay you every cent I owe you."

"When?"

"Next week—at the very latest. I've got a plan."

"You *had* a plan. Talk about counting your chickens before the fuckers hatch."

"I'll get it right this time, Wardell. Just give me one more week. That's not too much to ask, is it?"

Tharp got up and went over to the sofa, eyeing Ben as though trying to decide where and how hard to hit him. "No, I suppose not," he finally said, his expression softening. "You won't disappoint me again, will you?"

"No, sir. Absolutely not."

Wardell smiled. "I like that, calling me 'sir.' At least you know how to show some respect. Your old man was sorely lacking in that department." He stuck out his hand. "No hard feelings?"

Hardly believing his good fortune, Ben stood up and reached for the mahogany-colored hand. "None at all."

Quick as a snake, Wardell grabbed Ben's little finger and snapped it backward. There was a cracking sound and Ben let out a scream. He dropped to his knees, moaning and writhing in pain.

"You bastard," he blurted through his tears. "You didn't have to do that. I was gonna pay."

"You still are. Don't think for a second that broken pinkie entitles you to a free ride."

Ben rocked back and forth on the floor, cradling the throbbing finger in his left hand as if it were a wounded bird.

"But I'll be reasonable about this. I'll give you the week you're asking for and I'll throw in an extra one. You've got exactly fourteen days to come up with the money." Wardell turned and headed for the door, his movements agile for such a large man. "Better get moving on that plan of yours, whatever the fuck it is. This time it better be more than wishful thinking."

The door opened quietly and closed with a dull thud. The sound of footsteps receded down the hallway.

For a long time Ben sat on the floor, grimacing and nursing his throbbing finger. "How could you do this to me?" he moaned, his anger no longer directed at Wardell Tharp but at his own father. "I hope you rot in hell for giving what was rightfully mine to a goddamn golf course."

Chapter 6

The Shenandoah Inn might not be luxurious, but at least it was quiet—or so Abby thought as she turned out the lights and climbed into bed. It seemed as though she had hardly closed her eyes when she heard people enter the adjacent room, a young couple it sounded like. They clomped around for a while, and when they finally got settled, they had a long discussion about whether to take the Blue Ridge Parkway tomorrow or get back on the interstate. Then, after watching loud TV for what seemed like forever, they serenaded Abby with a symphony of wild pleasurable moaning accompanied by a plethora of squeaking bedsprings. By midnight, she'd had all she could stand and banged on the wall. "*Stop making so damn much noise!*" she yelled.

After that, the couple was quiet, but Abby slept fitfully, slipping into and out of painful dreams. The final one featured Will Ramsdell. He was standing between the tee markers on Pinecroft's seventeenth hole, staring in horror at his assailant who had just fired at him. A deer slug had just exited the gun barrel and was traveling in slow motion, the same speed as Abby, who was moving as fast as she could, desperately hoping to save her friend by pushing him to one side. She was too late. The bullet ripped into Will's chest and he crumpled to the ground. Kneeling beside him, Abby pressed her hand against his wound to staunch the bleeding. "Get away from me!" Will said. "Don't you know enough not to disturb a body before the police can examine it? Why are you here anyway?" When Abby tried to explain that she wanted to make sure his assailant was brought to justice, Will laughed. "The joke's on you," he said, and even though his face was contorted in pain, he continued to laugh, his chest heaving with the effort. Suddenly his body stiffened, his eyes glazed over, and his breathing stopped.

When her alarm clock went off at six-fifteen, Abby was tempted to reset it. Dragging herself out of bed, she remembered the couple in the next room and switched on her TV to give them a dose of their own medicine. Realizing she might disturb other people as well, she switched the set back off. She splashed cold water on her face, put on sweatpants and a sweatshirt, and did some limbering up exercises. After lacing up her running shoes, she opened the door on a bright, cold December morning. The mountains to the east hid the sun, but those to the west glowed orange, clearly indicating its presence.

Abby's plan was to go jogging, shower, eat breakfast, and be at Maltby's Department Store shortly before it opened at nine, so she wore her watch, something she rarely did when exercising. She stopped at the motel's front office to complain about the noisy couple next door, only to be told by the clerk that the rooms on either side of hers were vacant.

"Are you sure?"

"You're in number fourteen, right?"

"Yeah, that's right."

"Only four other rooms were occupied last night, and none are even close to yours."

Abby glared at the clerk. "I know what I heard. About ten-thirty a young couple entered the room next to mine and made a hell of a racket. They talked loud, they played the TV loud, they even had loud sex. You wouldn't believe all the moaning and squeaking of bedsprings."

"I don't know what to tell you," the clerk said just as the telephone began ringing. "Apparently you were dreaming." Turning away from Abby, the clerk picked up the phone. "Thank you for calling the Shenandoah Inn. This is Cindy. How may I help you?"

No way was I dreaming, Abby told herself as she headed outside. I hadn't even gone to sleep yet. Either that woman is lying or people she doesn't know about have a key to that room. As Abby began jogging, a third possibility occurred to her, and it was not a pleasant thought: maybe the noise she heard had occurred only in her mind.

It took Abby less than ten minutes to get to the veterinary clinic, which she found with no difficulty, having noticed it yesterday on her way to dinner with Marty. According to a handwritten sign on the front door, the clinic was open just three days a week—Monday, Wednesday, and Friday—and only from nine to eleven AM. Relief settled in on her when she remembered that today was Wednesday.

Although Marty had made it clear last night that he didn't consider Ned Copeland a suspect, Abby wanted to reserve that judgment for herself. To that end, she had pressed Marty for more information as they were finishing dinner.

"All I know is what Will told me," he had said. "Dr. Hux and Ned Copeland had a falling out that escalated to the point Will had no choice but to intervene. He wouldn't give me any specifics, but he said if Copeland ever figured out what he did, the guy probably wouldn't rest until he got his revenge."

When Abby suggested that maybe Copeland had figured it out and extracted the ultimate revenge, Marty shook his head. "All this happened a long time ago, Abby. If he was going to retaliate, it wouldn't have taken him all these years."

"Did Dr. Hux leave a wife behind?" Abby asked, still not convinced that Ned Copeland shouldn't be considered a suspect. "Or anybody else who knew him well enough to know what was going on between him and Copeland?"

"His wife is dead. Nelson Lang was his partner at the YMCA's weekly bridge tournaments, but I don't think they were close. The only person I'm aware of besides Will who might have been close to Dr. Hux after his wife died is Leona Figgins. She was his assistant at the veterinary clinic. As far as I know, she still works there. Last I heard, a vet from Hawthorne comes over a few days each week to keep things going."

✑✒✑

After eating breakfast at Sullivan's Diner, a small restaurant converted from an old trolley car, Abby drove across town to Maltby's. She pulled into its parking lot just as a tall blonde woman was getting out of a black Chevrolet Spark. Abby parked in the closest available space and exited her Corolla.

"Jamie?" she called, hurrying toward the woman. "Jamie Lang?"

"Yes?"

Abby identified herself and thanked Jamie for lending Marty her car last night. When Abby said she had some questions about Will Ramsdell, Jamie's face clouded with concern.

"I don't have time to talk now. I'll be late for work."

"I can come back during your break. Or maybe we could have lunch together, whichever would be less inconvenient for you."

"Well," Jamie said, clearly not pleased with Abby's suggestions. "I usually take a break about ten-thirty. If you want to come back then, I suppose I could give you a few minutes."

"I'd really appreciate it. See you at ten-thirty."

Back in her car, Abby looked up the Augusta County Sheriff's Department on her smart phone and dialed the number. She told the deputy who answered that she would like to make an appointment to see Sheriff Grice.

"What seems to be the problem, ma'am?"

Abby explained that she worked for a small North Carolina newspaper and wanted to find out the latest in the Will Ramsdell murder case. When there was a pause at the other end, she added, "I was a friend of Will's. He helped me with my first investigative assignment."

The deputy told her the sheriff was out of the office and wouldn't be back until after lunch. "He's got a meeting at one. I can put you down for a two o'clock appointment if you want."

"I do," Abby said and gave her name.

After ending the call, she drove to the veterinary clinic where she found several vehicles in the parking lot, the latest a mini-van driven by a woman who was in the process of extracting a full-grown collie from the passenger side. Abby parked and followed them into the clinic.

The waiting room was full—three dogs, including the collie, a black and white cat with half a black mustache, and something inside a cardboard box that an elderly woman seemed to be guarding with her life. The receptionist, a heavy-set black woman, was clearly too busy to talk. Deciding that now would be as good a time as any to visit Will's grave, Abby returned to her car.

The cemetery proved difficult to find, even though Marty, at Abby's request, had driven past it the previous night. That part of town looked different to Abby in daylight, but eventually she saw a large wrought-iron gate and the access road to the graves. It didn't take long to find Will's, which, as Marty had said it would be, was near the back of the cemetery on the right. The many baskets of flowers around his grave were also a give-away. The plot was shaded by mature maple trees, or would have been if most of their leaves hadn't already fallen, covering the ground with a russet blanket.

When Abby read the words inscribed on the headstone, *An Honest Man Is The Noblest Work Of God*, her eyes filled with tears. She wished she had done a better job of keeping in touch with the man who had done so much for her.

ᇬᏆᏇᏇᏆᇬ

When Abby pulled into Maltby's parking lot at ten twenty-five, she noticed that the Chevrolet Spark was gone. Inquiring inside the store, she learned that Jamie Lang hadn't been feeling well and had left about ten minutes earlier. "Damn," she said as she headed back to her car. "That woman is definitely trying to avoid me."

This time, there were only three vehicles in the veterinary clinic's parking lot. The woman and her collie were at the counter, the dog straining at his leash as his owner paid the bill.

Abby sat down on a bench across from an old man in bib overalls who was holding a calico cat on his lap. As soon as the woman and her dog left, Abby approached the counter.

The black woman was making notations on an oversized, well-used note card. "Won't be long," she said without looking up. "You can bring your pet in unless he or she doesn't get along with cats."

"I'm not here about a pet," Abby said in a low voice,

hoping to keep their conversation private. "I need to talk to you about Will Ramsdell."

The woman gave her a suspicious look. "You from the Sheriff's office?"

Abby shook her head. "Will was a friend of mine. I understand there was a problem between Dr. Hux and Ned Copeland that was serious enough Will had to intervene. I'd like to know what that was all about."

"You sound like police to me."

"Actually, I'm a reporter, but that's not why I'm here. Like I said, Will was a friend, a really good friend. I'd like to make sure his murderer gets what he deserves."

The black woman glanced at the old man and his cat. Then she focused again on Abby. "You want the short version or the long one?"

"Excuse me?"

"What Mr. Ramsdell did for Dr. Hux is a long story. I can cut to the chase now if you like. Or you can wait until Dr. Hughes and I finish up, which will take another half hour or so. It all depends on how much time you've got and how much detail you want me to go into."

"I've got an appointment in Hawthorne at two," Abby said. "Before I drive over there, I'd like to reach some kind of conclusion about Copeland, whether to rule him out as a suspect in Will's murder or add him to my list. I'd appreciate anything and everything you can tell me in that regard."

"Then have a seat. I'll be with you soon as I can." The woman finished filling out the note card and inserted it into a small wooden file. "Sorry to keep you waiting, Mr. Norfleet," she said, turning to the old man on the bench. "You can bring Oda May on back now."

Chapter 7

*A*s he drove the fifty miles that separated his daughter's dairy farm from Wisteria, Walter Hux felt more forlorn than he had ever been in his life. It wasn't that he missed all the activity of the last few days—a steady stream of visitors to the farm; Bonnie volunteering his services to look at a neighbor's ailing cow, another's lethargic horse, a third's sluggish pig; her husband requiring his assistance in Culpeper, not once but twice, to help with supplies. Even his grandchildren had gotten in the act, hauling him around to see this friend's pony, that one's litter of kittens, another's pet rabbit, as though a veterinarian of over forty years needed contact with animals every waking minute. A month earlier he would have relished the activity. Not now. It just made him all the more depressed.

"Next time you invite me for a quiet weekend in the country, you might consider holding the festivities at Richmond International Airport," he had told his daughter, trying to hide his despondency behind a veil of humor. "It won't be nearly as hectic there."

Bonnie smiled. "I know how unhappy you've been lately, Dad. I was hoping all the hustle and bustle would lift your spirits."

"It did," he lied. "I feel better about things now."

She gave him a strong goodbye hug. "You'll feel a lot better still. Remember what Mom used to say—time heals all wounds."

Not this one, he wanted to tell her, disappointed that she hadn't grasped the enormity of the incident or the intensity of his reaction to it. But how could she? Bonnie had her own family to think about, her own life to lead. It wasn't like she'd been there to witness the atrocity, or could have done anything about it.

Will Ramsdell had been there, though. And as Wisteria's police chief, he could and should have done something. Will had watched him pull back the blood-soaked blanket, had seen the result of the cruelty first hand. "What kind of warped son-of-a-bitch would do that?" the police chief had muttered, turning away.

"Who else but Ned Copeland—in retaliation for closing down his puppy mill?"

Will had nodded. "You're probably right. He waited just long enough so it wouldn't be obvious."

"That puppy was alive when I found him, Will. He'd been skinned and left on a cold concrete slab. You can't let Copeland get away with that."

"I'll do what I can, Walt. But Ned's a shrewd one. He's probably covered his tracks."

"Aren't you going to arrest him?"

"I will if I can come up with evidence linking him to the crime."

"What if you can't?"

"It'll depend on how he reacts when I question him. If he says something incriminating, I'll lock him up. But if he denies everything and doesn't slip up in the process, there's not much I can do."

A week went by and the police chief admitted he was no closer to arresting Ned Copeland than on the day Dr. Hux had reported the crime. "I haven't found a soul who saw anything suspicious at Ned's place or at the clinic," he said. "I haven't even located anyone who lost, sold, or gave away a German shepherd puppy."

"Why don't you lock him up anyway, Will? You know as well as I do he's guilty."

"What I know and what can be proved are two different things. Without some hard evidence, the county prosecutor would laugh me out of his office. There's other possibilities, Walt. Someone you had a run-in with years ago could've done it. So could a person you don't even know, some sicko who gets his kicks from doing things twisted and sadistic."

"But why leave that puppy on the clinic steps unless the act was directed at me?"

"Somebody might've found it and wanted to help but was scared you'd think he was the one responsible."

"It didn't happen that way and you know it."

"Maybe. But that's a reasonable explanation if you're looking at it from the outside, which is what a judge would do. An arrest wouldn't hold up just because he's got a motive and a bad reputation. Sure, I'm convinced he's guilty. I knew him in his younger days when he did a lot of things decent folks don't do. He was mean then and I doubt he's mellowed with age. I know how much this bothers you, Walt, but my hands are tied. This kind of crime is almost impossible to prosecute. You need a witness or a confession. Unfortunately, I haven't been able to come up with either."

"Then I guess I'll just have to take care of this myself."

"Oh? What exactly have you got in mind?"

"You'll see."

എഇഩ

That afternoon Dr. Hux drove to Ned Copeland's house

on the edge of Wisteria, parking behind a white Cadillac convertible, a model nearly ten years old but in immaculate condition. Hearing the periodic pop of a .22 rifle as he got out of his own car, the veterinarian walked around back where he found Copeland taking target practice at tin cans sitting atop wooden posts, all that remained of what once had been a large dog pen. He was a wiry man with a ruddy complexion and salt and pepper hair pulled back in a ponytail.

"Well, well, would you look who's here? You paying a social call, Doc, or checking to see if I'm still in the puppy business?"

"I'm here to find out if you're responsible for the one left on my clinic steps."

"Couldn't have been me. Hasn't been a pup around here since you and Ramsdell closed me down."

"The one I'm talking about was skinned alive."

"You don't say. Well, I wouldn't know anything about that."

"I think you do. I think you know plenty."

Copeland raised the rifle to his shoulder and squeezed the trigger. A tin can tumbled from a post, skipping end over end along the ground. "If I was the one responsible, I'd be a fool to say so, now wouldn't I? If you think it was me, fine. Next time, maybe you'll think twice before bringing somebody up on a bullshit cruelty charge." In a quick, fluid motion, Ned cocked the rifle and fired again, sending another can spinning to the ground. "Deer season's just around the corner, Doc. You oughta get yourself a gun and try being a real man for a change. Hunting's a lot more wholesome than minding other people's business."

"Funny you'd say that. I am going to buy a gun. But it's not deer I plan to shoot."

"Oh? What then?"

"You."

"Me! Because of what happened to that pup?"

"You're going to answer for that, one way or the other. Turn yourself in and accept whatever punishment a judge gives you, or I'll administer the punishment I think you deserve."

The incredulity on Ned's face turned to amusement. "You expect me to confess because of a dumb-ass threat like that?"

"I don't expect anything. I'm just telling you what I'll do if you don't confess."

"Don't you know it's against the law to go around threatening people, Doc? I could have you arrested."

"Cruelty to animals is against the law too, but that didn't stop you. You're going to pay for what you did. Either the court will punish you or I will. It's your choice. You've got exactly one week to decide which it's going to be."

Ned guffawed. "You wouldn't know which end of a gun to shoot. If you ever did figure it out, you wouldn't have the balls to pull the trigger. You think you can bluff a confession out of me, you're crazier than a goddamn loon."

Dr. Hux turned and walked away. Raucous laughter followed him all the way to his car.

附

The following afternoon Will Ramsdell stopped by the veterinary clinic. "What's this I hear about you threatening to kill Ned Copeland?"

"I'm glad he's finally taking me seriously."

"Actually, I don't think he is. One of my officers heard him laughing about it last night at the Shamrock. You're not serious, are you, Walt?"

"I'm dead serious. One way or the other, Copeland is going to pay."

"Killing him would be a mighty stiff punishment, don't you think?"

"Not for the suffering he caused. But I gave him a choice. I'm willing to let a judge decide his punishment."

"A judge can't do that if Ned doesn't confess, and you know he won't."

"Then I'll be the one to punish him."

Will shook his head in disbelief. "What's gotten into you, Walt? You're the last person I'd expect to hear talking like this."

"The bastard went too far this time—way too far. He can't be allowed to get away with it."

"Then make him pay some other way. Hire somebody to break his knee cap or trash that Cadillac he takes such pride in. But don't kill him."

"If I did something like that, the cycle would just start all over again. You saw what he's capable of. Next time, his vengeance could be directed at my daughter or one of my grandchildren. I'm not willing to play that kind of game."

"But you are willing to throw you own life away just to see him get punished? That doesn't make sense."

"I can forgive and forget a lot of things, Will, but not the agony Copeland caused that puppy. It was a monstrous act that simply can't go unpunished. I couldn't live with myself if it did."

Will gazed at the wall calendar behind the veterinarian's desk, a flock of Canada geese flapping across a cold November sky. "Give me two weeks," he said, glancing at his friend, then back at the calendar. "Actually, I might need a little longer. Give me until November twenty-third."

"For what?"

"Bringing Ned Copeland to justice."

"And just how do you plan on doing that?"

"I've got something in mind. It'll take until the Sunday before Thanksgiving to see if I can pull it off. You'll give me that long, won't you, Walt?"

Dr. Hux looked at the calendar. "I gave Copeland a week. I suppose another few days won't matter in the scheme of things. But if he isn't locked up by the twenty-third..."

"Then do whatever you have to do. Keep in mind I'll have to arrest you, assuming Ned doesn't kill you first."

ೞೞ

The next morning Dr. Hux bought a .32 caliber pistol and two boxes of cartridges at a gun shop in Hawthorne. That afternoon found him taking target practice in a secluded area next to the Shenandoah River, firing at stumps and tree trunks along the bank and rocks out in the water. Although he hoped Will would find some way to put Copeland behind bars, he doubted it would happen. He really didn't think Will had a plan. He's just stalling for time. He'll put me off as long as he can, hoping I'll back down. Well, it's not going to happen.

The days passed quickly, each seeming to blend with the next. Dr. Hux spent much of his free time taking target practice. Since his mind was made up, there was no agonizing over whether he had made the right decision. The only thing left to do was wait for Will's self-imposed deadline. In the meantime he would get his veterinary practice caught up and become as proficient as possible at using his pistol.

Near the end of the second week, Dr. Hux's daughter called to invite him to spend the weekend at her farm, telling him they wouldn't be able to have him Thanksgiv-

ing day this year because she and her husband had won an all-expense-paid trip to Dallas, plus tickets to the Cowboys' game.

"Thanksgiving in Dallas? When did you and Bob ever give a hoot about football?"

"We rarely go anywhere, Dad. This trip is exactly what we need. It's completely paid for. Our neighbors have agreed to take care of the farm while we're gone."

In the end Dr. Hux accepted the invitation. Actually, he was glad it had worked out this way, knowing that if everything went as expected, he wouldn't be spending this or any other Thanksgiving with Bonnie.

On Thursday, he called Tim Hughes, the young Hawthorne vet with whom he had an agreement that each would take care of the other's practice in case of an emergency. He asked if Tim considered their agreement to cover a situation where one of them was incapacitated for a lengthy period of time, possibly permanently.

"Of course, I'd look after your practice until somebody could come in full time. I hope you'd do the same for me. You're not having health problems, are you, Walt?"

"No, but at my age you never know what might happen."

Dr. Hux didn't see or talk to Will Ramsdell that week, but Friday morning, two days before the deadline set by his friend, he did catch a glimpse of Ned Copeland. As they passed each other near the post office, Ned tooted the horn of his Cadillac. Then, momentarily taking both hands from the steering wheel, Ned pointed with his right index finger toward his left wrist. Dr. Hux couldn't tell if the son of a bitch was wearing a watch or not, but he was definitely sporting a smug grin.

It was dusk when Walter Hux got back to Wisteria from his daughter's farm. He stopped at the clinic to check on the animals, finding them well cared for, their cages clean and their food and water in abundant supply. He had a good crew at the clinic, and he regretted that he probably would never work with any of them again. Since they all knew about the skinned puppy, he felt they would understand.

He checked his answering machine in case Will had tried to contact him. There were no messages. To be on the safe side, Dr. Hux called the police station, identified himself to the officer who answered, and asked if Ned Copeland had been arrested.

"No, sir," the young man replied. "Why would we arrest him?"

"That's all I need to know." Ending the call, Dr. Hux went to the hall closet where he kept his pistol. He loaded bullets in the chamber and headed for his car.

Driving through Wisteria, he thought about his wife, knowing she would have been appalled at what he was planning to do. "Same old Walt," he imagined her saying. "When will you learn to cut folks some slack and concentrate on things you can actually do something about?"

"There's a difference between folks and monsters," he replied. "There comes a time when monsters need to pay."

"You'll be the one who pays. Give it up for Bonnie's sake, if not for yours."

"She's a big girl now. She'll be all right, regardless of what I do."

When his wife didn't say any more, Dr. Hux felt that this time he had bested her, a rare occurrence since she was such a wise, level-headed person. He felt a sense of accomplishment until struck by the realization of what he'd been doing, something he'd done on a regular basis for the past several years, talking to and for a dead woman. "Maybe Copeland's right," he muttered. "Maybe I am crazy as a loon."

He thought of Bonnie, wishing there had been more

opportunity the past two days for them to talk. But there was nothing he could have told her, no way he could have prepared her for what he was about to do. She probably wouldn't have understood anyway, any more than Will had. A really first-rate police chief wouldn't have tolerated Copeland's atrocity. He'd have found a way to make the bastard pay.

"You don't understand," Dr. Hux said in frustration, his words directed at his wife, Will, even his daughter. "This is a wrong of such magnitude it has to be redressed. If the law won't do it, then somebody has to, even if it means paying the price." The price, he knew, would be his own life or prison, depending on whether his aim was good and he got off the first shot.

It was dark as he approached Ned Copeland's house. When he realized the lights were off and the Cadillac was gone, he felt both relief and disappointment, the two conflicting emotions leaving him in a quandary as to what to do next. Pulling into the empty driveway, he decided to wait. Better to get it over with tonight, he decided. To-morrow I might not have the nerve.

As he waited, Dr. Hux thought of his grandchildren. Being cut off from them, assuming he survived, would be a terrible punishment. He'd miss them sorely. Of course, he'd miss the animals too, the creatures that had been a source of enrichment for as long as he could remember. They had, in fact, been the one thing since his wife's death that made him feel connected to whatever divine or positive force might exist in the universe. At sixty-eight, he wasn't nearly ready to call it quits. As far as he could tell, his skills as a veterinarian hadn't diminished, nor had the pleasure he took from seeing a sick or hurt animal get better. He'd planned to keep practicing as long as his health allowed.

"What about the creatures?" he heard his wife ask. "You'll be abandoning them, you know."

"I've made arrangements for them to be taken care of until Wisteria can get another vet." He wasn't altogether pleased with his reply, but it would have to do.

As the evening wore on, Dr. Hux twice got out of his car and walked around, trying to stay warm and keep from getting stiff. He considered starting the car so he could turn on the heater but quickly rejected that idea. The last thing he wanted was for Copeland to find him dead of carbon monoxide poisoning.

During his wait, Dr. Hux had seen only four vehicles, three of them heading away from Wisteria. None had slowed down. Around nine-thirty, lights from a fifth vehicle appeared, and this one slowed as it approached the house. Dr. Hux was surprised at how calmly he watched the car pull into the driveway. It'll be over soon, he thought with only a modicum of anxiety. Headlights curtailing his vision, he picked up the pistol from the seat, opened the door, and got out.

As he started to take aim, Dr. Hux realized the car was neither white nor a Cadillac. It was a black Ford with a flasher on top. Quickly he lowered the pistol, trying to hide it behind his right leg.

"You better put that thing away before you hurt yourself," a familiar voice called.

"What're you doing here, Will?"

"If you really want to put more holes in Ned Copeland, you'll find him at Hawthorne General."

"More holes? What're you talking about?"

"He's recuperating from a deer slug in the butt. Somebody tried to make a trophy out of him. Get in and I'll tell you about it."

After Dr. Hux got in the car, Will explained that yesterday was the opening day of deer season and that Ned

Copeland had gone hunting as usual, only to end up get-ting shot himself. "Obviously whoever did it had a score to settle because he or they also shot up Ned's car. There's so many holes in it, I doubt it's going to live."

"Who did it?"

"Beats the heck out of me. Nobody saw a thing, in-cluding Ned."

Something about the way his friend spoke reminded Dr. Hux of a little boy describing in anonymous terms a prank he had successfully pulled off.

"You did it, didn't you, Will?"

"What makes you think that?"

"The way you're talking. You can't lie worth a damn."

"Well, if I hadn't, you would have…or more likely gotten yourself killed trying."

"But you didn't kill him. It sounds like he'll recover."

"I didn't intend to kill him. But he'll be laid up a while. And he won't ever drive that Cadillac again. That'll hurt him more than any bullet wound. Ned loved that car, and he'll never be able to replace it. Hell, after the medical bills he's going to have, he'll be lucky to afford a bicycle."

For the first time in what seemed like years, Dr. Hux felt like laughing. The noise started low in his throat, sounding at first like a cough or an angry squirrel chat-tering, but it soon grew louder and more natural. Will joined in, and the car fairly rocked with laughter.

"How about handing over that pistol, Walt. You won't be needing it anymore, will you?"

"I might when Copeland gets out of the hospital. He'll think I'm responsible for what happened to him."

"I've already discussed that with him. I told him you were the first person I suspected, so I checked into your whereabouts and found there's about thirty people who place you in the Culpeper area at the time of the shooting. I also explained there's a lot of folks around here who

think he's responsible for what happened to that puppy. Any one of 'em could've shot him. I think he'll leave you alone."

Dr. Hux recalled the hectic pace of activity at his daughter's farm, all the people he'd been in contact with during the visit.

"You even got Bonnie involved in this, didn't you?"

"I didn't want Ned to have any reason to think it was you. There was also the possibility I could've killed him. If that happened, I wanted you to have an airtight alibi."

"How'd you manage to get close enough to wound him without being seen?"

"You forget I was a darn good hunter at one time, Walt. Back before you shamed me into giving up the sport. A lot of folks used to say I was the best shot in the county." Will chuckled. "Turns out I still am."

ⓔⓢⓔⓢ

When Leona Figgins finished explaining how Will Ramsdell had interceded on behalf of Walter Hux, there were tears in Abby's eyes. For a while, all she could do was sit silently next to Leona on the waiting-room bench and marvel at the lengths Will had gone for a friend.

"Guess it's time I checked on the critters," Leona said and got up from the bench.

Abby also stood up. "Does Ned Copeland still live around here?" she asked.

"Last I heard he was the caretaker at that hunt club a few miles east of town. Holly Oak I think they call it. If it turns out Copeland did kill Mr. Ramsdell, I hope you nail his sorry ass to the wall."

"I'll do what I can," Abby said and extended her hand. "Thank you for sharing all that with me, Leona. I really appreciate it. Good luck with your search for a new vet.

Whoever he turns out to be, he's got a tough act to follow."

"You got that right." Leona shook Abby's hand. "They don't make 'em like Dr. Hux anymore—Mr. Ramsdell either."

Chapter 8

A tall, angular man who wore tinted glasses and whose dark brown hair was parted on the right, Quentin Grice reminded Abby of someone. After she introduced herself and explained that she had been a friend of Will Ramsdell's, it came to her. The sheriff looked like a scruffy version of North Carolina's 74th governor, who, for good reason as far as Abby was concerned, had been defeated in his attempt at re-election.

For a moment she found herself wondering if this was the same person, or possibly a close relative. Stranger things had happened. She was on the verge of asking if Grice was kin to the ex-governor when he nodded toward a semi-circle of folding chairs in front of his large mahogany desk and told her to have a seat.

"What exactly is on your mind, Ms. Burlew?"

"I'd—uh—I'd like to know if you've made any progress in—in identifying Will's killer." Sitting down in the chair directly in front of the sheriff, Abby told herself that she had to be sharper than this. Focus, girl. Focus on the reason you're here.

Grice eased himself into the leather swivel chair behind the desk. "That would depend on how you define *progress*. If you mean are there any suspects in the case, the answer is *yes*."

"I'd like to know who they are."

The sheriff smiled. "You should know I can't release that kind of information. If for no other reason, it could hamstring our investigation."

Abby nodded. "Actually, I probably have a good idea who your suspects are. There's one in particular I wanted to ask you about. From what I learned today, Ned Copeland should be at the top of your list."

Grice chuckled. "So, you've been in the area all of one day and you've already solved Will's murder. That's mighty fast work, Ms. Burlew. You're to be commended."

"I gather you don't think Copeland killed Will?"

"I didn't say that. I know there's history between those two, including the fact that Will came to Walter Hux's rescue when the good doctor got himself in a bit of a fix. I assume that's what you learned today."

"It is," Abby said, not sure how she felt about Grice's already knowing this. One thing she was sure about—she didn't like the sheriff's supercilious attitude.

"It's amazing someone could pull that off without Copeland actually knowing who did it, don't you think?" Grice continued. "The question is did he finally figure it out and extract his revenge. The fact that Ramsdell was killed on the first day of deer season suggests maybe he did."

"Then why isn't Copeland behind bars?"

"Same reason he wasn't arrested for dumping that skinned puppy at the veterinary clinic—a lack of evidence. Right now there's not enough evidence to arrest Ned Copeland or anyone else. Murder cases aren't always solved as fast as people might like, Ms. Burlew. But eventually most do get solved. Sixty-five percent, as a matter of fact. I'm confident Will's murder fits that category."

At least the smug son of a bitch doesn't think it was a

hunting accident, Abby thought. "Will helped me with my first investigative assignment," she said, working hard to maintain her cool. "He actually saved my life in the process."

"I can appreciate that. But other than assuring you that my deputies and I are doing all we can to catch his killer, I'm not sure what I can do for you."

"You can start by telling me if Ned Copeland is your primary suspect. And if he is, how close you are to making an arrest."

Grice picked up a ball point pen from the top of his desk and seemed to study it. "I'll start by reiterating that it's inappropriate for me to share that kind of information with the press, Ms. Burlew."

"I'm here as friend of Will's, Sheriff, not as a reporter. I want to make sure his murder doesn't slip through the cracks. He meant a lot to me."

Returning the pen to the desk, Grice leaned back in his chair and cupped his hands behind his head, interlocking his fingers. "Tell you what I'll do. Since you've apparently done some investigating on your own, how about sharing with me who else besides Ned Copeland is on your suspect list."

"Why would you want to know that?"

"It's remotely possible you've come up with something my deputies and I might have missed. If you tell me who your suspects are, I'll tell you whether each is or isn't on my list. Can you live with that?"

Abby wasn't sure what to make of the sheriff's proposal. "I suppose so," she said, her instincts telling her to be wary of this man and whatever deal he might be offering.

"This is strictly off the record, right?" Grice asked, leaning forward again.

"If you want it to be."

"I do. Who's the next person on your list behind Ned Copeland?"

"Ben Ramsdell."

"His motive?"

"Inheriting his father's estate."

Grice nodded. "From all indications, Ben was a good kid until the drugs got hold of him. Do I think he could have killed his father? I do, especially since Ben probably didn't know he was not the beneficiary of Will's estate. I assume you know who the beneficiary turned out to be?"

"Yes—Pinecroft."

"Then the Langs must be on your suspect list too?"

"They are."

"Who else is on it?"

"Wardell Tharp."

The sheriff raised an eyebrow. "May I ask why?"

"Will had already put him in jail once and would have done it again if the situation called for it. Am I correct in assuming you knew Will had been offered his old job back and had agreed to take it?"

"Yes. And I can't argue with your assessment of Tharp. I haven't ruled him out either. Who else is on your suspect list?"

Abby wondered if the sheriff was benefiting more from their little exercise than she was, though she couldn't imagine what good it would do him since all her suspects, aside from Ned Copeland, should have been obvious. "Mel Taggart," she said, not sure why she had left him for last. "With Will out of the picture, the police chief's job would probably go to Mel."

Grice nodded again. "You've done your homework, Ms. Burlew. I haven't ruled out Mel Taggart as a suspect either. Is there anybody else on your list?"

"Not at the moment. Is there anybody else on yours?"

The sheriff chuckled. "That wasn't part of our agreement. I will say that for all intents and purposes our lists are the same. I'm telling you this because I don't want you thinking we're working at cross purposes. We're not. My office won't rest until whoever Will Ramsdell's murderer turns out to be is behind bars."

"I'm glad you feel that way," Abby said, not altogether sure the man did. "I'd like to touch base periodically to check on your progress. Do you have a problem with that?"

"Not at all. How long will you be staying in the area?"

Wondering if the question was calculated or simply an innocent pleasantry, Abby paused before replying. "I haven't decided."

"Well, regardless of how long you're here, I hope you won't contact Ned Copeland or do anything that might tip him off that he's under suspicion. The same goes for Ben Ramsdell, Wardell Tharp, and Mel Taggart. You haven't talked to any of those people, have you?"

"No."

"I hate to sound melodramatic, but contacting any of them could make my job a lot harder. If you'll agree to stay away from them, I'll notify you as soon as there's a break in the case."

Yeah, right, Abby thought, having decided she wouldn't trust this man as far as she could throw the governor of New Jersey. "You don't have a problem if I talk to the Langs?"

"I'd be surprised if you haven't already. To know as much as you do, you must have communicated with Marty Stith. By the way, I'm a little surprised you didn't list Marty as a suspect. Didn't he tell you he's part owner of Pinecroft?"

"He did, but that doesn't make him a suspect as far as I'm concerned."

"Well, in fairness to him, he seems like a standup guy,

not the sort you'd expect to commit murder. Neither is Mel Taggart or Ben Ramsdell, for that matter, but I hope I can count on you not to mention anything about this case to either of them or to Wardell Tharp or Ned Copeland. Will you give me your word on that?"

No way, Abby said to herself, a plan beginning to take shape in her mind. "Sure," she said and crossed her fingers. "By the way, I'd like to do some early Christmas shopping while I'm here. Is there a Toys R Us in the area?"

"There's one right here in Hawthorne."

"What about a Radio Shack?"

"Sorry. Ours closed quite a while ago."

"How about a Staples?"

Grice nodded. "We do have one of them. It's in the same mall as Toys 'R' Us."

"Then I should be in business," Abby said and stood up. She felt good about the fact that, after a shaky start, she had focused herself on the task at hand and, as far as she could tell, hadn't done her investigation any harm in the process. "Would you mind giving me directions to that mall, Sheriff?"

"I'll be glad to."

Chapter 9

Most of the time, Ned Copeland had the run of the place—the banquet hall, the spacious kitchen, the massive living room replete with fieldstone fire place and large-screen TV, even the upstairs bedrooms normally reserved for hunters—as long as he picked up after himself and kept things clean and neat. During debutante parties, wedding receptions, and other social events hosted by Holly Oak members, however, he was expected to confine himself to his living quarters, which consisted of a small bedroom, an even smaller utility room, and a bathroom, all located at the rear of the lodge just off the kitchen. He could still use the kitchen, after first making sure none of the club members or their guests needed it.

Ned understood the rules and abided by them. Whatever resentment he might have felt about the arrangement was more than offset by the fact that he could hunt the two thousand acres of property to his heart's content. Some members considered him one of the more knowledgeable outdoorsmen around and often asked his advice about the best places to look for deer, coon, rabbit, pheasant, wild turkey, whatever might be in season at the time. A few even asked him to be their guide and tipped him handsomely for his services.

An even more important advantage to being Holly

Oak's caretaker was the fact that it wasn't a full-time job, thereby allowing Ned to pursue what he considered his true calling. Although intensely proud of his accomplishments in that regard, he never mentioned them to anyone, not even his girlfriend Bernadette Fossum, a nurse at Hawthorne General Hospital who viewed the world the same way he did. He explained his periodic absences from the area as visits to an ailing sister in Tennessee.

Ned spent much of his free time in his utility room surfing the internet. Though tiny, the room contained exactly what he needed: a computer, a desk, a recliner he used mainly when reading, and a bookcase filled with hardcovers and paperbacks. In this room he also kept a Browning ten-gauge shotgun and a Remington deer rifle with a cantilevered scope mount. His pistol, a Glock he'd purchased as a young man, rested in the top drawer of his bedside table.

Most of Ned's books pertained in some way to military history. Those that didn't included *The Turner Diaries, The Federal Siege at Ruby Ridge, A Brief History of the Ku Klux Klan,* and treatises on David Koresh, Timothy McVeigh, and Buford Furrow. On the wall above his bookcase was a fading caricature of Janet Reno attacking a mother and child with a flaming sword. On the opposite wall was a plaque with his favorite Randy Weaver quote: "My job is to be a burr under their saddle until the day I die."

After the FBI killed Randy's wife and son in 1992, the diminutive white separatist became a hero to Ned, more than just a kindred spirit. In 2004 Ned had the privilege of meeting him at a gun and knife show at the National Guard Armory in Roanoke. He bought one of Randy's $15 T-shirts bearing the phrase "Freedom At Any Cost" and an autographed copy of his second book *Vicki, Sam and America*. A year later, though, after learning that Randy disapproved of Timothy McVeigh's bombing of the Albert E. Murrah Building in Oklahoma City and that he no longer believed God loved white people more than any other group, Ned lost respect for the man. And more recently, when he found out that Randy had actually become an atheist, Ned felt betrayed. He could forgive a lapse in judgment concerning Tim McVeigh, but turning his back on the Almighty was inexcusable.

Although Sunday mornings usually found Ned sitting next to Bernadette Fossum in a pew at the First Baptist Church in Hawthorne, his heart lay with the Christian Identity sect because of its belief that white people are God's chosen and all others are doomed to hell. Eric Rudolph, the person he most admired after Randy Weaver's fall from grace, was a member of that sect. The fact that Eric had been captured while dumpster diving behind a food market in western North Carolina didn't sit well with Ned, but that didn't detract from Eric's overall accomplishments. Like Tim McVeigh, Eric was a true crusader, striking blows against a corrupt, overreaching government and the unholy practices it tolerated. The one blemish in his otherwise exemplary record of service in God's army, as far as Ned was concerned, was his failure to keep out of the government's clutches.

Quite a few years ago, Ned had followed with great interest the exploits of Ralph "Bucky" Phillips, who had escaped from jail in upstate New York and for almost six months had thumbed his nose at the authorities, shooting three police officers and stealing eighteen vehicles in the process.

Although Bucky was more of a career criminal than a crusader, Ned had pulled for him anyway, hoping he'd avoid capture indefinitely. Bucky's thirst for freedom seemed so intense that Ned figured the man would never be taken alive, and yet, when cornered by police near the

New York-Pennsylvania border, Bucky had given up without a shot being fired.

Ned long ago had vowed that such a fate would never befall him. If the time came when capture was inevitable, he, like another of his heroes Benjamin Nathaniel Smith, would turn the gun on himself.

Ned ate most of his evening meals at Sullivan's Diner in Wisteria, but tonight he fixed himself a T-bone steak and ate it in Holly Oak's living room, watching Fox News on TV and thinking about Bernadette Fossum, hoping she would drop by after her shift and spend the night. Although she was nowhere near the prettiest woman he'd ever slept with, Ned knew a man his age couldn't be but so choosy, and Bernie did have a decent figure for someone in her sixties.

After Ned washed, dried, and put away his dishes, he retired to his computer in the utility room. For a while, he read some of the more recent threads on his favorite gun forum and checked out the latest on the NRA's website. Finally he googled a name he had lately come to equate with the anti-Christ. He was about to read a review of this man's latest book when he heard the telephone ring. Taking his time, he returned to the living room and picked up the receiver.

"Is this Ned Copeland?" an unfamiliar raspy voice asked, a woman who seemed in the grips of a bad cold.

"Yes, ma'am."

"I'm calling to let you know that Sheriff Grice has you in his crosshairs," the woman said. "He plans to stick you with Will Ramsdell's murder."

Feeling his heart begin to race, Ned took a deep breath and slowly exhaled. "Who's this?" he asked, not as calmly as he would have liked.

The woman coughed. "It's the message that's important, not the messenger. Grice needs to arrest someone.

He knows you and Ramsdell go way back, so it looks like you're it."

"Why are you telling me this?"

The woman cleared her throat. "I'm on your side, Mr. Copeland. I'm just hoping you can stay out of Grice's clutches. Do you think you'll be able to do that?"

Ned set the phone back on its cradle. He began pacing the room, wondering who had made the call and why. Was it that female deputy of Grice's disguising her voice and trying to scare him into doing something stupid? But what? Incriminate himself? Make a run for it? If Grice really was planning to arrest him for Ramsdell's murder, why provide advanced notice?

Maybe the call was legit, Ned thought. But if so, what was the point of the warning? There was no evidence that needed destroying. There was no reason to contact a lawyer prior to getting arrested. It had to be something else. But what?

Finally Ned returned to his utility room, having decided there was nothing he could do about the call other than be on guard for whatever might happen. That was his normal approach to life anyway, so he didn't need to do anything differently.

Back at his computer, he decided he had better things to do than read about a blasphemous author who, in another few days, would be history.

He exited the book review and went back to AOL's home page. Spotting an article about Sarah Palin, a woman he admired and whose husband he considered a lucky man indeed, Ned clicked on it.

Maybe somebody is trying to put a burr under *my* saddle, he mused as he waited for the article to appear. If so, let 'em give it their best shot. He recalled something his father had told him early on: If you're going to dish it out, you damn well better learn to take it.

Ned had always prided himself on being able to do both.

Chapter 10

Dusk had almost faded into night when Abby parked her Corolla next to a vacant lot two blocks from Will Ramsdell's house. Turning off the engine, she took the flashlight from Marty and got out of the car, shutting the door behind her. Marty got out on the passenger side, slipping a small crowbar into his jacket pocket after he closed the door.

"If we hold hands, people won't have reason to be suspicious," he said a moment later. "They'll think we're a couple out for a walk."

"A couple of what?" Abby said, reaching for his hand. "I just thought of something, Marty. You said Dr. Hux died last summer. What was the cause of death?"

"Old age as far as I know. He was pushing ninety."

"Were you still a cop then?"

"I'd just resigned. Why?"

"I'm wondering if there was an autopsy."

"You think Dr. Hux was murdered?"

"Maybe Ned Copeland killed him *and* Will."

"That's quite a stretch, Abby. I know Will didn't suspect foul play, so there was no reason for an autopsy."

A few of the houses they passed had already been decorated for Christmas. Inside the front window of one of them, a large tree laden with multicolored lights reminded

Abby of her promise to Kevin that they would get a real tree this year instead of putting up their tired old artificial one.

"If Will had known how his own life would end a few months later, I bet he'd have been more suspicious. If we explain to Quentin Grice exactly what Leona Figgins told me, maybe we can get him to request an autopsy."

"It's a moot point, Abby. Dr. Hux was cremated."

"Really? You know that for sure?"

"Nelson Lang told me. He was at the funeral."

Most of the houses in the next block had their blinds drawn, including the colonial directly across from Will's ranch at the end of the street. As expected, Will's house was dark. When Abby saw his pickup truck in the driveway, she had the sensation that the man himself was inside the house, most likely in the basement working on his layout. All they had to do was ring the bell and wait for him to come upstairs and open the door.

Marty gripped her hand tighter. "Are you okay?"

"Yeah. Why?"

"I thought I heard you sigh."

"I was just thinking about Will."

As they approached the darkened house, Abby noticed that the street, instead of ending at a wooden barricade as she remembered from the previous year, continued for another fifty feet or so, having been expanded into a circular turn-around area. Will wouldn't have had to worry about cars turning around in his driveway anymore, she thought.

"Let's keep walking to the end of the street," Marty said. "That way, we won't be as noticeable when we cut over onto Will's property, and we'll have a better view of anyone who might be watching us."

"All right," Abby said, working hard to keep back her tears.

A minute or two later, they crossed Will's side yard and stepped up onto the stone patio at the back of his house. Abby withdrew the flashlight from her coat pocket as Marty tugged at the screen door, easily pulling it open.

"Okay, I need some light," he said in a low voice.

Positioning herself as best she could to shield the beam from potential onlookers, Abby pointed the flashlight at the door knob and turned it on, immediately noticing that the wood surrounding the locking mechanism had been splintered.

"Somebody beat us to it," Marty said. Slipping the crowbar back into his jacket pocket, he took the flashlight from Abby and slowly pushed open the door. "Be careful. Whoever did this might still be inside."

Sticking close to each other, they examined the rooms on the main floor, finding no sign of an intruder, nothing out of the ordinary. At the landing area separating the family room from the garage, Marty checked to make sure that door was locked. Then he began his descent to the basement, alternating the flashlight's beam from the steps below to those above so Abby could see where she was going. Holding the railing for support, she slowly followed him down the stairs. At the bottom she watched as he played the flashlight beam across the familiar O-gauge train layout that was so large only a portion of it was visible at any one time.

"Here's the light switch," she said. "Want me to turn it on?"

"You're sure there aren't any windows down here?"

"I don't recall any."

"All right, go ahead."

Abby flicked the switch, activating florescent bulbs in the ceiling, some of which took longer than others to brighten. Even before the layout was fully illuminated, she knew something was wrong.

"It's gone," she said and pointed toward several silver and blue passenger cars coupled together on a siding next to a Rico station. "The C and O engine. It was right there in front of those cars." Abby moved closer so she could see the tracks on the far side of the station. "It's not here, Marty. Neither is the shifter."

"The what?"

"The little steam switcher Will ran right before he let me run the C and O steamer. Everything else looks the same, but those two engines are gone."

"Whoever broke in must have stolen them. But why leave everything else?"

For the next few minutes, Abby and Marty searched the train room, looking beneath the plywood tables and examining the shelves that lined the walls. Then they checked the rest of the basement, including a combination laundry and furnace room that opened off the far end of the train room. Finding no other engines, they turned off the lights and went back upstairs.

"I figured by now we'd have a pretty good idea who killed Will," Marty said as they made their way through the darkened family room to the slightly lighter kitchen.

"We do anyway," Abby reminded him. "I'd be amazed if whatever Will put in that tender doesn't point directly at Ned Copeland."

"And I'd be amazed if it does."

"Why?"

"Just a gut feeling. I can't really explain it."

Marty opened the door to the patio and held it for Abby. Then, as she held the flashlight, he carefully closed the door, fitting it as snugly as he could into the surrounding molding. A second or two after Abby switched off the flashlight, she heard a muted click just as a beam of light caught her full in the face.

"Put your hands up, both of you, and don't make any sudden moves. You're under arrest."

The beam shifted from Abby's face to Marty's, and she was able to make out a man in a police uniform standing at the edge of the patio. He held a flashlight in one hand and a pistol in the other.

"Take it easy, Mel. It's me, Marty Stith. This is Abby Burlew. She was a friend of Will's. We can explain everything."

"I sure hope so," the cop said. "Otherwise, you've both stepped in some extremely deep shit."

Chapter 11

Nelson Lang and Maggie Calahan had been partners at the Hawthorne YMCA's bridge tournament ever since the death of Walter Hux, Nelson's previous partner. Not having a regular partner herself, Maggie had mentioned her availability at Dr. Hux's calling hours, and Nelson had agreed to give it a try. The pair quickly meshed, becoming a force to be reckoned with on Wednesday nights. The first time they won the tournament, Maggie gave him a long, wet kiss on the mouth, leaving no doubt in his mind that their chemistry extended to more than bridge.

Graham Calahan didn't play bridge and was glad, at least at first, that his wife had something to keep her occupied on Wednesdays. His law practice kept him busy, and as Wisteria's mayor, he needed an evening he could set aside for working on matters relating to the town.

Jamie Lang had mixed feelings about Nelson's new bridge partner. Sometimes she was glad she and Nelson spent Wednesday nights apart, even though he was in the company of another woman. It usually depended on his mood at the time. If Nelson was in one of his funks, it was nice to have a break from him. But if his depression seemed under control, she wanted to be with him. In spite of her husband's foul moods, Jamie did love him, and she knew she had more than enough faults of her own.

Until recently, she had never played bridge, but after Maggie became Nelson's partner, Jamie decided to learn. When Nelson showed little interest in teaching her, Marty Stith volunteered for the job, telling her that in college he spent almost as much time playing bridge as he did studying. Marty turned out to be an excellent teacher, and after a few weeks Jamie had mastered the rudiments of the game. She considered suggesting that she and Marty take on Nelson and Maggie some evening, but once she began suspecting that her husband and Maggie were having an affair, such an evening was out of the question.

℘℘℘

After making love for the second time that night, Nelson lay on his back and gazed at the motel room's ceiling, thinking about the moths that periodically got inside at Pinecroft and met their demise in the halogen lamp next to the sofa. Although he felt more alive than he had in years, he wondered if he, like the moths, might be getting a little too close to the flame.

"How was that on a scale of one to ten?" Maggie asked with a coy smile.

"An eleven. Maybe even a twelve."

She leaned over and kissed him lightly on the lips. "We're a good fit, don't you think?"

"Too good. I can't seem to get enough of you."

"Like to try for the hat trick?"

"I'm pushing fifty, Maggie, not thirty."

She leaned in even closer. "Want to bet that tired little private of yours won't make five-star general before I'm done with him?"

Later, as they lay exhausted in each other's arms, Maggie told him that she and Graham rarely had sex anymore. Their age difference—her husband was almost twenty years older than she—wasn't a factor early in their marriage, but it was now. Graham had turned into a slug, she said, no longer interested in much of anything except his law practice and politics. "He seems more like my father than my husband. You wouldn't believe how loud he snores. It's like trying to sleep next to a sawmill."

"I snore when I sleep on my back," Nelson told her. "Jamie has to turn me over all the time."

Maggie leaned closer and kissed him again. "At least you've got nice breath. I won't let Graham near me unless he's got a Tic Tac in his mouth." She grimaced and rolled over on her back. "I've got a question for you. Tell me when you're ready."

"For what?"

"My question, silly."

"I'm ready now."

"When you're snoring, who would you rather be turned over by—me or Jamie?"

The question surprised Nelson, though considering how direct and to the point Maggie tended to be, he knew it shouldn't have. "That depends," he said, trying to come up with a response he wouldn't later regret.

"On what?"

"On how things go with our respective marriages."

Through the wall Nelson heard the sound of a door opening and closing. A moment later a television set blared dramatic music followed by a woman's screaming. The sound shifted to a basketball game, then to a stand-up comedy act replete with laughter. Finally the room's occupant settled on a cop show.

"There goes the neighborhood," Maggie said, rolling her eyes. She sat up in the bed. "I think Graham and I are a lost cause. Under the right circumstances, I'd probably ask for a divorce."

"The right circumstances?"

"Sir Lancelot comes along and sweeps me off my feet. What about you? Any chance you'd ever leave Jamie?"

The roar of car engines and periodic bursts of gunfire blasted through the wall.

"I can't see myself leaving Pinecroft, especially now that we've got the money to make it into a really good course."

"Does Jamie have to be there for that to happen?"

"She's part owner."

"What if you bought her out?"

"There wouldn't be enough money left over to improve the course."

Maggie gave him a knowing look. "Yeah, there would," she said, her voice loud enough to compete with the sound of screeching tires and gunfire.

Nelson raised himself up on an elbow and looked at her. "And where exactly would that money come from?"

"Graham and I aren't exactly paupers, Nelson. If we divorce, I'd be entitled to my fair share of our assets." Maggie brushed a strand of hair from her eyes, hooking it behind her right ear. "If it so happens that I end up marrying a certain golf course owner, the lucky schmuck would have access to enough working capital to do whatever he wanted with his course."

"Schmuck, eh? I thought you were looking for Sir Lancelot."

Maggie climbed on top of Nelson, pulled herself to a sitting position, and pressed her thighs against his. She leaned down and kissed him, her breasts bobbing against his chest, her hair dangling in his face. "I think Guinevere has made her intentions clear. Just in case she hasn't, let me put it another way. Eventually I'd like to fuck your eyes out in our own bed, not in some noisy Motel 6."

She kissed him again and rolled over on her side of the

bed. "The ball's in your court, Lance. I don't need an answer now, or even want one. But eventually it's going to come down to my original question. Would you rather be lying next to me or Jamie in bed, whether or not you happen to be snoring?"

The television set was blaring a commercial, some jerk screaming his head off about a product's benefits. Nelson didn't hear a word of it. The moth, he thought, was flying dangerously close to the flame.

Chapter 12

The jail cell had whitewashed cinderblock walls, a cot, a toilet, and one window, too high up for Abby to see anything but a few dim stars. As she sat on the edge of the cot, she thought about her telephone conversation with Ned Copeland, which hadn't gone nearly as well as she had hoped, mainly because he had hung up before she could get him to say anything incriminating.

Now that her telephonic approach had failed, Abby decided that she needed a face-to-face conversation with Copeland. This, she knew, would require some serious planning and could be dangerous. At least she'd had the foresight to buy a cheap pre-paid cell phone at Staples, so her name wouldn't have appeared when Copeland answered the phone at Holly Oak. She had hoped to locate a voice-changing device at Toys 'R' Us (Kevin had wanted one for a previous birthday so he could prank his friends, a purchase Abby had nixed), but the store in Hawthorne didn't have such an item in stock. As a result, Abby had improvised by clamping her nostrils shut and lowering the pitch of her voice, thereby making it extremely unlikely, she hoped, that Copeland would recognize her voice when they met. Now if she could just come up with a credible reason for visiting Holly Oak—

The cell's door rattled open, the noise snapping Abby

back to the present. A woman wearing a rumpled sweat-shirt and baggy jeans entered the cell and closed the door behind her. She looked about forty and might have been pretty if her auburn hair hadn't been in rollers.

"I'm Tracy Taggart," she said in a tone that made it clear she was not the least bit happy to be there. "My husband wants me to search you. I'd like you to strip down to your underwear. Don't worry. I'm not going to molest you."

"What are you looking for?"

"I'll let you know that if and when I find it."

After searching Abby's clothes, the woman told her to unhook her bra and pull down her panties.

"What the hell for?"

"If it was me, that's where I'd hide something I didn't want anyone finding."

Reluctantly, Abby did as requested.

Eventually the woman thanked Abby for cooperating, mumbled something about missing *Antiques Roadshow* because of an overworked husband who damn well better get his promotion, and exited the cell.

A few minutes later, there was a knock at the cell door followed by the entrance of Mel Taggart. "Glad we could resolve this little incident without having to take any of-ficial action," he said, handing Abby her handbag and flashlight. "I'll drive you and Marty back to your car. In the future I hope you'll leave the police work to those of us with badges."

 espe

Wisteria resembled a ghost town as Abby drove through the downtown area. Except for the 7-Eleven, which had a single car in its parking lot, nothing was open. Traffic was nonexistent.

"I told Mel everything," Marty said as they passed a darkened Sullivan's Diner. "He was going to charge us with breaking and entering, which meant we'd have to spend the night in jail. Even after I showed him Will's poem and explained it, he was skeptical. He thought we might have found what we were looking for and had it on our possession."

"A Lionel train engine?"

"The message we hoped to find in the tender. I got searched thoroughly. I assume you did too."

"With a fine-tooth comb. At least Mel had the decency to have his wife do it. Did he say how he happened to be waiting for us?"

"He knew Will's house had been broken into, and he'd asked the neighbors to keep an eye on it and report anything suspicious. One of them noticed us on the patio and called the police station."

"So now Mel knows as much as we do."

"If he wasn't involved in Will's murder, that shouldn't be a problem—unless he shares what he knows with Quentin Grice, or decides to pursue the matter himself. As I see it, whoever stole those engines did it for one of two reasons. Either he knew there was something incriminating in one of them and didn't want anybody else finding it, or he needed money and figured the engines were big ticket items."

"The fact that more than one engine was stolen suggests the latter, don't you think?"

"Probably. The question is, what do we do next?"

Abby slowed for a black and white cat that almost ran in front of her car before changing his mind and scampering toward a nearby house. "Do we really need to know what's in that tender? Why can't we assume Will's message would tell us the same thing we already know—that Ned Copeland had good reason for wanting him dead?"

"I hate to keep beating a dead horse, Abby, but I don't think Copeland killed Will. Whether he did or not, I think it's important we find that engine and see exactly what Will wanted us to know. Depending on how bad the thief needs money, it'll probably show up soon, most likely at a hobby shop. It might be there already."

"So what do we do now—start calling hobby shops?"

"That's a start. I'm going to be tied up tomorrow, at least for much of the morning. Any chance you could make those calls?"

"How wide a radius should I check?"

"I'd say within forty, maybe fifty miles. There's at least one hobby shop in Hawthorne, probably several in Charlottesville. Other towns in the area might have one as well. The yellow pages would be the place to start. Look under hobbies, model trains, subjects like that. If anyone has a big silver and yellow Lionel steamer with C and O markings, ask them to hold it for us. I hate to put this all on you, Abby, but we need to get moving or somebody—Mel Taggart, Quentin Grice, or whoever else might know about Will's poem—could beat us to the punch."

The Shenandoah Inn swung into view and Abby slowed down. "Who else could possibly know about that poem?"

"Graham Calahan and/or his secretary could have read it. Or Will might have mentioned it to somebody we haven't thought of."

Abby turned into the motel's parking lot, maneuvering her car between the "VACANCY" sign and the lighted office. "I've been meaning to ask you about Jamie," she said as she pulled in next to Marty's motorcycle. "She was supposed to meet with me this morning during her break. When I got to Maltby's, her car was gone. One of the clerks said she left because she wasn't feeling well."

"She didn't say anything about being sick, and she got home at her usual time. Why was she supposed to meet with you?"

"I wanted to get her take on who might have killed Will."

Marty shook his head. "Jamie won't be able to tell you anything you don't already know, Abby. She's really stressed over Will's death as it is. If she thinks her father might have killed him, it could send her over the edge. I hope you'll hold off talking to her, at least until we find that engine. Whatever Will put in the tender could shed a whole new light on things."

More convinced than ever that Jamie had been trying to avoid her, Abby wondered why Marty was protecting someone whose actions seemed so bizarre. She decided not to press the issue. "Okay, I'll give her some space. I'll start calling hobby shops first thing in the morning."

She thought about mentioning her telephone conversation with Ned Copeland, but she couldn't imagine Marty thinking that was anything but a very bad idea. As they got out of her car, she considered inviting him in but thought better of that too. So far, the two of them seemed to have a good working relationship. No reason to jeopardize that by spending more time together than was reasonably necessary.

"I'm glad we don't have to spend the night in jail," she said as Marty climbed on his motorcycle.

"Me too. Sweet dreams, Abby. I'll call you tomorrow soon as I finish my chores."

Chapter 13

Abby slept fitfully, twice waking up with Ned Copeland on her mind, wondering how she might go about meeting him face to face. Toward morning she found herself enmeshed in one of her recurring dreams. She was playing for her high school basketball team, and her whole family was at the game—her father, her mother, and her brother Matt. Abby could hear them cheering, especially Matt, whose distinctive voice carried above all others. After stealing the ball from the opposing team's point guard and racing the length of the court for a layup, Abby glanced into the bleachers to see if she could catch Matt's eye. He wasn't there. The only person she recognized was her mother, and the woman was sitting alone. Then, as invariably happened in Abby's dream, she realized that neither Matt nor her father could possibly have been at the game: by the time she reached high school, both of them were dead.

As usual after waking from this dream, Abby felt depressed. She had planned to go jogging later in the day, but she decided to do it now, having long since learned that depression should be dealt with at its onset and that the most effective way to combat it, assuming an adjustment in medication wasn't required, was exercise. She splashed cold water on her face and spent several minutes stretching her muscles and limbering up her body. Then she put on her jogging clothes and opened the motel room's door, quickly realizing that the temperature was at least ten degrees colder than it had been yesterday morning and so foggy she couldn't even see the hill across the road. She felt an overwhelming urge to go back to bed.

One foot in front of the other, she heard a familiar voice say. *One step and then another.*

"That's easy for you to say, Dorene."

Nothing easy about it, Abby. But it can be done. It has to be done.

Shivering in the doorway for a long moment, Abby finally stepped outside and closed the door. She began pounding the pavement, hoping that once she got moving, it wouldn't take long to get warm.

She took a different route this time, away from the downtown area. She jogged through a cluster of modest ranch houses, past a park almost socked in by fog, and into the empty parking lot of an elementary school. She sped up when she reached the playground area, running around its perimeter several times before slowing to a fast walk. After catching her breath, she resumed her normal jogging speed, heading toward a part of the neighborhood that seemed less mired in fog. The cold no longer bothered her.

When she got back to the Shenandoah Inn, the sun was shining, people were out and about, and Abby's depression, like the fog, had begun to lift. A shower made her feel better still, and by the time she ordered breakfast at Sullivan's Diner, she felt almost human.

Back in her room, she called her mother to make sure things were okay at home. Then she started calling hobby shops. She began each inquiry the same way, telling the person who answered the phone that she was looking for a particular Lionel engine to give her husband for Christmas, a large silver and yellow Chesapeake & Ohio steamer. Most people she talked to were familiar with the engine, but none had it in stock. All were courteous except one woman who sounded put upon to be fielding questions so early in the day.

"What's the numba?" she asked in a Brooklyn accent before Abby could finish describing the engine.

"The what?"

"The numba. All Lionel items have a four or five digit numba."

"I didn't know that."

"Is it a Hudson, a Berkshire, a Northern?"

"All I know is it's big and it's sometimes called a yellow belly."

"We don't have it," the woman said and hung up.

After exhausting the possibilities in the immediate geographical area, Abby broadened her search, calling hobby shops in Winchester and Culpeper and finally in Charlottesville. Just as she was about to give up, she tried the Whistle Stop.

"We got that engine in yesterday," the man who answered the phone told her. "It's a beauty. Not a nick or scratch anywhere, and it runs great. It'll be the best Christmas present your husband ever got."

"Set it aside for me," Abby said and asked directions to the store. "I'll be there as soon as I can."

She called Marty's cell phone and left a message saying she had located the C&O steamer in a Charlottesville hobby shop which had taken possession of it yesterday.

Less than a minute later, Marty called her back. "Great work, Abby. Ready to go check it out?"

"The two of us?"

"Yeah. Most of my chores are done, and the rest can wait."

"Who's driving me?"

"Unless you want to ride on the back of my Harley. I'll

fill up your car with gas and buy your lunch. We'll go to the restaurant of your choice."

"Does Charlottesville have a Ritz-Carlton? Just kidding. I'll be there in twenty minutes."

℘℘℘

The Whistle Stop was sandwiched between an art gallery and a credit union in an upscale strip mall just east of the Farmington Country Club. Behind the plate glass window was a display featuring a diesel switcher in red and black Seaboard livery pulling four freight cars and an orange Atlantic Coast Line caboose around a dog-bone-shaped layout.

"I had the Santa Fe version of that engine when I was a kid," Marty said as he held the door open for Abby.

A plus-sized woman with a pleasant face and an abundance of premature white hair stood behind the counter reading a newspaper. "Mornin', folks. Can I help you find something?"

Abby told her she had called about a particular Lionel engine. "The man I talked to said he'd set it aside for me."

"That would be my husband. I'll get him."

The woman disappeared into the rear of the shop, reappearing a moment later pushing a frail-looking man in a wheelchair.

"You made good time, Ms. Burlew. I'm Jim Fergus. We talked earlier on the phone."

"Nice meeting you, Mr. Fergus. This is Marty Stith."

"Not the person you're buying the engine for, I presume."

"I'm afraid I misled you," Abby said as Marty shook hands with the man. "I am looking for the C and O engine I described, but not for the purpose of buying it. It belonged to a friend of mine who was murdered. We have reason to believe he put a note in the tender that might shed light on who killed him."

"Will Ramsdell," the man said, his voice containing more than a tinge of sadness.

"How did you know?"

"He was one of our better customers. We felt terrible when we learned he'd been killed."

"There's something fishy about this," Fergus's wife said. "If that engine belonged to Will and there's a note inside, why should we show it to them instead of the police?"

Abby explained that she worked for the *Scarboro Gazette* and that Will had helped her with her first investigative assignment. "He was a really good friend. I want to make sure his killer pays for what he did."

"I worked for Will when he was Wisteria's police chief," Marty added. "We'd rather not involve the local cops just yet because we're not sure how trustworthy or competent they are."

Fergus nodded. "What makes you think Will left a note in the tender?"

Marty withdrew a sheet of paper from his shirt pocket. "I got this in the mail yesterday. It was forwarded by the law office handling Will's estate."

Fergus chuckled as he read the poem. When he finished it, he turned to Abby. "You owned this engine at one time?"

She shook her head. "Will let me run it last year when I stopped at his house."

"Any idea why he didn't say straight out what he wanted you folks to know?"

"Will never had a lot of faith in lawyers," Marty replied. "I think he was guarding against this one being privy to information he wanted reserved for people he knew for sure he could trust."

Fergus handed the poem to his wife, whose expression grew quizzical as she read it. Finally, she nodded and gave the poem back to Marty. "I'm willing to trust these folks if you are," she said to her husband. "Want me to bring you a screwdriver?"

"A small flat head and a small Phillips. I'll also need something soft to set the tender on."

Motioning for Abby and Marty to follow him, Fergus wheeled himself toward the far end of the store, leading them down an aisle with various types and gauges of track and switches on one side and model buildings on the other. He stopped near a display case that contained HO-gauge engines, both steamers and diesels. Attached to the nearby wall were several shelves, the lower ones featuring O-gauge steamers, the upper ones O-gauge diesels. Prominently positioned in the center of the lowest shelf was a large silver and yellow Hudson in Chesapeake & Ohio livery.

"Is that the engine you're looking for?"

"It sure is," Abby said.

"Lionel made hundreds of 'em. Unless Will's had something unique about it, a noticeable scratch or some sort of discoloration, there's no way you'll know for sure if this was his. Like I said on the phone, it's in perfect condition. Except for the wheel marks, nobody would know it's been run."

The man's wife returned and handed him a towel and two screwdrivers.

"One more not-so-small favor," Fergus said.

"I know—lift down that heavy beast. Good thing you married a farmer's daughter and not some scrawny city gal."

"Just the tender. And you're right. I wouldn't trade you for any man's daughter—unless he threw in that set of Milwaukee Road passenger cars I've been lusting after."

The woman gave him a mock look of disgust. Declining Marty's offer to help, she hoisted the tender from the shelf and placed it on the towel Fergus had spread on his lap. Fergus turned the tender upside down and unscrewed the four Phillips screws holding the casting to the frame. After turning it right-side up again, he lifted off the casting, exposing a maze of circuit boards, diodes, and wires but nothing resembling a message of any kind. He held up the frame and then the casting for Marty and Abby to see.

"I'd have bet the farm there was a note inside," Marty said, clearly disappointed.

When Abby finished her examination, Fergus put the casting back onto the frame, turned the tender over, and began re-inserting the screws. "There's one other place we can look," he said. After tightening the screws, he set the tender upright on the towel and, with the end of the flat-head screw driver, gently pried off the plastic coal pile, revealing a rectangular compartment that contained a nine-volt battery. He lifted out the battery so Abby and Marty could see inside the empty cavity. "Nothing in there either. No note, no scratches or markings of any kind."

"I guess we struck out," Marty said. "Either this isn't Will's engine or somebody found the note and took it."

"I hope you don't think we did," Fergus's wife said as her husband began replacing the battery. "We wouldn't do something like that."

"I was thinking about whoever sold you the engine. I assume somebody brought it in off the street."

"That's correct," Fergus said, snapping the coal pile in place. "Kind of a scruffy-looking young guy. Early twenties maybe. He seemed nice enough. Said he had a layout as a kid but had lost interest in trains and needed the money. About the only thing unusual about him was the little finger on his right hand. It was in a splint."

Abby's attention was focused on something she had

just noticed. "That little engine on the middle shelf," she said. "Did you get it from the same guy who sold you the C and O Hudson?"

"How'd you know that?"

"It looks like the one Will ran right before he let me run the Hudson. He called it a shifter. It's a replica of one that worked the switchyard when he was a boy. His father would take him there and let him climb up on it."

"I think I know who stole those engines," Marty said, withdrawing his wallet and taking out a twenty-dollar bill. "I'm not a train buff, Mr. Fergus, or I'd buy something from you. Hopefully this will help pay for your time."

The man waved away the money. "Best payment we can get is if you catch Will's killer."

"We'll do what we can. You two have been a big help and we appreciate it." Marty turned to Abby. "Ready to go get some lunch?"

"Not quite." Abby eyes were still focused on the small steamer. "How much do you want for that shifter, Mr. Fergus? I think it was Will's favorite engine. I'd like to buy it for my son."

Chapter 14

When Graham Calahan realized how many people were in the park, he wished he had chosen a more private location for his meeting with Wardell Tharp. "Piss on it," he said and pulled his BMW into the nearest parking space. The mayor should be able to eat lunch wherever and with whomever he damn well pleases.

Holding a yellow Taco Bell bag in one hand and a capped Styrofoam cup in the other, Graham ambled across the street and into the small park. To his left an elderly couple sat at a bench feeding peanuts to a skittish gray squirrel and several pigeons. To his right a white girl with various tattoos and piercings was holding hands with a black guy whose dread locks cascaded to his shoulders. Both were watching a light brown toddler toss pennies into a concrete pool with a softly gurgling fountain in the middle.

Nearby, sitting at a picnic table on the far side of the pool, Wardell Tharp was finishing the first of his three Burger King Whoppers. A large order of French fries and two slices of cherry pie waited next to his large chocolate milkshake.

"Sorry I'm late," Graham said as he approached the table. "My last client took longer than expected."

"No problem. Just got here a couple minutes ago myself."

Graham set his lunch on the wooden table and eased his bulky frame onto the attached bench. "That spread of yours makes me wish I'd stopped at Burger King," he said as he withdrew four tacos, several packets of sauce, and a handful of napkins from his bag.

"Trade you a Whopper for those tacos," Wardell offered.

Graham poked a straw through a slit in the top of his cup. "Make it three tacos and you've got a deal. My cardiologist would have a fit, though, if he knew I ate one of those Whoppers. He told me to cut back on the cals if I wanted to reach a ripe old age."

"Can't see the sense of getting old if you don't enjoy the trip. Three tacos it is, Counsellor."

Graham slid three tacos and three packets of sauce across the table. "One thing about us ex-athletes—we know how to pack away the food."

The black man pushed a Whopper in Graham's direction. "Yeah, whole lot of talent sitting here, feeding our faces."

"You might find this hard to believe, Wardell, but back in the day I was a pretty darn good baseball player. My last two years at UVA I was the Cavaliers' starting centerfielder. Hit over three-fifty my senior year and led the team in stolen bases."

"Was that before or after Jackie broke the color barrier, Mr. Calahan?"

"I'll remember that the next time you need a lawyer." Graham reached into his shirt pocket and pulled out an envelope. "What did you find out last night?"

"Same thing I did last week and the week before that. Only difference was they skipped the bridge game this time and went straight to Motel Six."

Graham rolled his eyes. "Your money is inside," he said and handed Wardell the envelope. "Four one hundred dollar bills."

"You don't owe me that much."

"The last hundred is a retainer in case I need your services at a later date. Have you got something in writing for me?"

Wardell handed him a small folded sheet of paper. "Dates, times, and places. You want me to follow her again next week?"

"I've got all I need for now," Graham said and took a bite of his Whopper. "Damn that woman. I've worked too hard and too long to let her ruin things."

Wardell attacked a taco, practically inhaling it. "Dee-licious. Next time I get fast food, it'll be at Taco Bell. Four wouldn't cut it for me, though. I'd need at least ten."

Graham chuckled. "You remind me of what my college coach used to tell us every spring. Boys, he'd say, unless you've got the skills and the constitution of a Babe Ruth, there's three ways you can run yourself right out of baseball. You can eat your way out, you can drink your way out, or you can screw your way out."

"All three sound like a lot more fun than playing baseball," Wardell replied and guzzled some of his milkshake.

Graham ate more of his Whopper. "Wardell, if I decide I'd like a certain person to disappear, do you think you could arrange it for me?"

The big man shoved another taco into his mouth. "We talking permanent disappearance?" he asked.

"We are."

"I'm not in the murder business, Mr. Calahan."

Graham fixed him with his courtroom gaze. "You have uh…dispatched…at least one person during your illustrious career, though, haven't you?"

Wardell began unwrapping his final taco. "I don't think we need to go there."

"I wouldn't necessarily expect you to do it yourself. Actually, I'd rather not know who did it, or when, or how. I'd just want it done right—no way it could ever be traced to me."

"Afraid that kind of thing is out of my league, Mr. Calahan."

Graham sipped his cola. "When Barry Bonds got called up to the Pittsburgh Pirates in 1986, he didn't say he'd rather keep playing for the Prince William Pirates, did he?"

"The Prince William Pirates?"

"They're the Potomac Nationals now, but they still play in Woodbridge. I practiced law there before I moved to Wisteria. Met my first wife there too, bless her heart. If I'd stuck with Libby, I wouldn't be in the fix I'm in now. But that's ancient history. Have you ever been to the baseball park in Woodbridge, Wardell?"

"Don't think I've ever been to Woodbridge period."

"The seats are aluminum, which means on a hot day the place is like a sauna. I can still remember a rocket that Bonds hit there. You know how he used to stand at the plate and admire his home runs? Well, he didn't have more than a couple seconds to watch this one. It disappeared over the scoreboard in a flash. Next guy up was Bobby Bonilla. Ever heard of him?"

"Played for Pittsburgh too, didn't he?"

"He did. Damn if Bobby didn't homer on the very next pitch. His didn't go as far as Barry's but it had a higher arc. Those two boys could flat out hit."

Having finished his last taco, Wardell was working on

his final Whopper. "What's that got to do with making a certain person disappear?"

"The connection is I never figured you for a minor leaguer, Wardell. The one thing I've learned from our association over the years is you've got major league talent. If you wanted someone to disappear, I have no doubt you could arrange it."

"If the price was right, yeah, I probably could."

"No probably about it. When it comes to getting things done, you da man as they say. That's why I picked you to do the surveillance on my wife."

Wardell nodded almost imperceptibly, his primary focus on the Whopper.

"I'm not sure what to do about my predicament," Graham continued. "If I decide the woman needs to…uh…vanish, how much would you charge for the job?"

"We're still talking hypothetical, right?"

"That's correct."

"Best I can do is give you a ballpark figure. Can you make do with that?"

"A ballpark figure will be fine."

"Fifteen thousand dollars."

"Holy shit! It's not like I'd be asking you to assassinate the president."

The last of the Whopper disappeared into Wardell's mouth. "Considering the shithead in the White House now, I probably wouldn't charge as much for that."

"Now, now, Wardell. He got there fair and square."

"Yeah, right. I've got some prime swampland in Russia I'm selling cheap, Mr. Calahan. You interested in buying some?"

"No thanks." Graham finished his Whopper and sipped more cola. "Fifteen thousand, huh?"

The black man dabbed at his chin with a napkin.

"That's my best gestimate. You plan on eating that last taco, Counselor?"

⌘⌘⌘

After Wardell left the park, Graham got up from the bench, dropped his trash in a nearby plastic container, and ambled back across the street. Maltby's was having a sale on a fur coat his wife had expressed interest in several months earlier. Although Graham intended to lay down the law about her adulterous behavior, he knew from experience that when it came to Maggie, ultimatums were more effective when coupled with incentives.

As he approached Maltby's entrance, an idea came to Graham, something that might make a more suitable gift for his wife. Although much more expensive, what he had in mind now would bring more joy than any coat possibly could to Maggie's cheating heart—and, therefore, might make her more amenable to his wishes. It would also be something Graham could use himself if things didn't work out between them. If Maggie continued down her current adulterous path and he was forced to bid her a not-so-fond farewell, a fur coat would be a waste of money.

Graham turned around and headed for his car, confident that he had made the right decision. It was a judicious decision, he told himself as he slid in behind the steering wheel of the BMW—one worthy of a Virginia Supreme Court justice.

Chapter 15

A smile playing across Ben Ramsdell's face, he leaned back in his new La-Z-Boy recliner and watched marijuana smoke coil toward the ceiling. Ben felt good about himself, especially now that he'd figured out how to keep from paying Wardell Tharp. Taking a final toke on his reefer, he crushed it in the free-standing ashtray next to the recliner and extracted a sheet of paper from his shirt pocket. Unfolding it for perhaps the twentieth time, he began reading the handwritten note.

"Not everyone will be pleased to learn I'm getting my old job back. Unless I'm a poor judge of character, or grown paranoid in my old age, both of which are certainly possible, some people might start thinking they would be better off with me dead. Wardell Tharp's reason for wanting me out of the way should be obvious...."

Not needing to read any further, Ben refolded the note and slipped it back in his pocket. Leaning his head against the soft leather of the recliner, he reflected on his new-found prospects. The three hundred and fifty dollars he owed but had decided not to pay Wardell Tharp would get him started in business for himself. With money coming in to augment the meager trust fund his father had set up, he could pay off the recliner and start enjoying some of life's

pleasures. If he played his cards right, he might even become a factor on the local drug scene. It would serve
Tharp right to lose a chunk of his business. Nobody gets
away with breaking Ben Ramsdell's finger, regardless of
how much money he's owed.

Ben turned toward the lanky young man stretched out
on the sofa. "Got a question for you, Mitch."

"I'm taking a nap, dude."

"Shake off the cobwebs, son. This is important."

Opening one eye, Mitch Folby slowly inclined his head
in Ben's direction. "Yeah?"

"What are the chances of me getting hooked up with
that Richmond connection of yours?"

Mitch opened his other eye then blinked both of them a
few times. "You thinking about changing dealers?"

"I'm thinking about becoming a dealer myself. Can
your supplier handle that kind of traffic?"

"I don't know, man."

"How about calling him and finding out. Don't mention
my name. Just say there's a potential seller in the Wisteria
area who's looking for a supplier."

Rubbing his eyes, the gangly young man pulled himself
to a sitting position. "You'd be horning in on Wardell
Tharp's territory. He won't take kindly to that."

Ben snorted. "That big jerk won't have a choice.
There's something in my pocket'll ward him off like garlic
does a vampire. Here I've been badmouthing my old man
and it turns out he left me something after all. It could be
my ticket to financial independence."

"What're you talking about, Ben?"

"I'll explain later. How about making that call, Mitch.
By the way, I need to borrow your wheels this afternoon.
Got some important business to attend to."

⌘⌘⌘

Ben spent the next hour composing a letter to Raymond Patterson, a name he had found by calling the toll-free number listed for Virginia State Police headquarters. After going to the library and making copies of the letter and of his father's note, he drove to Graham Calahan's office where he sat in the waiting room until there was a break in the lawyer's schedule.

"I thought I explained everything the other day," Graham said.

"This doesn't have anything to do with my father's estate," Ben replied, holding out a stamped, sealed envelope. "If something bad happens to me, I'd like you to mail this letter."

Graham gave him a quizzical look. "Something bad?"

"Somebody hurts me real bad, maybe even kills me."

"You're pulling my leg, aren't you, Ben?"

"I'm completely serious, Mr. Calahan. That letter is all stamped and ready to go. Will you mail it if something bad does happen to me?"

"Of course. I must say this is a strange case of deja vu. Not long ago your father asked me to do the same thing for him."

"Oh, yeah? Who was his letter addressed to?"

"Legal ethics prevent me from telling you that, Ben. Suffice it to say my secretary mailed your dad's letter as instructed. I hope she won't have to do the same for you."

"Same here. How much I owe you, Mr. Calahan?"

"Nothing. It's on the house."

Ben shook his head. "I mean to pay you. I want this to be official."

Graham shrugged. "Suit yourself. How about ten dollars?"

"Make it twenty." Ben reached for his wallet, took out a twenty-dollar bill, and handed it to the lawyer. "I'd like a receipt if you don't mind."

After leaving Graham's office, Ben went to a pay phone down the street and dialed Wardell Tharp's number. "This is Ben Ramsdell," he said. "We need to meet this afternoon."

"Have you got the money you owe me?"

"Every penny of it."

"Then I'll stop by your apartment and pick it up."

"Wrong. I don't want you coming there anymore. Tell me when you'll be available, and I'll tell you where we'll meet."

"You must be high on something, talking to me like that."

"I am. But it's not any of that shit you've been pedaling."

❧❧❧

The fact that Tharp was late gave Ben a chance to enjoy the scenery. Below the overlook where he sat, hundreds of birds—mostly Canada geese, mallard ducks, and seagulls—bobbed up and down in the shimmering water of the Shenandoah River. A long-legged heron lifted from the shallows and began flapping downstream just as a brown Hummer wheeled into the turn next to the community center and rumbled toward the overlook. Ben watched the heron until it disappeared past a bend in the river, and then he got up from the bench and strode over to the parking area. The Hummer came to a stop a few feet from Mitch's car.

"Real pretty up here, don't you think?" Ben said as Wardell climbed to the ground. "That's why I picked this spot. It's got a nice view, plus there's nobody around this time of year to overhear our conversation."

"No need for a confab. Just give me the money. And I don't take checks."

Ben unzipped his jacket, reached into his shirt pocket, and pulled out an envelope similar to the one he had given Graham Calahan. "First things first," he said, removing two sheets of paper from the envelope. He unfolded one and handed it to the big man.

"What's this?"

"Something my father wrote shortly before he was murdered. Don't read it so fast you skip over your name."

The puzzlement on Wardell's face turned to anger. "This and two dollars might put enough gas in that piece of crap you're driving to get you back to your apartment. Stop playing games with me, Ramsdale. Where the fuck is my money?"

"The answer to that question is right here." When Wardell reached for the second sheet of paper, Ben pulled it back. "In case you decide to destroy this without reading it, I'll read it for you. You need to understand exactly what's at stake here." Ben looked down at the paper. "Dear Mr. Patterson. This letter is to inform you that an ex-Ferrum football player named Wardell Tharp has been operating a drug ring in the Wisteria area ever since he got kicked out of college. As a user of illegal substances myself, I've had dealings with Tharp, not all of them pleasant. For instance, he recently broke one of my fingers because I didn't pay my drug bill within what he considered a reasonable amount of time."

"You must be out of your fucking mind saying shit like that."

Ignoring the comment, Ben continued to read. "Because of what Wardell did to me, I've decided not to pay him a single red cent. He'll want to hurt me real bad for this, Mr. Patterson, maybe even kill me. If something bad does happen to me, I want you to know the person responsible, beyond a shadow of a doubt, is Wardell Tharp."

Ben handed over the letter. Wardell stared at it for a

moment and then tore it and the other sheet into tiny strips. "You're going to eat those words, Ramsdale—literally. And if you don't, I'm going to do something that'll make that broken pinkie of yours seem like a mosquito bite."

"Those were just copies," Ben said. "The originals are inside a stamped envelope addressed to Mr. Patterson, who's the head of the Virginia State Police's Criminal Division. The letter is on file in my lawyer's office. I've already paid him to mail it if anything happens to me. So if you want a herd of state troopers roaring up your ass like a highballing freight train, go ahead and do whatever you've got in mind. But if you so much as touch me, you over-grown sack of shit, your gravy train here in Wisteria is over."

Wardell's face was livid. "This is bullshit!" he roared, but he didn't move any closer.

Ben smiled. "As long as you leave me alone, you won't have anything to worry about. That letter will stay right where it is, and nobody'll be the wiser. Hurt me, and you'll just be hurting yourself." He gave the big man what he hoped was a knowing look, and then he turned and headed for Mitch's car.

"You'll regret this, Ramsdale. Just as sure as the sun rises in the morning."

"I don't think so, fatpockets," Ben said, feeling a rush of pride at the way he had handled things. "And it's Ramsdell, not Ramsdale."

തയ

Several minutes later, his anger still not completely under control, Wardell Tharp pulled out his cell phone and dialed a number. Getting the person's voice mail, he left a brief message: "We got ourselves a big problem. Let me know when and where we can meet to discuss it."

Chapter 16

Mel Taggart spent the morning wrestling with what, if anything, he should do about the possibility that Will Ramsdell had left behind a clue to his killer's identity. After dropping off Marty Stith and his friend the reporter at her car, Mel had returned to Will's house and spent an hour searching for a Chesapeake & Ohio steamer, finally satisfying himself that if such an engine existed, whoever broke into the house must have stolen it. That the engine might show up at a hobby shop or a train show occurred to him, an angle he planned to look into the next few days. No need to tell the other officers, he decided. God only knows what they might find in the engine, or what they would do with the information.

Most likely nothing would come of this, Mel told himself. Still, what he had learned last night could be relevant to Will's murder, and because of that, he would be expected to inform Sheriff Grice, who had jurisdiction in the case.

The more Mel thought about it, the more he realized that sharing the information with Grice was the prudent thing to do. With future funding for Wisteria's police department in doubt, whatever he could do to ingratiate himself with the sheriff made sense. Sooner or later, Mel might need to apply for a deputy's job.

That afternoon, while patrolling Wisteria's west side, Mel called Quentin Grice on his car phone.

"I've got information that might have a bearing on the Ramsdell murder," he said. "If you want me to, I'll drop by and give you a briefing."

Twenty minutes later, Mel was seated in the same chair Abby Burlew had occupied the previous day. "Last night, I caught two people coming out the back door of Will's house," he told the sheriff. "One was Marty Stith, an ex-cop I used to work with. The other was a young female who works for a North Carolina newspaper. Apparently Will helped her out with one of her assignments."

"What were they doing at Will's house?" Grice asked.

"Looking for a model train engine, a big Lionel Chesapeake and Ohio steamer to be exact. Trains were a passion of Will's. He had a basement full of the darn things."

"I know. My deputies and I scoured that house from top to bottom looking for clues. Why were Stith and the reporter interested in that particular engine?"

"They thought Will left a message in the tender saying who might've killed him."

Grice raised an eyebrow. "That's a mighty strange thing to do. But go on."

"I thought Marty was bullshitting me until he showed me this." Mel handed the sheriff a copy of Will's poem.

As Grice read it, the only change in his expression was a slight narrowing of his eyes. "Did Stith say how this came into his possession?" he asked, handing the poem back to Mel.

"Graham Calahan's law office mailed it to him. Marty called there to inquire, and Graham's secretary told him Will wanted the letter sent if he should die of unnatural causes. She said neither she nor Graham knew anything about the letter's contents."

"Took them long enough to mail it. Ramsdell's been dead two weeks."

Mel nodded. "One other thing you should know, Sheriff. Will's house had already been broken into when Marty and the reporter got there last night. The engine they were looking for was gone." Mel explained that a few days earlier Will's next-door neighbor had reported seeing someone hurrying from the back of the house with a box in his arms. When an officer checked the house, he discovered that Will's back door had been jimmied.

"You're sure neither Stith nor the reporter took that engine?"

"They didn't have it when I arrested them. We searched 'em both. Afterward, I went back to Will's house and made sure the engine wasn't there."

"Did the neighbor get a good look at the person running from the house?"

"She said it was a young white male, probably in his late teens or early twenties. It was too dark for her to get any more of a description."

Grice leaned back in his chair and for a moment seemed lost in thought. "I'm going to level with you, Mel," he said and sat up straight again. "I know who stole that engine."

"You do?"

"I also know this person found the note Will referred to in that poem. I even know what the note says."

"How the hell could you know all that?"

"I have my sources. Would you like to know what Will said in the note?"

"Well, yeah. I would."

"He said now that he'd been offered his old job back, there were three people who had good reason for wanting him dead—Wardell Tharp, Ned Copeland, and you."

Mel looked stunned. "Me! I'd like to see that note."

"I'm afraid that's not possible at the moment. But I can assure you it does exist."

Taking several deep breaths, Mel leaned forward in his chair. "I hope you don't think I killed Will. Why would I?"

"Well, there's the chief's job. Since Will is no longer around to claim it, it'll probably go to you."

"It hasn't so far. Even if it does, that job is hardly worth killing for. I'll be lucky if the police department lasts another three months. From what I hear, the town council is going to pull the plug on the funding."

"I've heard that rumor. Whether it's true or not remains to be seen. But I know you didn't kill Will. I don't think Tharp did either."

Relief washed over Mel's face. "You think it was Copeland?"

"I do. Unfortunately, there's only circumstantial evidence." Grice paused, as though trying to decide whether to elaborate. "Do you recall an incident involving a veterinarian named Walter Hux that happened several years ago? It was a few months after he and Will closed down Copeland's puppy mill."

"Yeah, I remember that. Somebody dumped a skinned puppy on the veterinary clinic steps. Dr. Hux thought it was Copeland and threatened to kill him. Fortunately, he cooled down after a while."

"He had help in that regard—a lot of help. If you've got a few minutes, I'll tell you what I know about that incident and why it's clear to anyone who knows all the facts that Ned Copeland is most likely the person who killed Will Ramsdell. Before I get started, though, how about a cup of coffee, Mel?"

"Sure. If it's not too much trouble."

"No trouble at all." Grice got up and went over to a small corner table that contained a coffee pot, a sugar bowl, and some non-dairy creamer. "What would you like in it, my friend?"

‹›‹›

As Mel Taggart left Quentin Grice's office, he thanked the sheriff for sharing information about Ned Copeland. "I can't imagine you won't get a conviction. If I was on the jury and the prosecutor presented things the way you just did, I'd vote guilty in a heartbeat. Any way I can help out, just let me know."

"I appreciate that. And I appreciate what you've shared with me, Mel. That speaks well of you." Grice stuck out his hand. "I wouldn't worry too much about Wisteria's police department losing its funding. If that happens, my office will be expected to pick up the slack, which means I'll need at least one more deputy. If it gets to that point, and you're interested in working for me, I don't see why that can't be arranged."

Driving back to Wisteria, Mel felt as though a great weight had been lifted from his shoulders. Regardless of what happened to Wisteria's police department in the next few months—or even the next few years—he now had some job security. With that worry no longer gnawing at him, he turned his attention to the other matter that had been troubling him, the fact that he had not been promoted to police chief.

Why hadn't Graham Calahan mentioned the promotion after resuming his mayoral duties? "If for some reason Will can't or won't take the job," Maggie had told Mel, "it will probably be offered to you." Had she been trying to spare his feelings when she said that, thinking it was a foregone conclusion that Will would once again become Wisteria's police chief?

As long as Will's murder remained unsolved, Mel had

been reluctant to mention the promotion—the mayor might think Mel valued the chief's job enough to kill for it. The longer Mel went without hearing from the mayor, the more he feared that Graham was waiting to see whether the town council would fund the department for another year, and if it did, Graham would do the same thing he did the first time Will vacated the job, bring in someone from the outside.

To Mel's way of thinking, it would be a damn shame if that happened. Anyone with a lick of sense would know that all things being equal—or even almost equal—the candidate already familiar with the town and the people he'd be serving would be the best person for the job. And Mel knew Wisteria and its residents better than most anyone. There wasn't much that went on there that he didn't know about.

He thought back to his high school days when the biggest scandal in town was the fact that Jamie Copeland had a kid out of wedlock and nobody knew who the father was. Most people thought it was Rudy Teague, even though Rudy denied it. Nobody was surprised when word spread that the baby had been put up for adoption and the identity of the adoptive parents was to remain secret, even to Jamie.

That baby would be all grown up now, Mel mused. He wondered how much it bothered Jamie to know she had a daughter out there somewhere and no way to find her, especially since she and Nelson Lang never had kids of their own. *Probably not nearly as much*, he decided, *as finding out that her father is a murderer*.

Chapter 17

*H*OLLY OAK—MEMBERS ONLY
The sign, its old English lettering etched in *severely* weathered wood, guarded the entrance to the hunt club's property. Her nerves jangling, Abby turned at the sign onto a dirt road barely wide enough to accommodate two passing cars. For nearly a mile she followed the road as it twisted and turned through a forest that occasionally thinned enough to provide glimpses of the mountain top on her left and farmland far below on her right. Finally she came to a clearing with a large two-story log house in the middle, practically a mansion. Between the house and a much smaller outbuilding, also built of logs, sat a pickup truck with a rear bumper sticker that said *Guns Don't Kill People, Abortion Clinics Do*. Abby parked a little farther from the truck than she needed to.

"If you're not a member, you're trespassing," a gravelly voice called as she got out of her car.

A man with white hair tied back in a ponytail stood next to a wood pile near the outbuilding. His wrinkled face suggested he was in his seventies, but his wiry, muscular physique could have belonged to a much younger man. His right hand held an ax.

"A member of what?" Abby asked, feigning ignorance and hoping Copeland wouldn't make the connection between her normal voice and the one she had used on the phone with him yesterday.

"Holly Oak Hunt Club, just like the sign said. This is private property."

"Sorry, I didn't see a sign. I'm looking for a golf course called Pinecroft. According to the directions I was given, it should be pretty close to where we're standing."

The man's expression softened. He set the ax on the ground and walked over to Abby. "You turned left when you should've turned right, assuming you came from Wisteria or somewhere thereabouts."

"I'm from Emmett's Corners," Abby said, naming a town she and Marty had passed through on their way to and from Charlottesville. So far so good, she thought; her voice alteration seems to have worked. "I could've sworn Mr. Lang said to turn right. Are you sure there isn't a golf course somewhere close by?"

"Depends on what you mean by *nearby*. Pinecroft is five miles due south."

Abby rolled her eyes. "That figures. I never was very good at directions." She stuck out her hand. "I'm Molly Finch, Mr. uh…"

"Copeland. Ned Copeland."

"Nice meeting you, Mr. Copeland. I'm the newly-elected president of Bogie Bustin' Babes, a women's golf league looking for a course to play next year. It's got to be within reasonable driving distance for most of us and, more important, it can't be crowded. We don't want guys getting all bent out of shape because we don't play as fast as they do. This year was a disaster for us. We paid top dollar to join a course near Charlottesville, and guess what? They treated us like second-class citizens. Do you play golf, Mr. Copeland?"

"No, ma'am, I don't."

"Reason I ask is I was hoping you might know something about Pinecroft. The less play it gets, the better we'll like it."

"Well, I do pass by there occasionally. Never seen more than a handful of cars in the parking lot."

"I'm sure glad to hear that. If the setting is anywhere near as nice as what you've got here, us Babes will feel like we've died and gone to heaven." Pleased with her performance and hoping it didn't deteriorate over the next few minutes, Abby glanced at the huge log house. "You live here, Mr. Copeland?"

"Yes, ma'am, I do. I'm caretaker of the place."

"You've got some mighty beautiful surroundings. You must love it out here. I know I would." *No need to overdo it*, Abby told herself. *Just get to the point when the opportunity presents itself.*

"Don't let those logs fool you, ma'am. The inside is just as nice as the outside. It's like a palace. Come on in and I'll show you around."

There was something creepy about the man that made Abby reluctant to accept his invitation. "I'll take a quick look," she said. "But I can't stay long. I still have to check out Pinecroft."

As soon as she entered the spacious living room, she realized Copeland wasn't exaggerating. The furniture included a classic dark brown tooled leather sofa with nailhead trim, a matching oversized chair and ottoman, several overstuffed club chairs done in either dark brown leather or green Tartan upholstery, three wing chairs upholstered in solid dark green, and a mahogany coffee table and end tables. In one corner of the room stood two mahogany card tables with matching chairs, each table with a sealed double deck of playing cards resting on top. A deer's head with a massive rack was mounted over the nearby stone fireplace.

After showing Abby the living room, Copeland took

her upstairs and pointed out the five bedrooms, each pleasantly decorated and comfortably furnished. She worried that he might try to get her into one of the beds, but he made no attempt to do so. After escorting her back down the winding staircase, he showed her the kitchen and the adjoining banquet hall, which contained as much table space as many restaurants.

"Quite a place," Abby said, genuinely impressed. "A lot more classy than I'd expect a hunting lodge to be."

"I like it. Can I get you something to drink?"

"No thanks." She decided now was a good time to broach Will's murder. "I—"

"Step this way and I'll show you my living quarters."

Against her better judgment, Abby followed the man back through the kitchen to what turned out to be a small neatly-kept two-room apartment. "Nice," she said, taking a quick look around before focusing on the books. "Judging from these titles, I'd say you're not exactly a fan of big government."

Copeland chuckled. "I'm not even a fan of small government. How about letting me fix you a toddy. There's Scotch, bourbon, vodka—you name it. There's even champagne if you're so inclined. We can celebrate your golf league finding the course of its dreams."

Yeah, right, thought Abby. "Thanks anyway," she said and glanced at her watch. "If I'm not home soon, my husband will start worrying about me."

Copeland's aura of courteous attentiveness faded. "Isn't one of your fingers missing something?"

"Excuse me?"

"The third finger of your left hand."

"Oh that," Abby said. "My ring's at the jeweler's getting re-sized."

"Shrunk up on you, did it? Must be one of those cheapies."

The contempt in Copeland's voice made Abby nervous, and she decided it was time to begin making her exit. "Guess I've trespassed long enough. Oh, I almost forgot. A couple of weeks ago I saw in the paper that a man was killed while playing golf at Pinecroft. Any idea what that was about?"

Other than a slight narrowing of his eyes, Copeland didn't react to the question. "The Langs will know a lot more about that than I do," he said and moved past Abby into the hallway. "I'll show you out."

Disappointed, she followed him back through the living room to the front door. "I still don't have a clear idea how to get to Pinecroft," she said, hoping to salvage something of the visit. "Could you refresh my memory?"

"Go back the way you came," Ned said and opened the door. "When you get to Highway 64 where you should've turned left instead of right the first time, keep straight. Pinecroft is about two miles further down the road on your right."

Abby stepped past him onto the porch. "Thanks. I think I've got it."

Copeland chuckled. "Oh, you've got it all right. You're just not interested in sharing it. If you're ever in this neck of the woods again and feel different, stop by."

As Abby crossed the clearing toward her car, she had the creepy sensation that she was a rabbit being eyed by a rattlesnake.

ひらひら

Ned Copeland watched the red Toyota recede into the forest. "You're no more married than I am," he muttered. "And you're not from Emmett's Corners either. Folks from there don't have Carolina plates."

As he headed toward the outbuilding, Ned wondered if

the woman was working for Quentin Grice and had made the phone call he got last night. If so, what was the purpose of her visit? To see how he'd respond when she mentioned Ramsdell's murder? Short of a confession, it wouldn't really matter how he reacted. Grice wasn't fool enough to think he'd volunteer a confession, was he? Maybe the woman was a distraction, someone whose purpose was to divert his attention long enough for a deputy to slip inside and plant a listening device.

Ned gazed back at the lodge, trying to recall if he'd locked up before going out to cut wood. He remembered leaving through the back door, and yes, he had locked it behind him. He also remembered having to unlock the front door before he and the woman entered.

He walked around the lodge's perimeter, making sure each window was locked and none had been jimmied. Satisfied that no one had broken in, he returned to the woodpile and picked up the axe.

Before resuming his chopping, Ned thought about the woman who supposedly had strayed onto Holly Oak property. Somebody from the sheriff's office wouldn't have been so quick to leave. Maybe this Molly Finch really was who she said, some airhead out looking for a female-friendly golf course. Whatever her reason for being at Holly Oak, she had the kind of body Ned liked. With a figure like that, she could wrap herself around a man and make him think the rapture had come.

Ned visualized her standing before him, at first as he had actually seen her earlier, and then as he imagined her to be if she were naked…

She gave him a coy smile and came closer. Slowly she unbuttoned his shirt and unzipped his pants. Then she got down on her knees in front of him. "I'll be yours for as long as you want, Ned Copeland. Do me however you like.

Whatever suits your pleasure, Ned, and the rougher the better. And then do me again and again and again..."

Ned smiled and swung the ax at an elongated piece of white birch lying on the ground in front of him, splitting it from end to end.

Chapter 18

The sun had just dipped below the western horizon when Abby pulled into the gravel parking lot of Ye Olde Barn Apartments, the address listed in the phone book for Ben Ramsdell. As she picked her way across the uneven terrain toward what in an earlier incarnation had been a large barn, a rat scurried across the concrete floor of the garbage area and disappeared under a dumpster. Abby was too preoccupied with thoughts of Ned Copeland to notice the furry creature.

She knew that her decision to telephone Ned Copeland had been a mistake. She had hoped he would let something incriminating slip, either by his words or the tone of his voice, that she could use to convince Marty that the man should be considered a suspect in Will Ramsdell's murder. The call hadn't accomplished a thing, and it might actually have been counterproductive, giving Copeland reason to be on his guard during her subsequent visit to Holly Oak. The only good thing about the visit, she decided, was that she had emerged from the hunt club grounds unscathed.

As she entered the apartment building, the aroma of something tomato-based caught Abby's attention, reminding her that if she planned to eat supper and still be ready for her date with Marty, she would need to hustle. She knocked on the first door she came to, deciding what she smelled was lasagna, one of her favorites. The door cracked open a few inches, and an elderly woman eyed her suspiciously.

"Sorry to bother you, ma'am. Can you tell me which apartment is Ben Ramsdell's?"

"Never heard of him," the woman said and closed the door.

Abby had better luck across the hall where a young woman with a baby on her hip suggested she try the apartment directly above hers. As Abby climbed the rickety stairway, the smell of lasagna grew stronger, making her mouth water. She knocked on the door of the apartment the woman had indicated, softly at first, and then louder when there was no response. Finally a groggy-looking Mitch Folby opened the door. He stared at Abby with glazed eyes.

"You collectin' fer a cause, tryin' to convert the heathen, or just plain fuckin' lost?"

"None of the above. I'm looking for Ben Ramsdell."

"Right apartment—wrong time. He's on his way to Richmond. Might even be there by now if old Jezebel has cooperated. That's my car. She's a bit long in the tooth."

"Any idea when he'll be back?"

"Well, if he spends the night in the Big R, which I expect he will, it won't be before noon tomorrow. Ben's a late sleeper. If he ever does get a job, it'll have to be a night shift somewhere. You a friend of his?"

"You might say that. How's his finger?"

"His finger?"

"The one he injured. I understand it's all bandaged up."

"Oh, yeah. A dumpster lid fell on it when he was taking out the trash. At least that's what Ben claims. I'd sooner think Shannon did it. That's his girlfriend. She gets really pissed at him sometimes." Mitch reached for the door jamb to steady himself. "I'll tell him you stopped by. What'd you say your name is?"

"Phoebe…uh…Finch. I'll check back later."

"Not before noon," the young man reminded her.

⧈⧉⧈

Marty arrived at the Shenandoah Inn shortly after eight, this time on his motorcycle. Abby climbed on the back and they rode to the Shamrock, a bar in the downtown area about a block from the police station.

"Why Phoebe Finch?" he asked after Abby told him about her visit to Ben Ramsdell's apartment. "It sounds like you should chirp instead of talk."

"Just a name that popped into my head. I'd used Molly Finch with Ned Copeland, but I couldn't remember the Molly."

"You talked to Copeland?"

"I did. I told him I was lost and needed directions to Pinecroft. He seemed like a decent-enough guy until I refused his offer of what he called a toddy. Then he lost his manners."

"That was not a good idea, Abby."

"Why?"

"For starters, if Copeland did kill Will, you might have tipped him off that he's a suspect."

Abby dismissed Marty's concerns with a wave of her hand. "As far as he knows, I'm some dumb broad who got lost searching for a female-friendly golf course."

The waitress had brought them each a mug of beer, and Marty drank some of his. "What did you think of Copeland?"

"I got the impression he can be a mean son of a bitch when he puts his mind to it—or even when he doesn't." Abby went on to explain that although she was unsuccessful in getting Copeland to reveal anything that suggested involvement in Will's murder, he definitely didn't do or say anything that made her think otherwise. "Since Jamie Lang is Copeland's daughter, I'd have thought he'd have mentioned that to me, but he never said a word about her. I wonder why."

"Apparently there's some bad blood between them. From what I understand, Jamie got pregnant in high school and had a kid she gave up for adoption. Copeland might hold that against her."

Abby took a sip of her beer. "Well, he might not be on your suspect list, but he's definitely on mine."

Being a recovering drug addict, Abby normally stayed away from alcoholic beverages, but she would have felt silly accepting Marty's invitation to a bar and then ordering a soft drink. Besides, she didn't really like beer and knew from experience that she could hold herself to one, assuming she even finished that.

"I thought I recognized a familiar face over here. What are you doing in this neck of the woods, Luke?"

A heavy-set man with a short military-style haircut and a ruddy complexion stood next to their booth. Abby had noticed him earlier when he was sitting at the bar. He had been staring at them and had only looked away when she returned his stare.

"You've got the wrong guy. My name is Marty."

"You're kidding."

"Nope. Marty Stith."

The man shook his head in disbelief. "Well, you sure had me fooled. You're a dead ringer for a guy I met in Charlottesville by the name of Luke Dawson. The company I work for does a lot of government-related work. I could've sworn we met when I installed some software at—"

"It wasn't me," Marty interrupted. "Where I work

doesn't even have a computer. And no, I don't have a twin brother living in Charlottesville."

The man apologized, muttered something about getting senile in his old age, and returned to the bar.

"Wish I had a dollar for every time I've been mistaken for somebody else," Marty said. "Must be a lot of really handsome dudes out there with features similar to mine." He gave Abby an awkward smile. "Just kidding. What were we talking about anyway? Oh yeah, our suspects list. We'll just have to agree to disagree about Ned Copeland, don't you think?"

"I guess so."

"Now that we've got that settled, let's talk about something more interesting—you, Abby. Tell me about yourself. What is it that makes you different from the other young, bright, good-looking women out there?"

Surprised at how abruptly—and awkwardly—Marty had changed the subject, Abby shrugged. "Nothing really. Aside from winning the Miss North Carolina beauty pageant a few years ago and being one of the most talented female point guards the state ever produced, I'm pretty much an average, run-of-the-mill type of gal."

"You're kidding, right?"

"Why would I do that?"

Momentarily at a loss for words, Marty looked sheepish. "You were actually a Miss North Carolina?"

Abby chuckled. "Of course not. I did play basketball in high school and some in college, but nobody from the WBA ever came calling."

"Where did you go to college?"

"I started out at East Carolina. Hardly cracked a book there and flunked out my freshman year. Then I tried Chowan, which didn't work out either. Eventually I went back to East Carolina as a part-time student. I haven't got my degree yet, but I'm working on it."

"What are you majoring in?"

"English. If my job at the *Gazette* doesn't pan out, I have no idea what I'll do for a living."

"Any reason to think it won't?"

"Yeah. My boss and I don't exactly hit it off. I think she'd like nothing better than to fire me."

"How did you get to be a reporter without having a college degree?"

"The *Gazette* isn't exactly what you'd call a big-time newspaper. I hired on as a proof reader. Eventually I was assigned some puff features, you know, local interest stuff. It was a fluke I got to be a reporter. The *Gazette* needed somebody to look into a young woman's disappearance, and its real investigative reporter was in the process of leaving for a better job. What about you, Marty? You were wearing a Georgetown sweatshirt the other day. Are you a Hoya?"

"I am."

"Have you been a cop all your working life?"

Marty shook his head. "After I graduated from Georgetown, I didn't know what I wanted to do. I'd majored in history, so I took a job teaching at Fork Union Academy. You probably passed right by it."

"I did. Nice campus. All the students seemed to be wearing military uniforms."

"They do and so do the teachers. I didn't particularly like it there. I was trying to decide whether to look for another teaching job or try a different line of work when I noticed a newspaper ad for an entry-level cop's position in Wisteria. I decided to give it a try and Will hired me. The rest, as they say, is history. Not exactly a glorious history, I admit, but at least I get to work outdoors at Pinecroft, which I really enjoy doing."

They continued to exchange personal information, Abby giving the generic version of herself. She didn't mention her drug addiction or bipolar disorder, deciding that was information Marty didn't need to know, at least not at this stage of their relationship. He told her that he was divorced and had a six-year-old daughter, who lived with his ex-wife in Richmond. "Barbara would have been better suited married to a professional man instead of a ne'er-do-well like me," he said. "But our divorce was amicable. I got what I wanted, which was reasonable visitation rights with our daughter."

Abby enjoyed her evening with Marty. She had no trouble stopping at one beer, and he stopped at two. They left the bar a few minutes before ten and returned to the Shenandoah Inn.

"I'll call you in the morning as soon as I finish my chores," Marty said, remaining on his motorcycle after Abby dismounted. "We can firm up our plans for the day and decide when and where to meet. Personally, I think a talk with Ben Ramsdell should be our first priority. In the meantime I hope you'll stay away from Ned Copeland."

"I was planning on jogging out to Holly Oak and having breakfast with him."

Marty chuckled, then surprised Abby by leaning over to kiss her. Although she didn't resist, she did nothing to prolong the kiss.

"I hope you won't take this the wrong way," she said. "But I have a rule about not mixing my professional life with my personal life. I violated that rule once and almost didn't live to regret it."

Marty revved up his motorcycle. "I'd be interested in hearing the particulars sometime," he said and shifted into first gear. "See you tomorrow, Scully."

"What'd you just call me?"

"Didn't you ever watch *The X Files* on TV?"

"I used to watch it all the time."

"Well, I've decided that from now on, I'm going to

pattern myself after Fox Mulder. He and Dana Scully made a great investigative team, and their relationship was strictly platonic."

Smiling, Abby reached into her purse for her room key. "Sleep tight, Fox," she said.

Chapter 19

Ben Ramsdell treated himself to an Outer Banks Sampler at a Red Lobster on Richmond's west side. He had decided not to spend the night in Richmond after all. The people he could have stayed with lived in a bad neighborhood, and he didn't want to risk Mitch's car being stolen, especially with the trunk full of drugs. He left his waitress a generous tip, smoked a joint in the parking lot, and generally felt on top of the world as he climbed into Mitch's ancient Mercury Sable. Even though the temperature had plummeted during the past two hours and the Sable's battery hadn't been replaced since Mitch bought the car off a used car lot several years ago, old Jezebel started right up.

What an amazing vehicle, Ben thought as he guided the Sable onto Highway 64 and headed west. Fifteen years old and still going strong.

A few miles beyond the city limits, however, the engine began to knock. Mitch had said the Sable burned oil, so Ben stopped at the first gas station he came to and bought a quart. The knocking subsided, but after another few miles, the heater stopped working. It threw out plenty air but the air was freezing. Conversely, the temperature gauge registered a lot hotter than the last time Ben checked it. Something's wrong with the damn radiator, he thought, and made a mental note to pull into the next gas station. Unfortunately, he didn't see any, at least none that were open. The engine knocking resumed and was as loud as ever. Keep going, Ben told himself. Eventually, you'll come to a gas station that's open.

Ten miles later he did. The only person on duty, however, was a young woman who didn't know squat about cars. The mechanic had gone home hours ago, she told Ben, and wouldn't be back until tomorrow. When he asked if she had an additive for plugging radiator leaks, she gave him a blank look. At least she knew where the antifreeze was, and Ben bought a gallon along with another quart of oil. He managed to pour the oil into the crankcase without incident but almost scalded himself when he removed the radiator cap to add the antifreeze. The radiator took every drop, so he bought another gallon and poured in half of it. When he checked under the car and saw only a small puddle of liquid, which he decided was probably left by another vehicle, he breathed a sigh of relief.

A few miles farther on, the heater still didn't work. Ben tried to take comfort in the fact that his Richmond dealings had gone extremely well. He had spent almost five hundred dollars on illegal substances—marijuana and cocaine, plus a small amount of crystal meth with which he intended to test the Wisteria market—at prices he knew from experience would allow him a handsome profit. His source, a skinny guy with big ears and a goofy smile, turned out to be as easy to do business with as Mitch had suggested; he even provided a cell phone number so Ben could call ahead with his next order. There was no reason to think the two of them wouldn't enjoy a long and prosperous relationship.

The engine started knocking again, the sound curtailing Ben's efforts to take solace in his purchases. "What the hell's wrong with this car?" he groused.

Ben looked forward to the day he could afford wheels of his own, something not just reliable but stylish, worthy of a successful business man. Nothing so extravagant as Wardell Tharp's Hummer, of course, though a Corvette would be nice, even a used one. Ben didn't want to be ostentatious, though. He'd probably buy something small and foreign like a Honda or a Subaru or maybe a Mazda, though if he went that route, he'd insist on a moon roof. That would impress his girlfriend, whoever she happened to be. One thing for sure—it wouldn't be Shannon Pfeiffer sitting next to him under a moon roof. An up-and-coming entrepreneur could definitely do better than that.

Twenty miles east of Wisteria, Ben came to Emmett's Corners, the last town before the isolated stretch of road leading to the Blue Ridge Mountains. He knew the town had at least one auto shop, having noticed a Monro Muffler and Brake on his way to Richmond. When he spotted a motel with a vacancy sign, he almost decided to stop for the night and have Mitch's car checked out first thing in the morning.

"Old Jez has gotten me this far," he muttered. "Another few miles won't kill her—or me."

Ten of those miles passed without incident. The engine's knocking didn't get any worse, and the heater situation actually improved. After a series of gurgling noises, it started putting out enough warm air to take the chill off and even melt some of the ice that had collected on the windshield. The temperature dial eased back toward the middle of the gauge.

Now that he had put enough distance between himself and Emmett's Corners to make returning on foot impractical, Ben was keenly aware of how isolated and lonely this stretch of road was—almost no traffic, no moon to brighten the sky or the earth below, and very few houses. He could always ask Shannon to come get him. But how?

His cell phone was hooked to his belt, but that was for show, his service having long since been terminated for nonpayment of bills.

The windshield started icing up again. Glancing at the temperature gauge, Ben saw that the dial was back in the red zone, actually touching the H. "Shit," he said. "This is the last time I'll ever borrow this piece of crap."

Again he thought of Shannon Pfeiffer, wishing he'd asked her to drive him to Richmond. She might not be the prettiest flower in the garden, but at least her car was reliable and she wouldn't charge him an arm and a leg. A guy could do worse than Shannon, even one on the cusp of success. She could ride in his new Subaru. In fact, she would be the first person he'd show it to.

Bright lights suddenly appeared in Ben's rearview mirror. A vehicle that seemed to have come out of nowhere was moving up fast, making it nearly impossible to see.

"Use your dimmer, jerk!" Ben tried adjusting the mirror to alleviate the glare. It refused to budge then fell off in his hand. "Son of a fuckin' bitch," he said and re-focused his attention on the road ahead, periodically glancing at the side mirror to see what the other vehicle was doing.

It closed to within a few yards and then settled in directly behind him.

"Nothing's coming, asshole! Go ahead and pass why don't you?"

As though in response, a third light appeared, a surrealistic swirling of reds and blues emanating from the top of the vehicle. Fear shot up and down Ben's spine.

Glancing at the dashboard, he was relieved to see that he was only going fifty-three miles an hour, two miles below the speed limit, assuming the speedometer worked. What the hell was he being pulled over for?

Ben thought of the stash of drugs in the trunk and felt

sick to his stomach. *If a cop looks in there, I'm fucked.* He felt like crying.

He put on the turn signal—at least it worked—and slowed the Sable enough to pull off the macadam and onto the dirt shoulder. The other vehicle pulled in behind him, high beams assaulting Ben's eyes when he turned around in the seat to look. *Take it easy,* he told himself as he applied the parking brake. *The worst thing you can do is give this guy a reason to search the car. He probably pulled me over because this old clunker has a taillight out, something minor like that. No need to get all bent out of shape. Just keep cool and everything will be fine.*

Ben rolled down the window far enough so he and the patrolman could talk, and then he took out his wallet so he'd be ready to produce his license. He started to unhook his seat belt but quickly changed his mind, not wanting the cop to think he hadn't been wearing one. He thought about the Sable's registration and started to panic. Then he recalled Mitch saying it was in the glove compartment. Ben hoped an up-to-date proof of insurance would be in there too.

Hearing the dull thud of a door closing, he glanced at the side mirror and saw a figure moving up beside him, a large man walking slowly. This could be a blessing in disguise, Ben told himself. The cop might turn out to be a nice guy. *After I tell him how this rust bucket has been acting up, he might even volunteer to follow me to Wisteria, make sure I get home safe and sound.*

Actually, Ben thought, *this really could turn out to be my lucky day after all.*

Chapter 20

Abby woke up Friday morning with Ned Copeland on her mind, not a pleasant way to start the day. Yesterday's encounter with Copeland had left her more convinced than ever that he was Will Ramsdell's murderer.

There was something intrinsically malevolent about the man, she thought. If he believed he could get away with killing someone with whom he had a grievance, he probably wouldn't hesitate doing so.

Abby knew her perception of Ned Copeland would in no way hasten Quentin Grice's decision to make an arrest. What really concerned her was the possibility that Copeland might escape punishment altogether. Such an outcome, she felt, was absolutely unacceptable. There had to be something she and Marty could do to prevent it from happening.

After a quick shower, she dressed, took her morning dose of lithium, and slipped on her jacket. The sky was a robin's egg blue mixed with streaks and swirls of white, no sign of rain or snow. Having decided to postpone jogging until later in the day, she power walked the half mile to Sullivan's Diner, hoping to burn off some of the calories contained in the Big Mac and French fries she had eaten the previous evening before her date with Marty. By the time she reached the restaurant, she had worked up a hearty appetite.

There were two empty booths. Abby took the farther one from the small TV set suspended from the ceiling just to the right of where yesterday's waitress was working the griddle. The sizzling sounds and pungent aroma made Abby even hungrier.

The man who had been the cook yesterday brought her a menu. "Coffee, ma'am?" he asked with a slight foreign accent. He had a wide forehead and hair cut in a 1950s era flattop.

"Decaffeinated. I see you and the cook changed places."

"That's my wife. We switch off every so often. Promotes a better...how shall I say it?...partnership."

"Makes sense to me. I'd like the Farmer's Special. I almost ordered it yesterday but wimped out at the last minute."

"How you like the eggs?"

"Scrambled. I'll need ketchup to go with them."

"I'll bring a bottle. You like home fries or grits?"

"Home fries."

"Ham slices, sausage links, or sausage patties?"

"Sausage links."

"White, whole wheat, rye, or sourdough toast?"

"I'll take the rye."

"Orange or grapefruit juice?"

"Orange," Abby said, reminded of the rapid-fire way Quentin Grice had questioned her yesterday, except there was nothing condescending about the man standing next to her.

"A scrambled farmer from Orange County at home on the links and in the rye," he called. His wife responded with a momentary rolling of her eyes.

"Impressive," Abby said. "What if I'd ordered fried

eggs, grits, sausage patties, grapefruit juice, and sour-dough toast?"

"Not a problem. Try me again tomorrow."

The television was loud enough so everyone in the diner could hear it. The regional news was being shown, something Abby wasn't remotely interested in, and she tuned it out—until the words "son of Wisteria's recently murdered police chief" grabbed her attention. Looking up at the screen, she saw a young female reporter questioning Quentin Grice, both of them standing on the shoulder of a highway. In the background, diagonally across the road, an older model burgundy car had been cordoned off by police tape.

"Sheriff, it was barely two weeks ago that Ben Ramsdell's father was killed. What can you tell those in our viewing audience who might be wondering if the two murders are connected?"

"We'll be looking into that possibility," Grice replied, perfectly at ease as far as Abby could tell, as confident in this setting as he had been yesterday in his office. "So far, though, there's no evidence of a connection."

"This location seems like a strange place for a murder. Do you think Ben might have been killed somewhere else and the killer or killers parked the car here?"

"No, I don't. My forensics people think Ben was be-hind the wheel when that Mercury Sable left the highway. So far, there's no evidence suggesting anyone else was inside the vehicle within the last day or so."

"Then someone must have forced him off the road."

"That's possible. But according to the tire tracks, the vehicle pulled off in an orderly fashion and slowed to a stop. There's no sign of any contact between the car Ben was driving and any other vehicle—no broken glass, no recent bumps or scrapes."

"Then whoever shot him must have had some other

way to pull him over. Could a cop have done this?"

"Extremely unlikely. It could have been a hitchhiker, I suppose, or maybe someone Ben was planning to meet here. But that's pure speculation."

The reporter nodded. "Sheriff, a moment ago you said 'the car Ben was driving' instead of saying 'Ben's car.' Am I wrong to think that Mercury Sable might not belong to Ben?"

"It doesn't. At least it's not registered to him."

"Who it is registered to?"

Grice shook his head. "Sorry, but I'm not going to release a name until we've had a chance to talk to this person."

"Is this person a suspect?"

"Not at this time. Right now we don't have any suspects."

"I see," the reporter said and turned toward the cordoned-off vehicle. The camera zoomed in on it, focusing on a man in civilian clothes who had just opened the trunk and was leaning into the cargo space beneath the raised lid. "I assume that's one of your forensics people, Sheriff. What exactly is he looking for?"

"Nothing at the moment. He's getting ready to take a sample of a substance we found earlier in the trunk."

"What kind of substance?"

"A white powdery material. It could be heroin or cocaine, or it might be something perfectly innocuous. We won't know until it's been tested."

"How much of this material did you find?"

"About a teaspoon, I'd say. It was spread out over an area of about two square feet."

"If it turns out to be an illegal substance, what conclusion will you draw—that Ben's murder is drug related?"

"That it *might* be drug related."

"Could you elaborate on that?"

"Not at this point. It would be a waste of my time and yours, especially since the substance could be something perfectly legal—baking soda, for instance. No point in speculating until after we know for sure what it is."

"I understand. When do you expect to get those test results?"

"Probably tomorrow, though it's possible we'll know late this afternoon. Keep in mind that even if the substance turns out to be heroin or cocaine, that won't tell us a whole lot. Unless we've learned something in the meantime that we don't know now, we won't be any closer to knowing who killed Ben, or why he was killed. I hope I'm wrong, Carmen, but my feeling is we've got a long, hard road ahead of us." Grice glanced at his watch. "Sorry to have to end on that note, but that's all I've got for you now. When more information is available, I'll let you know."

"Thank you, Sheriff. There is one more thing I'd like to ask before you go. I think it's quite important."

"All right, what is it?"

"Earlier when we were setting up our camera equipment, I heard—or thought I heard—a deputy mention something about Ben's finger being severed. Did I, in fact, actually hear something to that effect?"

Clearly Grice hadn't anticipated this question, and he hesitated, as though trying to decide how—or even if—he should answer it. Finally he nodded. "Nothing wrong with your hearing, Carmen. One of Ben's fingers had been severed."

"Which finger was it?"

"The little finger of his right hand."

"The pinkie?"

"Some people might call it that."

"And where exactly was Ben's pinkie found?"

It was clear to Abby that Grice's aura of self-confidence had dimmed a bit and that he was working hard to restore its luster. The reporter had managed to pry information from him that he'd had no intention of revealing, at least not at this time, and now he had no graceful way to end the interview. "It was in the victim's mouth," he said, an undertone of frustration in his voice.

The reporter was silent for a moment, giving her audience a chance to react to what they had just heard. "Do you know if Ben's finger was severed before or after he was murdered?" she asked.

"I have no idea. The medical examiner can probably tell us that after the autopsy. Now if you'll excuse me, I have work to do."

"One more question, Sheriff. Any idea why the killer would have cut off Ben's finger?"

Grice shook his head. "Anything I say about that would be pure speculation."

Abby got up from the booth, in the process almost bumping into the waiter bringing her coffee.

"Is something wrong?"

"I need to make a phone call," Abby said, slipping into her jacket. "I'll be right back."

Grabbing her purse, she hurried to the restaurant's alcove, got out her cell phone, and dialed Marty's number. He answered almost immediately.

"Did you hear about Ben Ramsdell?" Abby asked.

"No. What happened?"

"He was murdered, apparently shot to death." Hearing only silence from Marty's end, Abby told him what she had learned from Grice's TV interview, including the fact that Ben's body had been found in what looked like an old clunker of a car registered to someone else and that there might have been drugs in the trunk.

"We need to get on this right away," Marty said. "Where are you?"

"Sullivan's Diner, waiting for a breakfast I never

should have ordered. No disrespect intended for Ben, but knowing what happened to his little finger, there's no way in the world I could eat a sausage link right now."

Chapter 21

W hat the fuck!" Graham Calahan muttered as he pulled into the parking area behind his law of-fice and saw that his reserved space was occu-pied. By a shit brown Hummer no less. Easing past the ugly vehicle, he noticed Wardell Tharp in the driver's seat reading a newspaper, apparently oblivious to his sur-roundings.

A moment later, though, after Graham pulled into the first available undesignated space, gathered up his brief-case, and exited his BMW, Tharp was waiting for him at the back entrance to the office building.

"Last time somebody took my spot, I had his car towed," Graham said. "Cost the guy a hundred and fifty bucks, not to mention the time he lost. Time is money, Wardell. You should know that."

"Just wanted to make sure I was your first client of the morning. We need to talk."

"Well, go ahead and talk."

"In your office if you don't mind."

In addition to Graham's secretary, there were two other people in the reception area, a young couple sitting next to each other on a plaid sofa. All three looked up as the door opened.

"Sorry I'm late," Graham said. "Got caught up in the

TV coverage about Ben Ramsdell. Did you hear what happened to him, Jennifer?"

The secretary nodded. "Never thought I'd be mailing his letter so soon. I never thought I'd have to mail it period. Ben must have known he was in grave danger, don't you think, Mr. Calahan?"

Treating the question as rhetorical, Graham looked at Wardell. "This won't take long, will it?" he asked in a low voice.

"It all depends on you, Counselor."

Graham turned back to his secretary. "I need to talk to Mr. Tharp before I do anything else," he said, and then he apologized again to the young couple for making them wait. "This shouldn't take long." Once inside his private office, Graham closed the door. "What's this about, Wardell?"

The big man sat down in the visitor's chair closest to Graham's desk and crossed one leg over the other. "That letter Jennifer just mentioned. I want it."

"You're kidding, of course."

"I'm dead serious, Mr. Calahan."

"Why would you want Ben's letter?"

"I've got my reasons. You're better off not knowing what they are."

The surprise on Graham's face turned to shock. "Y—You killed Ben?"

"You wouldn't believe me if I denied it, so I'll pretend you didn't ask that question. I need that letter, Mr. Calahan."

Graham took a deep breath and let it out. "I can't give it to you. It would be a breach of legal ethics, not to mention against the law."

"So is hiring a hit man to kill your wife."

"You don't think I was serious about that, do you? I was just asking a hypothetical question."

"Yeah, right. Ben Ramsdale is dead. He won't know what happened to that letter or give a flying shit."

"I'll know what happened to it. That's why I have to make sure it gets mailed."

Wardell leaned back in his chair and gazed at the ceiling, hands folded across his ample stomach. "We can do this the hard way or the easy way," he said. "It's your choice. Bottom line is I can't afford to have that letter mailed."

"Are you threatening me, Wardell?"

"I don't threaten. If I want something, I just do what it takes to get it."

Graham seemed to reflect on that statement for a moment. "You wouldn't go so far as to kill me for that letter, would you?"

Uncrossing his legs, Wardell leaned forward in the chair. "Let me put it this way, Mr. Calahan. I like you. I really do. I think we understand each other and have a good working relationship. I'd hate to see that come to an end."

Graham was the first to break eye contact. Slowly he got up from his desk and made his way to a metal filing cabinet on the far wall. Opening one of its drawers, he rifled through several folders until he came to the one he was looking for. He withdrew an envelope, closed the file drawer, and returned to his desk. "How much would you be willing to pay for this letter?" he asked, holding up the envelope. "You can see it hasn't been opened. I have no idea what's inside."

The big man gave Graham a quizzical look. "I wasn't planning on paying you anything."

"That's not the way things work, Wardell. If I let you have this letter, I'll be giving you something that's clearly of value. Don't you think it's reasonable for me to want something in return?"

"What have you got in mind?"

Graham went over to the window and gazed at the butt-ugly vehicle in his parking space. "If I decide I really would like a certain person to disappear, I'd like the job done at a reduced rate."

A smile slowly crept over Wardell's face. "How reduced?"

"I'd like you to give me your word you'll arrange things for ten thousand dollars, not the fifteen thousand you quoted me earlier."

"That wouldn't leave much for me."

"Take it or leave it."

Wardell got up from the chair. "You drive a hard bargain, Counselor. But you've got yourself a deal. Hypothetically, of course."

Graham handed him the envelope. "One more thing," he said and reached for his wallet. He withdrew a twenty-dollar bill and held it out.

"What's this for?"

"It's what Ben paid to have that letter mailed. I wouldn't feel right keeping it."

"That's all you charged the turkey?"

"I don't believe in gouging my clients, especially those who don't have much to begin with."

"A man of principle," Wardell said and took the twenty-dollar bill.

After the black man left the office, Graham asked his secretary to send in the young couple. He was pleased with the way he had handled this tricky situation. Had he done it any other way, Wardell Tharp sooner or later would have considered him a threat, a potential informant to the police. *I could have found myself in the same boat as Ben Ramsdell*, he reflected. *But now, that big miscreant will think of us as partners. And who knows, depending on how things work out, I might have saved myself five thousand dollars in the process.*

Chapter 22

S hannon Pfeiffer and Mitch Folby could have passed for siblings as they sat next to each other on the worn sofa. Both were skinny and had sun-streaked brown hair and blue eyes. There was one major difference, however, and Abby noticed it as soon as she and Marty entered the apartment. Mitch was high as a kite while Shannon seemed sober and alert.

"Did you know Ben broke into his father's house a few days ago?" Marty asked.

"I didn't," Shannon replied. "How about you, Mitch?"

The young man gave her a blank look. "What?"

"Did you know Ben broke into his dad's house the other day?"

Mitch closed his eyes, opened them, shut them again, as though blinking in slow motion.

"He stole two of Will's model train engines," Abby added. "We found them at a hobby shop in Charlottesville. The owner gave us a description of the person he bought them from, and it fit Ben to a T."

Shannon grabbed Mitch's shoulder and gave it a shake. "Focus, Mitch. You might be able to help nail the bastard that killed Ben."

"Don't matter who killed um. The dude's dead—stone cold dead. All the king's hearses 'n all the king's men—"

Shannon shook him harder. "Mitch, we need you to help out here. Pull yourself together and talk sense, or I'll get a glass of cold water and throw it in your face."

"Don't do that," Mitch said, his enunciation slightly improved.

"Then answer Mr. Stith's question like you've got a brain in your head and not a rotten cheese ball."

"It's hard enough answerin' the sherf's questions without you buttin' in, Miz Bitch."

Shannon sighed. "We talked to the sheriff earlier, Mitch, don't you remember? These people are friends of Ben's dad. Now get hold of yourself, and I won't need to butt in."

"Okay, okay. Just hold your horses, will ya." Slowly Mitch turned to Marty. "Fire away, Mr. uh…"

"Stith. I was wondering if you know anything about the model train engines Ben took from his father's basement."

Mitch sucked in a breath and blew it out. Then he shook his head as though trying to clear it. "I know the dude got five hundred bucks for 'em. I thought he was gonna use it to pay off what he owed Tharp, but he took Jezebel to the Big R to buy a load of drugs. Said he was gonna set himself up as a dealer."

"Good Lord," Shannon said, rolling her eyes toward the ceiling. "Good Lord in heaven."

"Who's Jezebel?" Marty asked.

"It's Mitch's car," Shannon said when Mitch didn't seem to hear the question.

"I shouldn't of let the dude take her. But his mind was made up. He'd of gotten to the Big R one way or the other."

"We think Ben's father put a note inside the tender of one of the engines," Marty said. "Did Ben mention anything about finding a note or a message of some kind?"

Mitch shook his head. "What'd the note say?"

"That's what I was hoping you could tell us. We have reason to believe it names the person or persons responsible for Will Ramsdell's murder."

Although Mitch still had a spaced-out look, he seemed to be trying to process what Marty had just told him. "What's all this gotta do with who killed Ben?"

Marty stepped closer to the young man. "To my way of thinking, there's a good chance the person who killed Ben's father also killed Ben."

Mitch's eyes widened. "Whoa. Now that's some heavy shit." His recent effort seemed to have exhausted him, however, and Mitch leaned his head against the back of the sofa and gazed at the ceiling, his breathing resembling light snoring. Except for the fact that his eyes were open, he seemed to have fallen asleep. Suddenly he sat bolt upright. "When I told Ben that Wardell Tharp wouldn't take kindly to competition, he said he had something in his pocket that would keep Tharp from being a problem. Maybe that's the note you're talking about."

"It very well could be. Any idea where Ben might have put it?"

"Don't have a clue," Mitch said and seemed to lapse back into semi-consciousness.

Marty turned to Shannon. "Did the sheriff search the apartment?"

"Him and a deputy. Said they wanted to check Ben's belongings for clues."

"Did you get the impression that they found anything?"

"Not really. They seemed kind of disappointed. At least the sheriff did. The deputy didn't seem to care one way or the other."

"Maybe Ben had the note with him when he was murdered," Abby suggested. "If so, the killer might have it now."

"Sounds to me like Wardell Tharp is the killer,"

Shannon said, as much to herself as to the others. "Help us out, Mitch. If Ben didn't have the note with him, where would he have put it?"

Slowly Mitch seemed to pull himself out of his stupor. "Ben was no dummy. He'd of kept a copy somewhere."

"But where?" Marty asked. "Apparently you two knew Ben pretty well. Where would he hide something important like that?"

"I gave him a stuffed animal for his birthday," Shannon said. "A real cute-looking platypus. It wouldn't have been hard to break the stitching and slide in a piece of paper. Then with a little glue—"

"Naw," Mitch said. "I know where Ben put it." He got up from the sofa, almost falling down in the process. Regaining his balance, he tottered over to the hallway. "Come along, little doggies, and I'll show you."

Abby, Marty, and Shannon followed Ben down the hall to a room that looked like a tornado had ripped through it. Clothes were everywhere—shirts, pants, a ragged-looking lightweight coat, a beat-up pair of running shoes. Some items lay on the bed, others in a folding chair next to a decrepit chest of drawers, still others on the floor. Books, papers, and magazines were scattered here and there. Boxes of all sizes and descriptions had been torn open, their contents strewn on the floor.

"This is Ben's bedroom," Mitch said in a sad voice. "At least it used to be."

Shannon noticed a stuffed animal lying in one corner, its insides ripped out. "Those bastards," she said, her eyes filling with tears. "What a kick in the ass." She sat down on the edge of the bed and turned her head to the wall.

Abby went over and sat down next to her.

"I don't know why I'm being such a baby," Shannon whimpered. "Ben didn't even like me very much. He wasn't exactly my Prince Charming either. But seeing that butchered platypus made me think of Ben lying there with a bullet in his head and his own finger stuck in his mouth. Why'd he have to die like that? Why'd he have to die at all? Ben wasn't a bad person. He really wasn't. He'd have straightened himself out eventually. It's just so…fuckin' sad." She began to cry.

Abby put an arm around her. "It's okay. Go ahead and let it all out if you want."

Resting her head on Abby's shoulder, Shannon began sobbing in earnest, her body heaving.

In the meantime Marty, at Mitch's suggestion, took apart the framed print of a race horse hanging above Ben's bed, hoping to find a note hidden between the matting and the print. When the search proved fruitless, Mitch had a new idea and beckoned Marty to follow him back down the hall.

A few minutes later Marty re-entered the bedroom. "Found it," he said, handing Abby a wrinkled sheet of paper. "It was inside the seat cushion of the recliner between the fabric and the padding."

Abby began reading the handwritten note, fully expecting Ned Copeland to be its subject matter.

Dear Marty,

Not everyone will be pleased to learn I'm getting my old job back. Unless I'm a poor judge of character, or grown paranoid in my old age, both of which are certainly possible, some people might begin wondering if they would be better off with me dead.

Wardell Tharp's reason for wanting me out of the way should be obvious.

Quentin Grice's is less so. Maggie Calahan can provide whatever information you need regarding Grice's motive.

I hope you never have the occasion to read this, Marty.

But if you do, I wanted to share these thoughts with somebody I know I can trust.

Happy trails, old buddy.
Will

Chapter 23

It's getting late, Jamie," Nelson Lang called from the doorway of their bedroom, the second time that morning he had come downstairs and made such an announcement. "Better get up."

Opening her eyes, Jamie slowly rolled over in the bed. As she sat up, a shaft of sunlight slanting through a gap in the curtains caused her to squint. "What time is it?"

"Almost noon. Your foursome tees off in half an hour."

With a sigh Jamie turned her head away from the sunlight. "Tell them I'm not feeling well and to go ahead without me."

"You're not sick, are you?"

"I don't have a cold or the flu, if that's what you mean."

"Are you depressed?"

"Give the man a kewpie doll."

Nelson didn't take offense, knowing how out of sorts he had been, and acted, during his bout with depression. "Want me to fix you something to eat?"

His wife shook her head. "I'm not hungry."

Nelson hovered for a moment in the doorway, and then, his face taking on a somber expression, he stepped closer to the bed. "I apologize for the way I acted the other night, Jamie. I was a real asshole."

She gave him a feeble smile. "It's not like I've been a model wife."

A wave of sympathy washed over Nelson. He wanted to tell her that she was a better wife than he had been a husband and that she should try to look on the bright side, which shouldn't be too difficult now that Pinecroft was no longer in danger of bankruptcy. There was no reason they couldn't work things out between them and still have a good life together. But he couldn't find the words, unable to get past the fact that Jamie, except for rare instances, had withheld from him what Maggie Calahan so joyously provided.

"I'll keep an eye out for the girls," he said and turned toward the door.

"Nelson?"

"Yeah?"

"Never mind." Lying back down on the bed, Jamie turned her head to the wall. "Make sure you give Bogie some fresh water."

෴

Since Maggie Calahan was busy with a customer, Abby took the opportunity to look for something to give her mother. It wasn't long before she found a suitable present, a Whiting and Davis mesh purse in a colorful Art Deco geometric design. During her drugging days, Abby had stolen a similar purse from her mother's collection and sold it to a local antique dealer, probably for a tenth of what it was worth. Purse in hand, she joined Marty in the adjacent booth where he was examining a Murano milifiore paperweight.

"Think Jamie would like this?" he asked. "She collects paperweights."

Abby studied the item. "It's beautiful, Marty. You can

probably get it for less than the asking price. Most antique shops give a ten percent discount if you ask for it."

"You sound like an expert."

Abby resisted the impulse to tell him that she had stolen enough antiques to fill a curio cabinet. "My mom is a collector," she said.

They waited until the customer left the shop, and then they took their items to the cash register.

"I was beginning to think you'd gone into hibernation, Marty."

"Not quite. Maggie, this is Abby Burlew. She's a reporter for a North Carolina newspaper, and she was a friend of Will's."

Maggie extended her hand. "Pleased to meet you."

"Same here," Abby said and shook the woman's hand. "Marty and I are investigating Will's murder. We think you might be able to help."

"Me? Why?"

Marty took out his wallet and withdrew Will's note. "This should explain," he said, unfolding the note and handing it to Maggie. "Let's take care of these purchases first, though. Can you do any better on this paperweight?"

Maggie glanced at it and then at the purse Abby was holding. "It just so happens I'm offering a twenty percent discount to all police officers, current and former, and whoever accompanies them to the shop."

"Works for me," Marty said, and Abby nodded her agreement.

After completing the paperwork and wrapping and bagging the two items, Maggie read the note, her face taking on a curious, surprised look.

"Where did you get this?" she asked, handing the note back to Marty.

He explained how they knew of the note's existence, how it came to be in Ben Ramsdell's possession, and where they had found it. "Apparently you have some pertinent information about Quentin Grice."

"I don't know how helpful it'll be," Maggie said and went to the front door, which she locked. Then she put a *Closed* sign in the window. "Let's talk in the back. Nobody will see us from the street and think I'll open up if they knock."

She led them to a booth filled with antique furniture, including a grouping that caught Abby's eye, a circular smoked-glass table surrounded by four white director's chairs. After pulling out two of the chairs for Abby and Marty, Maggie took one for herself.

"Nice set," Abby said. "It would look really nice in my apartment."

"I'll give you an even better deal than I did on the purse," Maggie said. "Think about it and let me know." She turned to Marty. "I've suspected all along that Quentin Grice had something to do with Will's murder. But unless he's a mind reader, I don't see how he could have known about Will's contingency plan."

"Contingency plan?"

"You knew he'd decided to take the chief's job, right?"

Marty nodded. "He told me that on the day he was murdered."

"Wisteria's finances are in sad shape, Marty. So bad, in fact, that the town council is considering abolishing the police department to save money. Will knew that, and he was reluctant to accept a job that might be temporary—until I suggested he could use it as a springboard for an even better job, namely Quentin Grice's."

"Will was planning to run for sheriff?"

"Only if the police department lost its funding. I told him if that happened, Graham and I would support him if he decided to run."

"What were his chances of getting elected?" Abby asked.

"Folks in Wisteria would have voted for him in a heartbeat. I think the rest of the county would have too once we got the word out about what a good chief he'd been and the fact that he'd resigned because he was grieving his wife's death."

"So Grice did have a motive," Marty said. "Assuming, of course, that he knew about Will's plans, or suspected them."

"But why resort to murder unless he knew for sure the police department would lose its funding?" Abby said. "That's not a foregone conclusion, is it, Maggie?"

"No. According to my husband, the issue could go either way."

"Then why kill a man when there's a good chance you won't need him dead?"

"As a preventative measure," Marty offered. "If Grice waited until after Will announced his candidacy, his motive would have been obvious."

Abby shook her head. "That seems like a stretch to me."

"Not necessarily. From what I understand about Quentin Grice, he isn't the kind to let someone stand in the way of his getting something or keeping it."

Maggie nodded her agreement.

❧❧❧

After giving Bogie fresh food and water and informing the three women golfers that his wife wasn't feeling well enough to play, Nelson Lang went to the kitchen and poured himself a cup of coffee. The telephone rang, and he hurried to answer it.

When the caller asked if the course was still open,

Nelson gave his usual spiel about Pinecroft never closing, even in the dead of winter.

He took his coffee to the living room, and after checking the parking lot to make sure no more golfers had arrived, he sat down on the sofa and tried to relax. Bogie sidled up against his leg.

"Glad you're not holding the other night against me," Nelson said and began stroking the cat's head. Bogie soaked up the attention for a while before wandering off to another part of the house.

Nelson thought of Jamie still in bed so late in the day. Although he suspected that she could use some professional help, he didn't know how to broach the subject when the likely cause of her depression was his own lengthy bout with the illness, his more recent affair with Maggie, or a combination of the two. Once he got his own depression under control, though, Jamie had seemed fine. Actually, she hadn't seemed really depressed until quite recently.

Nelson wondered if Jamie's depression had been caused by Will Ramsdell's death. She had told Nelson that she stayed at Will's house for the sole purpose of saving money and that she had not slept with him. Nelson had believed her at the time, but now he wasn't so sure. Clearly Will had had strong feelings for Jamie. Why else would he leave his estate to Pinecroft? And why would Jamie go into such a funk now if she hadn't felt the same way about him?

Again the phone rang. This time it was Graham Calahan's secretary calling to remind the Langs that they needed to sign some documents before the inheritance could proceed. Nelson told her they would come in on Monday.

He fielded two more calls and chatted with a pair of golfers returning the key to an electric cart they had rented.

Glad for the company, Nelson gave each a cup of coffee and eventually sold one of them a membership for next year.

After the golfers left, Nelson went to the kitchen for something to eat, though he wasn't really hungry. He was about to open a can of soup when he detected movement out of the corner of his eye. Turning, he saw Jamie standing in the doorway, naked except for the thong he had given her a few years earlier. Nelson had purchased the item only partly as a gag gift, hoping she would wear it. She never had until now.

"Here I am," she said in a low, almost apologetic tone. "If you still like what you see, why don't you put the we're-not-home sign on the front door and meet me in the bedroom."

❧❧❧

The meeting with Maggie Calahan did not convince Abby that Quentin Grice should be their number one suspect in Will Ramsdell's murder. Back in her car, she told Marty she had decided to return to North Carolina that afternoon. "My mom has taken care of Kevin for three days now and can use a break."

"Why leave when we're on a roll? We're a lot closer to nailing Will's killer than we were yesterday."

"I don't think we are. I'm not ruling out Grice, but I still think Ned Copeland did it."

"Even after hearing what Maggie had to say?"

"Especially after hearing what Maggie had to say. As far as I'm concerned, we're a long way from knowing for sure who killed Will. And we're even further from being able to prove it."

"My gut feeling is we're close to doing both."

"Then you must have in mind what our next step should be."

Marty shrugged. "I was hoping we could come up with something over dinner. The Mountain Top Inn has a fish fry on Friday nights. I thought we might give it a try."

"Some other time, Marty. Right now I don't have a clue what we should do next. Apparently you don't either. I for one could use some time to think about what we've learned so far."

"When will you be coming back?"

"I'd like to attend Ben's funeral. Any idea when it'll be?"

"I'd think Monday. I'll check and let you know. Maybe we can get together afterwards and discuss how to proceed with the investigation."

"Assuming we've come up with any fresh ideas in the meantime. Right now we can't even agree on the main suspect."

When they reached the Shenandoah Inn's parking lot, Marty told Abby that he would miss her. "In spite of our differences of opinion, I feel like we make a really good team," he said as he climbed on his motorcycle. "Maybe not quite as good as Scully and Mulder but we're close."

"We haven't solved anything yet," Abby reminded him. "Don't forget to call when you find out about Ben's funeral."

Chapter 24

Quentin Grice was livid. Not only had Wardell Tharp disregarded his advice about Ben Ramsdell but he was late. Grice hated waiting for people. For the past ten minutes, he had paced back and forth near the boarded-up concession stand at the abandoned outdoor movie theater, the location where he and Tharp had agreed to meet. Any way you cut it, the guy was getting too big for his britches.

Another few minutes passed before Grice heard the crunching of gravel on the theater's entranceway. As though the driver had all the time in the world, a brown Hummer eased around the corner of the concession stand and came to a stop next to Grice's police cruiser.

"We were supposed to meet at two," Grice said after Tharp opened the door and hopped to the ground.

"Got caught at a railroad crossing, Sheriff. If that train had been going any slower, it would've been standing still. I stopped counting coal hoppers at fifty."

Grice glared at the black man. "Why did you kill Ben Ramsdell when I asked you to hold off dealing with him until I figured out how best to handle the situation?"

"I didn't kill the turkey. Word on the street is that he made a drug run to Richmond and somebody saw the transaction and tailed him to that isolated stretch of road where his body was found. Whoever it was relieved Ben of his purchases and whatever was left of his money."

"Knowing what I do, I have no doubt that person was you. Our agreement was I'd look the other way when it comes to your transgressions if they aren't so serious no sheriff could ignore them. Ben's murder sure as hell fits that category."

"I told you I didn't have anything to do with that."

"And I don't believe you. Now I've got two high-profile murders on my hands."

Wardell shrugged. "Afraid I can't help you with that, Sheriff."

"That's where you're wrong. You can help me and you will."

"I didn't kill Ben Ramsdale, and nobody can prove I did."

"Forget about Ben for the time being. Right now I'm more interested in his father. Will Ramsdell was murdered by a guy named Ned Copeland. Do you know him?"

"Name's familiar. He the caretaker at that hunt club on the other side of Wisteria?"

"Yeah, Holly Oak. Several years ago Will did something to Copeland not many people know about. I'm surprised Copeland waited this long for his revenge. I'd throw his ass in jail, but all I've got is circumstantial evidence. It wouldn't be enough for the DA."

Wardell leaned over and picked up a discarded metal bottle cap. He poked at the cork insert with his index finger, then flipped the cap toward the concession stand and gazed at the expanse of rusted audio hookups that resembled a crop of ungainly metallic plants awaiting harvest.

"There's a way Copeland can be brought to justice," Grice said. "But it will take an effort beyond the capability of my present staff."

"I'm listening."

For the next few minutes, the sheriff explained what he had in mind. Tharp listened quietly, alternately gazing at the audio hookups and the movie screen that threatened to collapse into the encroaching weeds and bushes.

"Guess that's doable," he said, his eyes once again focused on Grice. "What do I get out of it?"

"A reasonable fee. Plus it will go a long way toward making me ignore the fact that the most obvious suspect in Ben Ramsdell's murder is you."

∾∾

Marty Stith was disappointed when he realized that Jamie's car was gone. Parking his motorcycle in its usual spot near the deck overhang, he carried the Bygone Daze bag up the back steps and into the house.

Nelson was in the living room reading the *Hawthorne Observer*, something he almost never did so late in the day.

"Where's Jamie?" Marty asked, setting the bag on the table next to the display case where she kept her collection of antique glassware.

"At the cemetery putting flowers on her mother's grave," Nelson said, getting up from the sofa. "I'm worried about her, Marty. She stayed in bed all morning and part of the afternoon. When she finally did get up, she...well, she acted really strange."

"In what way?"

"She wanted to make love."

Marty chuckled. "Nothing strange about that. You're a lucky man, Nelson."

"Under normal circumstances, I'd agree." Nelson walked to the window overlooking the golfers' parking lot. "Today is the first time she's let me touch her in months." He paused, gazing vaguely in the direction of the first tee. "I might as well have been making love to one of those floor mannequins at Maltby's."

"Give her time," Marty offered, not knowing what else to say. "She took Will's murder real hard. Then Will's son gets murdered. It's not easy dealing with a double whammy like that."

Nelson turned and faced Marty. "Our problems didn't start with Will's murder. I hate to say it, but Jamie has never been very interested in making love, at least not with me."

Marty tried to come up with something reassuring to say, but all he could think of was

Nelson's ongoing affair. "I know it's none of my business, but you've been spending a lot of time with Maggie. Don't you think that might contribute to the problem?"

"It probably does. And that concerns me too. I don't like being unfaithful to Jamie. But damn it, Marty, the fact is I've pretty much had to if I wanted any kind of sex life at all."

✑✑✑

Since the direct approach to her mother's grave meant having to pass Will Ramsdell's, Jamie took the long way, driving up the hill to the northwest corner of the cemetery and then cutting across to the opposite side. Parking next to an oak tree that still clung to most of its leaves, she slowly got out of her car, glad there wasn't another vehicle or person in sight.

Jamie hadn't visited her mother's grave in months and was surprised to find the floral arrangement she had put there in August still thriving.

Nevertheless, she gathered it up, replacing it with the arrangement of mums she had purchased a few minutes earlier at Turk's, the only garden center in the area still open.

"Hopefully these will get you through the winter, Mom," she said in as cheery a voice as she could muster. "I'm afraid it's the best I can do." She carried the older flowers to the edge of the cemetery and tossed them into the woods. Then she walked back to her mother's grave.

Jamie stood next to the stone marker for a long time before giving in to tears. The fact that she shed them more for herself than for her mother made her all the more ashamed.

Chapter 25

Marty had just turned on the microwave when he heard a vehicle pull into Pinecroft's back parking area. Glancing out the window, he saw Jamie get out of her Spark, her blond hair purple in the fluorescent light from the pole lamp. Her face looked drawn, almost haggard, as she climbed the steps, her left hand holding the wooden railing for support, her right clutching a McDonald's bag. Marty opened the door for her and stepped aside as she entered the kitchen.

"Sorry I'm late but I had things to do," she said and set the McDonald's bag on the counter between the sink and the refrigerator. "This isn't exactly a weight watcher's special, but who's counting calories, right? Whatever you don't want, just put back in the fridge. Nelson will probably be hungry after his nightly roll in the hay with Maggie."

It was the first time Jamie had mentioned her husband's infidelity, and Marty was temporarily at a loss for words. He went over and stood next to her. "I know for a fact that he still loves you, Jamie. He seems to think you've lost interest in him."

She put the McDonald's bag in the refrigerator and then pulled out a chair and sat down at the kitchen table. "I've lost interest in most everything," she said and began fiddling with a crease in the tablecloth, smoothing it. "I couldn't compete with Maggie anyway, even if I wanted to."

Marty sat down in the chair across the table from Jamie. "You're a very attractive woman," he said. "Maybe if you—"

A bell rang and the microwave went silent. Jamie pushed back her chair and stood up. "Your supper's ready. If you're hungry later on, don't forget the burgers and fries in the fridge."

Marty followed her into the living room. "I bought you something today." He picked up the bag he'd left on the table next to the curio cabinet and handed it to her.

Jamie peered inside, her face brightening when she saw the paperweight. "A Murano," she said and took it over to the halogen lamp next to the sofa for a better look. "Where did you get it, Marty?"

"Maggie's shop." The words were barely out of his mouth when he realized his mistake. "I'll take it back tomorrow and get you something just as nice in Hawthorne."

"You'll do no such thing." Jamie gazed at the paperweight, turning it this way and that. Opening the door of the curio cabinet, she began rearranging the items on the middle shelf. When everything was the way she wanted, she set the Murano in the center of the shelf, making sure it wasn't touching another piece. "The place of honor," she said and eased the door closed. "Thank you, Marty. It's a lovely gift."

She gave him a hug and then turned and slowly walked toward the steps leading to the lower level of the house. On the landing, halfway to the bottom, her head was briefly turned in Marty's direction, and he couldn't help but notice the sadness on her face.

ᴄ⁓ᴄ⁓

Abby had planned to eat a late supper at her mother's house. A few miles after she crossed into North Carolina, however, her appetite got the better of her. Spotting a lighted sign advertising a KFC in the distance, she slowed her car and took the next exit.

She had almost the entire restaurant to herself. As she ate, she thought about what she had learned in Virginia. Quite a lot for such a short period of time, she thought. And yet, as she had told Marty earlier, they were still a long way from identifying Will's killer. Ned Copeland, Quentin Grice, and Wardell Tharp all seemed likely candidates, but there were others who couldn't be ruled out: the Langs, Mel Taggart, even Will's dead son.

Abby wondered why Marty, after initially mentioning Ned Copeland as a possible suspect, had refused to believe the man could have killed Will. It's like he knows something about Copeland that he isn't sharing. But what? And why would Marty withhold information?

A reason suddenly occurred to Abby, one so troubling she put down the chicken breast she was eating and stared into space. Could it be that Marty Stith is a phony, not the person he appears to be? He seems like a genuinely nice person, a man committed to helping her identify the person who murdered Will, and yet...

Had Marty been orchestrating the information she received? Had he actually been trying to lead her away from, instead of toward, Will's killer?

Abby thought of the poem supposedly mailed from Graham Calahan's office. For all she knew, Marty had written that poem himself. The same applied to the note Ben Ramsdell supposedly found in the C&O tender. Marty could have written that too. He also could have stolen Will's train engines and given them to Jim Fergus in return for the man's agreeing to describe Ben as his supplier. Was that the way the scenario at the Whistle Stop had really played out?

You're letting your imagination run away with you, Abby told herself. *Bipolars tend to do that, you know. We get weird ideas in our heads, and then, to the detriment of ourselves and others, we act on them.*

And yet certain things about the case just didn't add up. Even the notion that Will would have left behind a message naming people who might have wanted him dead didn't ring true. Why would a level-headed man like Will Ramsdell go to such bizarre lengths to keep the names a secret from everyone except her and Marty?

The fact that Marty hadn't seemed troubled by Will's elaborate transmittal process made Abby wonder all the more if he had written the poem and the note himself. But why would he do such a thing? Had he been trying to shield Ned Copeland from suspicion? Had he been trying to buy time, cause her investigation to go around in circles and ultimately lead nowhere?

Abby thought of her conversation with Quentin Grice. The sheriff had been surprised that she hadn't included Marty as one of her suspects. Maybe she should have included him. Had she been wrong to assume that the Langs, as the major owners of Pinecroft, were the only real beneficiaries of Will's estate? Maybe Marty had sunk more money into the course than he'd let on. And since he and Will were friends, maybe Will had told him his estate was earmarked for Pinecroft. If that's what really had happened, then Marty Stith did have a motive.

Abby wondered if she was not only being paranoid but also getting manic. The news of Ben's death had shocked her. Ever since hearing it, she had been more revved up than usual, more impulsive. She hadn't really planned on returning home today; the idea just popped in her head and she went with it. She didn't feel manic, though. She felt lucid and in complete control. Was that in itself a sign that she was manic?

Stop worrying about it, she told herself. You'll drive yourself crazy if you're not there already.

"Are you the owner of that red Toyota out front?"

The voice seemed to come out of nowhere. Glancing up, Abby saw a scruffy-looking young man, probably still a teenager, wearing a hooded parka and rumpled, baggy jeans. Instead of looking directly at her, he seemed to stare at a spot just past her left shoulder, his eyes not completely in focus.

"Is there a problem?"

"Your lights are on. Lemme have your keys, and I'll turn 'em off for you."

"My keys?"

"Your car's locked, right?"

It took Abby exactly two more seconds to decide how to respond. "I'm an off-duty cop, and I've got a pistol in my handbag, a nine millimeter Glock to be exact," she said, enunciating each word. "Do you still want my keys?"

Without changing his expression, the young man turned and walked away.

"I didn't think so."

Abby took her time finishing her meal, and she enjoyed every bite.

When she left the restaurant, her "good Samaritan" was nowhere to be found. Her car's lights were off, and, just as she suspected, the motor started right up. No problem with the battery.

As she exited the KFC's parking lot, Abby goosed the engine, feeling a sense of exhilaration as gravel clattered against the Toyota's wheel wells. She blew past a slow-moving pickup truck and an even slower moving sedan. By the time she reached the interstate, she had located an oldies rock station on her car's radio and was singing along with Jim Croce in a wild, off-key rendition of "Bad, Bad Leroy Brown."

ಲ⊃ಲ

Relief washed over Nelson Lang when he saw Jamie's car in its usual spot. He parked beside it and hurried up the deck steps, anxious to talk to her. When Marty told him that Jamie had already gone to bed, Nelson was disappointed. He spent the next hour flicking TV channels, and when the local news came on at eleven, he turned off the TV and went downstairs.

Bogie was curled up at the foot of the bed, apparently asleep. Judging from the rhythmic rise and fall of Jamie's breathing, so was she. Nelson hoped she would wake up when he joined her in the bed, but she didn't stir. He wanted to talk to her about this afternoon. Since having sex with him had apparently become sheer drudgery, an unpleasant duty she occasionally forced herself to perform, he wanted to know if there was anything he could do to make their love-making less of a chore? If not, was there some sort of libido enhancer Jamie could try that might make the act at least somewhat pleasurable?

Jamie stirred when Nelson touched her shoulder. Then slowly she turned over on her side, her back to him, her breathing once again regular. Leaning closer, he started to say her name, but then decided not to wake her. More than likely, he reasoned, she wouldn't be in any mood to talk.

Nelson wanted to give his marriage every chance to work. If that meant going without sex for weeks, even months on end, then so be it. But if it meant being celibate for the rest of his life, that was a steep price to pay. "I don't know what to do," he wanted to tell Jamie. "I know I can't have a mistress and a good marriage too. I'm willing to

break off with Maggie if that will make things better between you and me. But if you'd rather scrub floors than
make love to me, maybe we really shouldn't be married."

As though in response, Bogie meowed softly, stretched,
and settled contentedly against Nelson's left foot.

Chapter 26

The fire next time…

Where had Jamie heard those words? Must be the title of a book, she thought, though she didn't remember having read it. She knew the phrase originated in the *Bible*, God's promise to Noah that He would not use a flood if He needed to punish the world again for its evil ways. Whatever its origin, the words kept echoing in Jamie's mind as she stood at the edge of the moonlit clearing and gazed at the sprawling log structure where she hoped her father would be sleeping.

So far, everything had gone according to plan. Other than an ethereal-looking possum that scurried across the road soon after Jamie got out of her car and a creature she couldn't identify that growled in the undergrowth a few moments later, there had been no surprises, nothing unexpected. An owl hooted as she stood watching the house, but the sound didn't break her concentration.

Jamie chose the first window to the left of the front door. Odds were that it gave on the living room and, therefore, was far enough from where her father slept that the noise she made breaking into the house would be less likely to wake him. Grasping the stool in one hand and the gasoline container in the other, she stepped into the moonlight and began making her way across the clearing, walking as fast as she dared without risking a fall.

The house had conventional windows, a big relief. Had they been the casement type, she probably couldn't have broken in and would have had to resort to her alternate plan of setting fire to the building and waiting for her father to emerge, a scenario that could prove disastrous if he chose the back door or slipped out a window beyond her view. Waiting for him outside the house also precluded giving him a dose of his own medicine, waking him from a sound sleep to a nightmare in progress.

Jamie clicked on the flashlight and examined the screen and the glass beyond, looking for signs of an alarm system. Noticing nothing out of the ordinary, she aimed the flashlight inside. The beam slid across a sofa, a coffee table, two upholstered chairs, a fireplace—an exceptionally large room with oversized furniture but otherwise unoccupied. She switched off the flashlight and set it on the ground. Then she reached in her backpack for the wire cutter she had purchased at the Do It Center. She began cutting the screen, first a horizontal slit across the middle, then three more cuts, one down each side and the final one along the bottom edge.

Once she removed the lower half of the screen, Jamie tried the window, not really expecting it to be unlocked. It wasn't. Playing the flashlight beam along the top of the sash, she located the latch. Then she slid the step stool closer to the window and carefully climbed on it. She dug in her backpack for the glass cutter she also had purchased at the Do It Center and began the process of cutting out the pane closest to the latch. The job proved tedious, but eventually she was able to break loose the rectangular piece of glass while still managing to hold onto it. After placing it and the glass cutter in her backpack, she reached through the hole and released the latch. Stepping back to the ground, she carefully pushed up on the sash, raising the window about two feet above the sill.

For nearly a minute, she listened for sounds that might indicate her father's presence. Hearing nothing, she retrieved a section of rope from her backpack and, using a knot she had practiced earlier, tied one end to the gas container. Holding onto the rope's other end, she climbed over the sill. Once inside the house, she hauled up the container, smelling fumes as she set it on floor. She untied the rope, returned it to her backpack, and eased the window shut.

For the next few moments, Jamie stood motionless, letting her senses acclimate to her surroundings, hoping to detect the sound of snoring. Among her many unpleasant memories of her father was the fact that he snored, sometimes wildly. Such a noise would make locating him easier, but the only sound she heard was that of her own shallow breathing.

ᑲᔕᑲ

Nelson rolled over on his stomach, thinking he had been snoring and Jamie was trying to turn him over. Again he felt his shoulder being shaken.

"Wake up, Nelson. It's me. Jamie just left."

Opening his eyes, Nelson raised up on one elbow. In the dim light from the hallway, he saw Marty Stith standing next to the bed.

"I heard a noise out back. When I checked to see what it was, Jamie was putting something in the trunk of her car. It looked like that step stool you keep in the pantry. Then she got in the car and drove off."

Nelson sat up in the bed, trying to make sense of what Marty was telling him. Glancing at the clock on the dresser, he saw it was almost one-thirty. "Where's she going at this hour?" he muttered, the urgency of the situation beginning to flood in on him.

"That's what I wanted to ask you. I checked the pantry and that stool is gone."

Nelson roused himself from the bed and hurried down the hall to the laundry room where he opened the metal storage container next to the washing machine. When he realized both shotguns were still there, he ran back to the bedroom and felt along the top shelf of the closet. "My pistol's gone," he said and quickly pulled on a pair of jeans over his pajama bottoms and a sweatshirt over his bare upper body.

Brushing past Marty, he hurried upstairs to the telephone and dialed Maggie Calahan's cell phone number. She answered in a groggy voice after four rings.

"Jamie left Pinecroft a few minutes ago, and she's got my pistol. She took our step stool too, so she might try to break in. Whatever you do, don't open the door for her or go near a window."

"Have you called the police?"

"You call them if you see her car or hear any strange noises. I'm not sure it's you she's after."

"Who else could it be?"

"Just take care of yourself, Maggie," Nelson said and ended the call. He opened the phone book and found Holly Oak's number. He started to dial it, changed his mind, and dropped the phone back on its cradle.

"I'm going out there," he told Marty, who had followed him up the stairs.

"Where?"

"Holly Oak. If she plans on killing herself, she might try to kill her father too. I just hope I can get there before it's too late."

"I'm going with you," Marty said and hurried for the stairs. "We'll take my car."

e/ɔe/ɔ

After her eyes adjusted to the dark, Jamie reached in her backpack for the pistol, which, along with the flash-light, was all she would need for the next phase of her plan. She began picking her way across the living room toward the hallway. Once there, she stopped and listened. There was a scratching noise, a tree branch, Jamie decided, that was brushing against the side of the house.

She wondered if her father was awake and knew someone had broken in. If so, he would have his pistol ready and would shoot as soon as he detected movement. *Be prepared to shoot back*, Jamie told herself. *If you're the one still standing, you can go back for the gasoline.*

The fire next time, repeated in her consciousness. She could almost see the words hanging in the darkness like a fluorescent sign an airplane might pull across the night sky. *Make a good title for a poem*, she reflected. As she gathered herself for this next-to-last phase of her plan, she thought of the opening lines for such a poem:

> *Cremate the bastard and yourself too*
> *'til there's nothing left of either of you.*

❧❧❧

Marty drove as fast as he dared. The traffic light at the Route 64 intersection was red, but the only reason he even slowed was an eighteen wheeler barreling down the hill, heading toward Wisteria. They didn't encounter another vehicle until shortly after turning on the access road to Holly Oak—Jamie's Chevy Spark parked on the shoulder.

"I'm driving up to the front door," he told Nelson. "No reason to be secretive at this point."

"I wish I'd brought my shotgun in case Copeland gives us trouble."

"I've got my pistol."

The lodge loomed ahead, dark except for the next-to-last window on the far left. Marty pulled up to the front porch and both men hurriedly got out.

"If it's locked, start knocking and ringing the bell," Marty said. "I'll see where that light is coming from."

"Don't shoot if there's any chance whatsoever you might hit Jamie!" Nelson called as Marty broke into a run, heading for the far end of the house.

As he approached the lighted window, Marty saw what looked like a large kitchen. There was a refrigerator, a stove, and then, off to one side, a long wooden table. Someone was standing next to the table, and when Marty moved closer, he realized it was Jamie. She was staring upward, toward the ceiling, a calm, almost serene look on her face. There was a pistol in her right hand. Slowly she raised it to her head.

"Don't do it, Jamie! It's me, Marty. Nelson is with me. Whatever you did to your father doesn't matter. The guy had it coming." Not knowing if she could see him or even hear him, Marty knocked on the glass. "Ned Copeland doesn't matter, Jamie! You do!"

Suddenly Marty realized there was someone else in the kitchen, a man who towered over Jamie. He seemed to be standing on something. The far end of the table? Slowly the man's head turned, just enough to reveal a ponytail and other familiar features.

At first, Marty couldn't comprehend what he was seeing. The man was upright, no question about it. Although in a vertical position and well above Jamie, he wasn't standing on anything. He seemed to be staring at the floor, as though wondering why there was so much space between it and his feet. Then Marty noticed the rope around the man's neck. Ned Copeland was dangling in the air, suspended from one of the kitchen rafters like an oversized ham hanging from a smokehouse ceiling.

Chapter 27

After arriving at her mother's house in Scarboro, Abby switched off her cell phone and didn't turn it on again until late the next morning after she and Kevin returned to their apartment. She had two messages, the most recent from Charlene Greer instructing her to report to the *Gazette* first thing Monday morning. "The Wardlaws' lawyer has scheduled a press conference at ten, and you need to cover it," her boss said. "And why didn't you leave your cell phone on after I specifically asked you to?"

The other message was from Marty Stith telling her that Ned Copeland was dead. "Apparently, he hung himself," Marty said. "There was a note near his body saying he knew the sheriff was closing in on him for Will's murder, and he had no intention of spending the rest of his life in jail."

Feeling like doing a victory dance, Abby dialed Marty's cell phone number. "Justice has finally been served," she said as soon as he answered. "And here you poo-pooed the idea every time I even suggested Copeland might be the killer."

"He was definitely capable of murder, Abby, but he didn't kill Will. He was a hundred miles away at the time. I

know that because I've been keeping him under surveillance"

"Why would you do that?"

"I'm an FBI agent."

"Yeah, right. And I'm Hillary Clinton."

"Remember that guy at the Shamrock who thought he
recognized me? Actually, he did. I had some dealings with
him while I was in the FBI's Charlottesville office."

"So you really are Luke what's-his-name?"

"Luke Dawson. Yeah, that's me."

Abby took a deep breath and blew it out in a prolonged
sigh. "What other lies have you told me, Luke Dawson?"

"None, except for saying I invested money in Pinecroft.
Even that wasn't a total fabrication. I've been paying the
Langs room and board."

"What about your ex-wife and kid?"

"I've got both. I kind of overstated the part about my ex
leaving me. I might be a neer-do-well, but the real reason
we divorced is we just didn't mesh. She's re-married now
and I'm still single. A year or so ago, Will asked the FBI to
investigate corruption in Augusta County government,
with particular emphasis on the sheriff's department. He
agreed to provide cover by pretending to hire me as one of
his officers, which worked fine as long as he was police
chief. When he resigned, he suggested I rent one of the
Langs' bedrooms and use Pinecroft as my base of opera-
tions. It was a win-win situation. The Langs needed the
money, and I had fresh cover as a guy dumb enough to
sink money in a struggling golf course."

Abby took a moment to digest what Luke was telling
her. "What's Ned Copeland got to do with corruption in
Augusta County government?"

"Nothing. Do you remember that Richmond doctor
who was murdered because he performed abortions? The
killer left a note claiming to be God's avenging angel."

"Yeah, I read about that."

"It wasn't the first time that kind of note had been left at the scene of a hate crime. By then, the FBI suspected Copeland was behind some of those crimes. My boss decided I could be better utilized keeping him under surveillance."

Although the explanation sounded plausible enough, Abby was still angry. "Why didn't you tell me the truth from the get-go?"

"I was going to last night, but you up and left town." Luke explained that Will and the Langs were the only people who knew his true identity and that even the Langs didn't know his real name. "They knew I was keeping track of someone. I was afraid they wouldn't let me live at Pinecroft if they knew it was Copeland—or even worse, tip him off. Turned out that wouldn't have been an issue. Jamie despised her father. Last night she went to Holly Oak intending to kill him. Apparently, she was planning to kill herself too. Nelson and I got there just in time."

"I thought you said Copeland hung himself."

"He did. At least it looked that way. He was dead when Jamie got there."

"Ned Copeland didn't strike me as the suicidal type. Are you sure Jamie didn't kill him?"

"He was hanging from the kitchen rafters. Jamie couldn't possibly have hoisted him up there. It would have taken two people—or at the very least, one exceptionally strong man."

Abby didn't know what to make of this new information since the person providing it had already proved himself a dissembler. Maybe she shouldn't be so quick to believe him now. "Marty—damn, it's going to be hard to stop calling you that. Luke, are you sure Ned Copeland didn't murder Will?"

"I'm one-hundred percent positive. He might have

hired somebody to do it, but there's no way he could have done it himself. Before I moved in with the Langs, I installed a tracking device on Copland's truck. By the way, that's why I never had a car of my own to pick you up in. Mine has electronic surveillance equipment that I'd have a hard time explaining. I kept it in the shed where the Langs store their mowing equipment, and I only drove it when I was tailing Copeland, which I was doing the day before Will was murdered. I followed him to a motel in Blacksburg and handed him off to FBI agents from the Roanoke office. They kept him under surveillance for the next day and a half. Copeland never left Blacksburg until several hours after Will was killed."

"I wish you'd told me all this from the start. Or at least not let me think Copeland was a legitimate suspect. I wasted a lot of time thinking he was our man."

"I apologize for that. When I mentioned the guy, I didn't realize you'd latch onto him like a bulldog. When you did, I tried to steer you in a different direction, short of actually telling you why he couldn't have killed Will. That would have blown my cover."

"Then why would you have told me the truth last night?"

"By then, I was convinced I could trust you."

Abby chuckled. "The shoe is on the other foot now, isn't it? I don't know how much I can trust *you*."

"Can't blame you for that. Listen, Abby. I've got a favor to ask. When you come back to Wisteria, I'd like you to keep calling me Marty. That's the name I've been going by around here. It might cause problems if people other than the Langs hear you call me Luke."

"You told the Langs?"

"I told Nelson. Jamie had a nervous breakdown last night. She's in the hospital."

Abby still wasn't convinced that Luke was being

straight with her. "Why do you need to maintain your cover now that Copeland is dead?" she asked.

"I've been put back on my original assignment. Quentin Grice was the main focus of that assignment and he still is. Since he's also a suspect in Will's murder, it's not like I'll be switching gears entirely. I'd like to get together with you soon, Abby—assuming you're willing to have anything more to do with me."

"I'll think about it. As far as I'm concerned, Mr. FBI Agent, you're on probation. One more awkward step and you're toast."

Chapter 28

Nelson Lang spent Saturday morning in Pinecroft's pro shop, answering the telephone and taking care of customers addicted to golf enough to brave the cold. Around noon he ate lunch, and then, having been assured that Luke Dawson would look after things until he returned, he drove to Hawthorne. He arrived at the hospital shortly before one, the beginning of the psychiatric unit's afternoon visiting hours.

After Nelson signed in, a nurse escorted him to a large room where there were two sofas, a television set with the sound turned low enough so people not interested in watching TV could talk, and three heavy-duty molded polypropylene tables, each surrounded by four matching chairs. The tables and chairs were bolted to the floor.

"Have a seat, Mr. Lang. I'll go get your wife."

Two of the tables were occupied by patients and their visitors, a three-handed card game being played at one of them. Nelson sat down at the empty table.

When Jamie entered the room a moment later, he hardly recognized her. Her face was pallid and her eyes puffy. Her hair, normally lustrous and full-bodied, was stringy and lifeless. She looked frail and much older than the woman he remembered.

"Never thought I'd end up here," she said in a weak

voice. "Sorry to have caused all this trouble."

Nelson stood up and hugged her, surprised when she actually put her arms around him. "How are you feeling?"

"Like something Bogie dragged in."

He waited for her to sit down, which she seemed to do in slow motion. "I sold another membership," he said in an effort to make conversation.

She nodded absently.

"Marty is taking care of the store. Actually that's not his real name. It's Luke. Luke Dawson. But he still wants us to call him Marty."

"Oh?" Jamie said, the word more of an automatic response than a question, spoken in an obligatory way by a person too troubled to care.

"If people hear us calling him Luke, they'll wonder what's going on. He's still on assignment and doesn't want to draw attention to himself."

Again Jamie nodded, her head barely moving, her mind clearly elsewhere. "You can add cowardice to the list of my failings," she said. "I wasn't planning on being alive today."

Nelson reached for her hand, which felt clammy and cold. "The list of your failings is shorter than the list of mine. I haven't been a very good husband."

"We both have our faults," she said and withdrew her hand. "I won't stand in the way of your getting a divorce."

"I never said anything about wanting a divorce, Jamie."

"You didn't have to. I have no intention of fighting it."

"Aren't you putting the cart before the horse?" Nelson asked, ashamed of himself for not saying something more meaningful, a heartfelt denial or at least some comforting words that might stretch the truth only a little. He wanted to tell her that divorce was out of the question, the farthest thing from his mind, but he couldn't bring himself to say it. Right now, he wasn't sure what he really wanted other than for Jamie to get well.

"No, I don't think so. You deserve someone who can make you happy."

Again Nelson reached for her hand. "You make me happy, Jamie," he said and almost meant it. "And I'll be happier still when you can leave here and come home. Pinecroft isn't the same without you."

He gently squeezed her fingers, hoping for a response but not getting one. *At least she's alive*, he told himself. *Thank goodness for that.*

☙❧

On his way back to Wisteria, Nelson felt more con-flicted than ever. The fact that Jamie had almost commit-ted suicide—indeed probably would have succeeded if Luke hadn't intervened—had come as a shock, reminding him just how much Jamie had meant to him. The possi-bility that the two of them might be separated by any-thing—divorce or death—had been unthinkable. Jamie, in spite of his relationship with Maggie Calahan, was still the most important person in his life.

And yet, this fact didn't lessen what Nelson felt for Maggie. He wanted to be with her, touch her, kiss her, make love to her. As he approached Wisteria's town lim-its, he wondered if he might actually love both women. He quickly rejected the idea as ridiculous. He might be *in* love with Maggie, but he didn't love her, at least not the way he loved Jamie. But there was no denying that Maggie Calahan had become a force in his life. Nobody, not even Jamie in her younger days, had ever done for him what Maggie had.

Nearing the Wisteria by-pass, Nelson maneuvered into the right-hand lane and remained there as the lane turned into Jefferson Avenue. Soon after he crossed the CSX tracks, the veterinary clinic swung into view.

"My life was a lot less complicated back when you were my bridge partner, Walt," he muttered.

At Church Street, Nelson turned south and drove another two blocks before pulling up in front of Bygone Daze. When he saw that the shop was open, he felt as much anxiety as relief.

Maggie had telephoned him that morning after seeing Quentin Grice's televised announcement that Will Ramsdell's murder had been solved. When asked why Jamie had gone to Holly Oak at such an ungodly hour, Nelson had explained that she hated her father and had come to the conclusion, as others had, that Ned Copeland was Will's murderer. "She went to Holly Oak to avenge that murder," he had told Maggie. "That's why she took my pistol and the step stool. When she broke in, she discovered that Copeland had hung himself. The sight of him hanging there must have sent her over the edge. After the sheriff questioned her, Marty and I took her to Hawthorne General."

What Nelson hadn't told Maggie—and had no intention of telling her—was that Jamie had planned to commit suicide after she killed her father.

"You don't look like the bearer of good news," Maggie said as Nelson entered the shop and approached the counter. "Is Jamie going to be all right?"

"It's too early to tell. Right now she's extremely depressed. She's going to need all the support I can give her."

"Of course. Is there anything I can do, short of…well, making the ultimate sacrifice?"

"The ultimate sacrifice?" Nelson asked, though he was pretty sure he knew what Maggie meant.

"Giving you up."

Nelson hesitated, knowing that his response might mean the end of their relationship. It would have been easier if he had detected a trace of sarcasm or mean-spiritedness in Maggie's voice, but he hadn't. She was just being herself, direct and to the point, a person who pretty much saw things as they were and faced them head on. "Maybe we should stop seeing each other for a while," he said. "At least until Jamie gets back on her feet."

Maggie took a deep breath and let it out in a slow, nearly inaudible sigh. "You still love her, don't you?"

The question surprised Nelson, even knowing Maggie's directness as he did. "Well, yes. Yes, I do."

Slowly Maggie nodded. "I respect that. I don't particularly like it but I respect it. We've had something really good, Nelson, you and me. I'd be lying if I said I wasn't going to miss you."

He wanted to take her in his arms and kiss her one last time before beginning their temporary separation. It was going to be temporary, wasn't it? "I'm not going to lose you, am I?"

Maggie looked at him as though not sure how to respond. "That will depend on you and Jamie. I wish her a speedy recovery. I really do. After she gets well, I'll give you a reasonable time to sort things out. But I won't wait forever, Nelson. You need to realize that."

He reached out and took both her hands in his. "I do," he said, giving her hands a prolonged gentle squeeze. Then, knowing there was nothing else he could say or do, he released her hands, turned, and exited the shop.

Chapter 29

Shannon Pfeiffer was parked near the entrance to Wardell Tharp's apartment complex when she got a call on her cell phone directing her to a fare at the county airport. "The guy was pissed he actually had to call for transportation," said Totem Taxi's dispatcher, who was also Shannon's mother.

When Shannon arrived at the tiny airport, the only person waiting outside the terminal was a tall young man with close-cropped red hair. She pulled to the curb and rolled down the window. "Taxi, mister?"

"It's about time you got here."

"Listen, bub, I'm not in the mood for any crap. You want a taxi or don't you?"

"I called for one. I need to be at Wisteria's veterinary clinic by two o'clock sharp. "

Shannon glanced at her watch. "Shouldn't be a problem. Normally, I'd load your suitcase, but if you want to save time, just toss it on the back seat and hop in."

"Okay if I sit up front with you?"

"Suit yourself."

As Shannon pulled away from the curb, the young man introduced himself as Dr. Charles Winslow. "I'm interviewing for Dr. Hux's job. I understand he won't be a tough act to follow."

Shannon ignored the comment. Barely slowing for the stop sign at the entrance to Highway 64, she merged with the traffic and headed east.

"Apparently, he kept practicing way too long," Winslow said. "Lost a lot of pets he shouldn't have."

"I wouldn't know about that. Personally I liked the man."

"Tell me about him. It's always good to know about the person you're replacing—assuming I decide to take the job."

Shannon didn't feel much like talking. She decided, however, that it might do her good to focus, at least for a while, on something other than Ben Ramsdell's murder.

"I was in high school when I first met him," she said, pulling out to pass an empty flatbed trailer. "My mom and dad were too busy starting up their taxi business to be hauling a cat to the vet's."

A brief smile came to Shannon's face as she recalled her conversation with Dr. Hux.

"Are you familiar with the word responsibility?" he asked, squinting through thick-lensed glasses that reminded Shannon of two pop bottle bottoms.

"Yes, sir. I know what it means."

"Then why wait until this cat is practically consumed with tapeworm before bringing him in? Didn't you notice his sluggishness and lack of appetite? And how could you possibly miss the worm segments around his anus?"

"To begin with, that's not my cat. He's a stray my mom took in. And in the second place, even if he was mine, I wouldn't go around checking his butt all the time."

"His coat is a disgrace," the old veterinarian continued, unfazed by Shannon's comment. *"Doesn't he get any attention at all?*

"I didn't come here for a lecture, Dr. Hux. All I want is—"

"Young lady, do you know another veterinarian?"

"I know there's one in Hawthorne."

"There are two over there, both capable as far as I know. I'll be glad to refer you to one of them."

"Seems like a long way to go just to have a cat checked out."

"Well, as long as you feel that way, you'll have to put up with whatever I tell you. Now, if you and your parents had used common sense and exercised some responsibility, I wouldn't have had to tell you anything."

Shannon told the young vet about the time she brought in an old hound that was lying on the side of the highway. After Dr. Hux realized nothing could be done, he spent a long time stroking the dog's head and speaking soft words of affection before administering the shot that put him down.

"It was good of you to bring him in, Miss Pfeiffer. Perhaps I underestimated you when you were here before. If so, I apologize. By the way, how is your mother's cat?"

"Not too good, I'm afraid. Actually, he's dead. Mom found him in the street the other day when she went out to get the paper."

Dr. Hux shook his head. *"They don't have a chance, do they?"*

"Cats?"

"Animals in general. If hunters don't kill them, careless drivers will. You should have kept that cat indoors where he would have been safe."

Shannon started to take issue with Dr. Hux, but he continued his diatribe before she could get in a word.

"I do everything I can to help them. I patch up their wounds, I treat their diseases, I plead with their owners to exercise good judgment and responsibility. What good does it do? Most end up victims of the busy monster man-unkind."

"Victims of what?"

"The phrase comes from a poem I doubt you'd under-stand. No offense, Miss Pfeiffer, but I don't think Mr. Cummings would be your cup of tea."

"What's a poem got to do with Mama's cat?"

"That cat had something precious until a careless human snatched it away—a life."

"It was an accident. They do happen, you know. Even people who care about animals have accidents. Most folks are decent enough if you give 'em half a chance. What about me? I stopped for that dog, didn't I?"

"Yes, you did. And I have no doubt you're a cut above the rest as far as human decency goes. Most people would have ignored that hound just as the priest and the Levite passed the wounded man on the other side of the road."

"Oh, I don't know. I—"

Dr. Hux waved away whatever Shannon was going to say. *"Spare me the platitudes about man's virtues, Miss Pfeiffer. The fact is the world is dominated by the ignorant and the inhumane. Bullfighting is still popular in Spain, France, Portugal, Mexico, and several other Latin American countries. Canada and Japan harvest seal pups. America has its bow hunters, slaughter houses, testing labs, dog fights, cock fights, rodeos, and a plethora of irresponsible pet owners. Cruelty to animals is our way of life."* Dr. Hux banged a fist against the table. *"And I can't do a damn thing about it."*

Shannon started to tell him he should lighten up, maybe take a vacation, or find himself a hobby, but she figured what's the use? The old vet wasn't going to listen to her or anybody else. Still, she couldn't let him get away with what he'd just said. *"Most people aren't cruel to animals. I know I'm not. Neither are my mom and dad."*

"By any chance is your father a hunter, Miss Pfeiffer?"

"He was before he had his stroke. Used to take me with

him. Last time we went I bagged a six-point buck."

"And you're telling me you and your father don't inflict pain and grief? What do you call killing a deer or a rabbit or a squirrel? Don't you realize they suffer just like people when they're injured? Don't you realize they feel sadness when they lose a mate or an offspring or a parent? What is it but inflicting pain and grief when you shoot an animal?"

"If people didn't hunt, there'd be way too many animals," Shannon replied. "A lot of 'em would starve to death."

"The same can be said of people. There are way too many of us. Why don't we have open season on human beings? Thinning our ranks would make it more pleasant for those who survive, don't you think?"

"There's a difference between animals and people, Dr. Hux."

"Of course there is. We should know better."

By that time, Shannon had had about all she could take of the man. "I gotta go pick up a fare," she said.

"Don't go just yet. This isn't a bad conversation, even if we don't see eye to eye. What's your first name, Miss Pfeiffer?"

She told him, surprised he wanted her to stay.

"There's a pot of coffee in my office, Shannon. How about having a cup with me? We can talk about something else."

"Well..."

"We'll talk about the weather or a book you've read lately, anything that comes to mind. I rarely engage in a good conversation, and I'd like to do more of it. Right now I feel an urge to sit down and have a cup of coffee with another human being—you, Shannon, even if you are a hunter."

Two miles from Wisteria, the traffic picked up. When the highway added a lane, Shannon gunned the taxi around a slow-moving car and in the process was able to slip through a yellow light just as it turned red.

"Nice move," the young vet said. "I might get there on time, after all. So what did you and the good doctor talk about?"

"Not much of anything."

"You must have talked about something."

"He asked how my dad was doing and whether my mom and I could make a go of the taxi business with him laid up. I asked if he liked to fish."

"We better steer clear of that subject, Shannon. Too close to what we were arguing about. Did your mother ever get another cat?"

"Not yet. I'm trying to talk her into getting a dog this time."

Shannon couldn't think of much else to say, and Dr. Hux seemed to have the same problem. After a few minutes she thanked him for the coffee and got up to leave.

"Thank you for caring enough to bring in that hound," he said and shook her hand. *"If more people were like you, maybe I wouldn't feel so…so down on the human race."*

"Did you have any more dealings with the guy?" the young vet asked.

"Nope. Our paths never crossed again."

"When I talked to Mayor Calahan on the phone, he said Dr. Hux went through a personality change the last year of his life. What was that all about?"

"Well, from what I heard, he started easing up on folks. Eventually, Mom did get a dog, and when she took him in for shots last year, she couldn't believe the change in the doc's personality. He was downright personable."

Wisteria's town limits sign appeared, and Shannon slowed the taxi, staying in the turn lane when Route 64 kept straight. A moment later, she pulled into the veterinary clinic's parking lot, stopping next to the only other vehicle there, an ancient Chevy Prism with a cracked windshield.

"It's exactly two minutes to one," she said, glancing at her watch and then at the meter. "Your fare is fourteen dollars and seventeen cents. Make it fourteen dollars even. No charge for my conversation."

The young vet took out his wallet and handed her a ten and four ones. "I'll need a ride to the Holiday Inn after the interview. You'll get your tip then."

"How long do you expect the interview to last?" Shannon asked, anxious to get back to her surveillance of Wardell Tharp.

"A half hour should do it. The mayor pretty much said the job is mine if I want it. He wouldn't be driving that old clunker, would he?"

"That belongs to Leona Figgins. She was Dr. Hux's assistant."

"I might as well go have a talk with her. Can I count on you being here when my interview is over?"

"I'll have to keep the meter running. It's fifty cents a minute when I wait. If you're done in a half hour, it'll cost you an extra fifteen dollars."

"I guess I can handle that. Don't expect a big tip, though."

Shannon shrugged, thoughts of Ben Ramsdell already creeping into her consciousness. A BMW arrived and Graham Calahan opened the door and got out.

"What's the matter, Shannon? You look like you've lost your last friend."

"Something like that. Dr. Winslow is inside. He wants me to take him to the Holiday Inn after his interview."

"Might as well come in and join us then. No need to stay out here in the cold."

Shannon followed the mayor into the building, lagging behind as he introduced himself to the young vet. After the two men chatted a while, Graham asked Leona Figgins to give them a tour of the premises.

When they came to the kennels out back, Graham did a double take.

"Can't be. That dog's been dead for months. Died after my wife brought him in with the broken leg he got when a neighbor's boy dropped him off the porch. Darn kid wanted to see if he'd land on his feet like a cat."

As Graham headed for the kennel to get a closer look, Leona bit her lip as though trying to stifle a smile, maybe even a laugh.

"It's Pepper. He's still wearing that fancy collar Maggie bought him."

The black woman chuckled.

"What's so funny, Leona? You know something about this I don't?"

"Here everybody thought Dr. Hux was failing and couldn't half do his job. Fact is he was doing his job and a lot more besides. The last two years he operated an underground railroad—for pets."

"An underground railroad? What the hell are you talking about?"

"He told their owners, the ones he felt mistreated 'em, that their pets had died. Then he took 'em out in the country or over to Hawthorne and gave 'em to people he knew would provide a decent home. He never got a chance to place Pepper."

The mayor and the young vet stared at each other as if they couldn't possibly believe such a story. "Well, I don't know," Graham said. "I wouldn't have thought even Dr. Hux crazy enough to pull a stunt like that."

For the first time in days, Shannon felt like smiling.

"I can't imagine there was much money in it," Dr. Winslow said.

Leona's smile dissolved. "He didn't do it for profit.

Most of the time he paid folks to take 'em. I sent out checks every so often to pay for their keep."

Graham shook his head in amazement. "Why, that old fox. The personality change was part of his scheme, wasn't it? He eased up on folks and started acting all friendly and nice to divert suspicion from what he was doing with their pets."

Leona's face was as sober as the young vet's, though in a different way, a melancholy sort of way. "That wasn't it at all. Once Dr. Hux figured out how to transfer pets from bad homes to good ones, it was like finally, after all these years, he realized that folks were...well, just folks, and there was no point staying mad at 'em."

"I still say it was to throw us off the scent," Graham said.

Dr. Winslow took a step forward. "If you ask me, that old man wasn't flying with all his colors."

Shannon glared at the young vet and then went over and stood next to Leona. "He wasn't crazy," she said. "Dr. Hux might've seen things different from other folks, but he wasn't crazy."

"What riled you up all of a sudden?" Graham asked. "Dr. Winslow is entitled to his opinion, and so am I."

Shannon thought about that for a moment and then she nodded. "That's true, and I'm sure you'll enjoy each other's company while you drive him to the Holiday Inn."

She turned and headed for the taxi. If Dr. Hux could devise and carry out such a plan on behalf of abused animals, she told herself, then she damn well ought to be able to come up with a way to avenge Ben Ramsdell's murder.

Chapter 30

By the time Abby crossed into Virginia, glimmers of sunlight were poking through the tree line. It had been pitch dark when she left Scarboro. Her mother's final words when they told each other good bye still echoed in Abby's head: '*You be extra careful, honey. You seem right on the verge.*'

The previous night, after Kevin went to bed, her mother had asked Abby if she was still taking her meds.

"Sure am, Mom."

"You haven't cut back?"

"Nope. Why are you asking?"

"You've been revved up all weekend, honey. You've been in motion practically every minute you've been here."

"So?"

"Don't you think you should have your blood tested?"

Abby had bristled then realized that such a response was not justified. That would have been the old Abby's reaction, an angry response to a well-meaning concern. "I'll do it when I get back from Virginia."

"I wish you'd do it before you go."

Abby sighed but managed to keep her cool. "I might have a slight touch of hypomania, Mom. It's not a big deal.

Actually, it's probably a good thing. It means I'll be performing at peak efficiency."

"It means you're in dangerous territory. You could slip over the line and not realize it. It's happened before."

"I'll watch myself."

It wasn't until the past year that Abby would have tolerated such interference, from her mother or anyone else. Any suggestion that she was getting manic would have elicited an angry outburst. "Stop trying to run my life," she would have snapped. "I've got everything under control."

Although Abby had been diagnosed with bipolar disorder while still in her teens, it had taken her until well into her twenties to fully accept that she had a mental illness *and* a major responsibility regarding its treatment.

"There are certain things you absolutely have to do," Dorene Milsap had told her. "Only if you do them religiously, will you be able to live a relatively normal life."

Abby had learned that her most important responsibility was to take her meds exactly as prescribed, with the understanding that the medication, and even the dosages, might need to be adjusting periodically to maintain therapeutic levels.

"It's my job to make sure your blood levels are tested on a regular basis," Dorene had said. "It's yours to be on the lookout for any changes in how you're feeling or acting—any indication at all that you might be cycling into mania or depression—and to bring those changes to my attention. I can't help you if you don't keep me informed."

Another of Abby's major responsibilities, Dorene had said, was to identify at least one person Abby trusted completely. It could be a relative, a friend, a lover, anyone she interacted with on a regular basis who had her best interests at heart. "If that person says you're off kilter, you need to take him or her seriously. Chances are, your meds will need adjusting. Ignore such a warning and you're asking for trouble."

Abby easily identified her mother as the person she most trusted, though it was not so easy to accept as gospel everything Lillian said. Abby knew, however, that her mother was right about her being in motion this past weekend. She had spent almost all of it with Kevin and was glad for the opportunity. Saturday she had taken him shopping for school clothes, played one-on-one basketball with him, organized and chaperoned a get-together with two of his friends (pizza followed by the movie of their choice, which Abby picked up at a video store after the boys voted). She had even played poker with them when the movie was over, winning most of their money but returning it before they went home. Sunday she had taken Kevin to the local IHOP for breakfast, helped him with his homework, fixed his lunch, played more one-on-one basketball with him, and taken him to Red Lobster, his favorite restaurant, for supper and to a movie afterwards.

Practically the only time Abby hadn't devoted to her son was the hour she spent convincing Charlene Greer that the news report about Will's murder being solved was erroneous and that a potential blockbuster of an exclusive awaited in Wisteria. Her boss had been skeptical that Luke Dawson was actually an FBI agent. "Make him show you some identification, Abby. And make sure it isn't fake." Reluctantly Charlene had agreed to assign someone else to cover the Wardlaws' press conference.

Although Abby didn't disagree with her mother's assessment that she had been hyperactive over the weekend, she didn't think she was on the verge of being manic. I haven't come close to crossing the line, she told herself as she sped north toward Richmond. And I'm not going to cross it. What I am going to do is nail Will's killer. That's just the way it's going to be.

That's the way you *hope* it's going to be, a voice whispered. Dorene's? Lillian's? Her own?

"Maybe so," Abby muttered. "But I sure as hell will give it my best shot."

She focused on the road ahead, already looking forward to seeing Luke Dawson again.

℮ℑ℮ℑ

Arriving at Pinecroft with little time to spare, Abby rode with Luke to the cemetery in his cobalt blue Dodge Charger.

The car contained an array of electronic gadgetry that, according to him, had showed the location of Ned Copeland's truck at any particular time.

"Are you sure it was Copeland you followed to Blacksburg?" Abby asked. "Couldn't somebody else have driven his truck and you just thought it was him?"

"I watched through binoculars when he registered at the Knight's Inn, and I saw him when he came back out for his suitcase. I got a good look at him, Abby."

"What was he doing in Blacksburg?"

Luke explained that Copeland's next target probably would have been a visiting professor at Virginia Tech, a Biblical scholar who had been a Christian fundamentalist early in his life but who was now an agnostic. Recently he had published a best-selling book that infuriated Christian evangelicals. "Copeland had been familiarizing himself with the professor's movements—where he was living, where his classes were held, where he went between classes, whatever could be learned to facilitate a successful hit and getaway."

"Are you sure those Roanoke FBI agents were following Copeland and not somebody else?"

"They knew what he looked like as well as I did. It's

time you rule him out as a suspect, Abby. Ned Copeland didn't kill Will."

Though not entirely convinced, Abby nodded. "So where do we go from here?"

"I've got a meeting with my boss tomorrow to discuss exactly that. Right now my inclination is to plant a listening device in Grice's office and one in Tharp's apartment and to tap both their phones. The phones should be easy, mainly a matter of getting a federal judge's approval. The bugs could be tricky."

"Maybe I can help you with that. I was planning to get Grice's take on Copeland's death, so installing a bug in his office shouldn't be a big deal. As far as Tharp goes, we could pretend I'm your girlfriend from North Carolina who needs her marijuana supply replenished. One of us could distract him while the other plants the bug."

Luke shook his head. "There's no reason for you to get involved any more than you already are. I'm getting help this time around."

"What kind of help?"

"Another agent to assist with the case. The bad news is this is her first time in the field."

"Her?"

"Pauline McCracken. She graduated from law school last year and just finished her FBI training at Quantico."

Abby frowned. "Well, at least it's not Dana Scully. She went to med school."

"Do I detect a note of resentment in your voice?"

"I thought we were going to keep working together on this, Luke. When is this Pauline supposed to show up?"

"She'll be at the meeting tomorrow. She'll probably be on the case soon after that."

ରେଓର

Ben Ramsdell was buried next to his father and mother in a simple graveside service attended by about twenty people. Shannon Pfeifer and Mitch Folby were there, as were Maggie and Graham Calahan, various other local residents, and a handful of relatives from out of town, including a craggy-faced old man who turned out to be Will's father. Abby went up to him after the service, introduced herself, and expressed her condolences.

"Thank you for coming," he told her in a shaky voice.

"Will was a wonderful man," she said and was on the verge of promising to do everything in her power to ensure his killer was brought to justice when it occurred to her that she better shut up. Like most everyone else at the funeral, Mr. Ramsdell would still believe Ned Copeland had murdered Will. Not only that, but this was Ben's funeral and, therefore, not an appropriate time to focus on Will. Noticing the profound sadness on the old man's face, Abby wished she hadn't mentioned Will at all, and she stepped aside so Luke could offer his condolences.

᷎᷎᷎

The sun was almost directly overhead when they left the cemetery, strong enough to make the Dodge's heater unnecessary. On their way back to Pinecroft, Abby asked if Luke planned to continue living with the Langs now that Ned Copeland no longer required monitoring.

"For a while anyway, assuming Jamie doesn't object. Nelson said it's okay with him."

"What about Pauline? Where's she going to stay?"

Abby felt foolish for asking. Three days ago she had insisted that she didn't want anything but a professional relationship with this man, and now she was jealous of his female partner. She hardly knew Luke Dawson and was acting like a jilted lover.

"My guess is she'll drive back and forth for a while. She'll probably end up getting a room or a cheap apartment somewhere in the area."

Abby envisioned the woman renting a room at Pinecroft, or worse, sharing Luke's bedroom. Angry at herself for caring, she tried to focus on what really mattered, identifying Will's murderer.

"The way Jamie avoided me makes me think she has something to hide," she said, expecting a negative response from Luke. "I don't deny that Grice and Tharp are the most logical suspects. I'm even willing to help you pursue them, but apparently you're not interested in my help."

"It's not that, Abby. The kind of help you're offering is dangerous. I'd be irresponsible to accept it. From now on, I'd like to do things by the book, which means I can't use a newspaper reporter to do an FBI agent's job."

Luke's comment angered Abby, even more than if he had chided her for being suspicious of Jamie. Up ahead, the Pinecroft sign swung into view. Abby remained silent until after Luke turned into the driveway and parked near her car.

"I guess the question now becomes: Do I wait for you and Pauline to find out who killed Will, or do I strike out on my own?"

"How about I make us some lunch and then we do a little sightseeing, maybe take a ride on the Blue Ridge Parkway."

Her anger deepening, Abby got out of the car. "I've got other fish to fry, Special Agent Dawson." She slammed the door and headed for her Toyota.

ℰↄℰↄ

Twenty minutes later, Abby stood at the Wisteria Police Department's front desk, telling a burly young man whose uniform shirt was a size too small that she needed to talk to Mel Taggart.

"He's out on patrol, ma'am. Something I can do for you?"

"Only if you know what was going on around here thirty years ago."

"I wasn't even born then. Mel should be back in a few minutes."

Fifteen minutes later, Mel Taggart returned, clearly surprised to see Abby sitting in the waiting area. "I thought you'd had enough of this place the other night."

"I'm hoping to pick your brain about Ned Copeland," she said, getting up from the chair and doing her best not to let her still smoldering anger at Luke Dawson impact her performance. "I'm thinking about doing an article on him."

Mel gave her a quizzical look. "For a North Carolina newspaper?"

Abby gave Mel the same spiel she had given her boss about Will helping with her first investigative assignment and saving her life in the process. "If the *Gazette*'s readers know all that, I think they'll have more than a passing interest in why he was murdered and by whom."

"Well, come on in my office, and I'll tell you what I know."

Once seated, Abby told Mel she had hoped to interview Ned Copeland's daughter for this story but Jamie was in the hospital. "By the way, I understand she had a baby while she was still in high school. Any idea who the father was?"

Mel paused in momentary reflection. "Most people thought it was a classmate of hers named Rudy Teague. He and Jamie had been pretty close. Yeah, I'd put my money on Rudy."

"Does he still live around here?"

"As far as I know. Last I heard he was an insurance agent over in Hawthorne."

"What about the baby?" Abby asked, hoping Mel wouldn't notice how far she was straying from the subject of Ned Copeland. "Apparently, she was put up for adoption early on, but nobody seems to know who adopted her, including Jamie."

"I've got a feeling Jamie knows."

"Oh?"

"My older sister was in high school at the time. During a sleep-over at our house, I heard one of the girls say the kid was being raised by a professor at Hawthorne College and his wife and that every now and then Jamie would slip over there and visit her."

Seek and ye shall find, Abby said to herself, surprised that Mel Taggart would share such information with her. "You wouldn't happen to know the name of that professor, would you?"

Mel shook his head. "I don't even know if the story is true. I thought your article was about Ned Copeland, not the whole Copeland clan."

"It is. I just thought it would be interesting to include some material about his relatives. My boss gets after me all the time for that sort of thing. Stick to the subject at hand, she keeps telling me." Abby gave Mel the same scatterbrained look she had used on Ned Copeland when he told her she was trespassing. "It's just so darn hard for me to do sometimes."

Chapter 31

Teague Insurance Agency occupied a modest portion of a strip mall within easy walking distance of Hawthorne College. Abby had no trouble finding it, having called and asked directions from the secretary, a petite white-haired woman much older than her voice had suggested.

"You can go right in," she said, nodding toward the open doorway between her desk and a combination copier, printer, and fax machine.

Although Rudy Teague's thinning hair and paunchy physique implied a middle-aged man, he had a boyish look that reminded Abby of Richard Thomas, the perpetually youthful-looking actor who had played John Boy on *The Waltons*. He gave her a warm handshake and indicated the closer of two visitor's chairs.

As she sat down, Abby noticed the picture on the corner of his desk. A younger, thinner version of the insurance agent had his right arm around a plump, freckle-faced woman. The two of them were standing behind a boy who appeared to be in his early teens and a girl who looked about ten. All four were smiling, but only Rudy seemed completely at ease.

"What kind of insurance are you interested in, Ms. Burlew?"

"Actually, I'm not here about insurance. I'd like to talk to you about Jamie Lang."

Surprise replaced the easy-going earnestness on Rudy's face. When Abby explained that she was investigating Will Ramsdell's murder, Rudy looked dumbfounded.

"Will stopped in here a month or so ago. Believe it or not, he wanted to talk about Jamie too."

It was Abby's turn to be surprised. "He did? Why?"

"Before we get into that, how about telling me the real reason you're here. It can't be to solve Will's murder. That's been solved. Or haven't you heard?"

"I know what the sheriff claims, but I have good reason to believe Ned Copeland didn't kill Will."

"Yeah? And you think Jamie did?"

"She definitely had a motive. The golf course she and her husband own was the beneficiary of Will's estate."

Rudy's eyes widened in surprise. "Are you sure about that?"

"Positive."

"So why exactly are you here, Ms. Burlew?"

"I was hoping you could give me some insight into the kind of person Jamie is, just how far she might go to speed up an inheritance process."

"Why would you think I could do that?"

"I was told you and Jamie had a relationship in high school and that you might be the father of her daughter."

Heaving a sigh, Rudy stepped over to the doorway. "Hold my calls, Mrs. Judson," he said and closed the door. He slid behind his cluttered desk and sat down in a swivel chair. "At the time, there wasn't any *might be* about it, at least as far as I was concerned. I thought for sure that kid was mine."

"Something convinced you otherwise?"

"You bet it did. My wife and I always wanted kids, but Lorraine was never able to get pregnant. We had ourselves tested a few years ago to see if there's a fertility problem. Turned out there is. I'm sterile, have been all my life."

Abby glanced at the picture on the corner of the desk. "Aren't they your kids?"

"Adopted."

"Then…"

Rudy nodded. "When Jamie told me she was pregnant, I thought my life was over. I figured I'd have to marry her, assuming her father didn't kill me first. But she didn't want to get married, at least not for a while. She said she wouldn't tell anyone else she was pregnant until it was obvious and she'd never reveal who the father was. That way if we stopped seeing each other right then, people wouldn't be so quick to think it was me. I couldn't believe my good fortune. Later on, of course, I felt like a heel. But when I found out I was sterile, I realized Jamie hadn't exactly been a saint either."

Abby took a moment to assimilate this information. "Who was the father?" she asked.

"Beats the heck out of me. Jamie meant it when she said she'd keep that a secret."

"Is that why Will came to see you, to find out if you were the father?"

"That's what he said. He told me he represented someone with an interest in the matter but wasn't at liberty to say who. I thought Jamie must have hired him to find out if I was telling the truth about being sterile."

"You told her about that?"

"Just as soon as I found out. I was all set to raise hell about what a phony she was. But after she reminded me how willing I'd been to let her assume the entire burden of a pregnancy I thought I was responsible for, I decided what the heck, I might as well let it go and call us even. You're not working for her, are you?"

"Why would you think that?"

"Maybe she's afraid I'll cause trouble. If she is, you can tell her I have no intention of contacting her again or bringing up the subject of our past relationship—to anyone."

Pleased with what she had learned so far, Abby reiterated that she and Will had been friends and that her sole reason for contacting Rudy was to find out whether Jamie might be capable of committing murder.

"I don't think she's a bad person," Rudy said. "Actually, she seemed like a really sweet girl, decent in every way—except, of course, for letting me think I was the father of her daughter."

"So what did you tell Will?"

"Same thing I'm telling you—that there's no way I could have fathered that kid, and I don't know who did."

It occurred to Abby that Will might have had more in mind than identifying the father of Jamie's child. "Did he question you about anything else?"

"No. That was it."

"He didn't ask if you knew anything about Jamie's daughter?"

"Nope. He just thanked me for sharing what I did with him and left."

Abby wondered who would have wanted to know the identity of the girl's father enough to ask Will to investigate. The daughter herself? The daughter's adoptive parents? "That's really weird," she said, more to herself than to Rudy. Then she asked him if he knew anything about Jamie's daughter. "Anything at all pertaining to her identity or present whereabouts?"

"Not a thing."

"What about the people who adopted her? Any idea who they might be?"

Rudy shook his head. "Children and Family Services would probably have a record, but I doubt they'd give out that kind of information."

"Children and Family Services?"

"The branch of the county Social Services Department that handles adoptions. My wife and I went through that agency when we adopted our kids."

"Have you got a point of contact there, somebody I could talk to?"

"Not any more. We haven't had any dealings with DSS in years."

⌘⌘⌘

The first question Abby asked once she was seated in Quentin Grice's office was whether Ned Copeland's suicide note was handwritten or typed.

"What difference does that make?" the sheriff asked.

"I had a talk with Copeland a few days ago, and he—"

"I asked you not to do that."

"I didn't say anything to suggest he was under investigation, by you or me," Abby said, not feeling the least bit intimidated by Grice. "Judging from our chat, he's the last person anyone would expect to commit suicide." Abby thought she detected a subtle change in the sheriff's expression, a slight flicker of concern in his eyes that made her think she had struck a nerve. If anything, she thought, she might be intimidating him.

Ever since her conversation with Rudy Teague, Abby had felt on top of her game. After leaving the insurance agent's office, she had called the sheriff's department on her cell phone, identified herself, and asked to speak to Quentin Grice. When the sheriff came on the line, Abby said she'd like to talk to him face to face as soon as possible and that it was very important. Grice had agreed to meet with her in twenty minutes.

"You think somebody killed Copeland and made it look like a suicide?" the sheriff asked.

"I think that's entirely possible. Now will you answer my original question?"

"The note was handwritten."

"Did you verify that it was in Copeland's handwriting?"

"I'm in the process of doing exactly that. I'm expecting a report from the FBI's handwriting expert in Charlottesville any day now. I'd be amazed if it turns out the note isn't in Copeland's handwriting, but if it isn't, I'll cross that bridge when I get to it. Right now, as far as I'm concerned, Will Ramsdell's murder has been solved."

"What about Ben Ramsdell's murder?"

"What about it?"

"Any idea who killed him?"

Grice leaned forward in his chair. "I think we need to get something straight, Ms. Burlew. I've bent over backwards to share information about Will Ramsdell's murder because you were a friend of his. But I'm drawing the line when it comes to other matters. All I'm going to tell you about Ben Ramsdell's murder is that my deputies and I are vigorously investigating it."

"Can you at least tell me if you think there's a connection between Ben's murder and Will's?"

Looking more relaxed now, the sheriff eased back in his chair. "I'm not aware of a connection. Is that all you wanted to talk to me about?"

"No. I've got a request to make. The *Gazette* has given me more time to investigate Will's murder. Rightly or wrongly, I plan to spend that time operating on the assumption that the killer is still at large."

Grice shrugged. "That's your prerogative. What's your request?"

"It has to do with Jamie Lang. Back when she was in high school, she had a daughter out of wedlock that she gave up for adoption. I'd very much like to know the daughter's identity, but I'd settle for the identity of her adoptive parents."

"I don't mean to be rude, but what business is that of yours?"

"As far as I'm concerned, Jamie is still a suspect in Will's murder. Her daughter or the people who adopted her might be able to provide some pertinent information. I was hoping you could give me a point of contact at Children and Family Services who might be willing to release some names."

The sheriff shook his head. "They won't give out that kind of information. If it isn't against the law, it would be against the agency's rules and regulations."

Confident that she was more than holding her own, Abby had no intention of giving up now. "I figured you for a man who could cut through red tape," she said. "Was I wrong about that?"

Grice looked at her the way he might look at a prisoner who just requested a key to his cell. Then the corners of his mouth lifted in the beginning of a smile. "There is someone at DSS who owes me a favor. If he agrees to help you, what would you give me in return?"

Abby recalled Luke Dawson's comment that for the right price Quentin Grice could be bought. "I hope you're not suggesting trading information for sex."

"You flatter yourself, Ms. Burlew."

Feeling on top of her game, Abby ignored the insult. "How about if I agree not to bug you any more about Ben Ramsdell?" she said.

Grice chuckled. "If you agree not to bug me anymore about *either* Ramsdell, I'll see what I can do."

Flush with pride, Abby nodded. "It's a deal, Sheriff."

Grice got up from his chair and made his way to the open door of his office. "Wait here and I'll see what I can find out."

The sheriff's use of the word *bug* reminded Abby of her latest conversation with Luke Dawson. As she waited for Grice, she thought how easy it would have been to plant a listening device. Too bad young motorcycle-riding Marty turned out to be old by-the-book Luke, she mused.

The sheriff returned a few minutes later, closing the door behind him. "Good news," he said. "The person I talked to at DSS is willing to provide you the name and address of the daughter's adoptive parents."

After providing Abby with directions to the Department of Social Services, Grice told her that at three o'clock sharp a paunchy middle-aged man with a bushy mustache and thinning gray hair would go for a walk behind the DSS building like he usually did during his afternoon break. "There's a big pecan tree that overhangs the far right corner of the parking lot. If you're standing under it when Tom walks by, he'll ask if you saw the big flock of Canada geese that flew over a little earlier. If you tell him one of them crapped all over your windshield, he'll hand you a slip of paper with the name and address of the adoptive parents on it."

"You're kidding, right? What do you think this is—a friggin' James Bond movie?"

Grice chuckled. "About the geese—yeah, I'm kidding. So long, Ms. Burlew. Don't forget your part of our bargain."

Chapter 32

"Are you in or not, Mitch?"

From where she sat, Shannon Pfeiffer had a clear view of Ben's recliner, the first object her eyes had focused on when she entered the apartment. She turned her head away and tried not to think about how empty the chair looked.

"One way or another I'm going to make Tharp pay," she said, keeping her voice low because of the paper-thin walls in Ye Olde Barn Apartments. "I'd like your help, but I'll do it without you if I have to."

"You really want to kill the guy?"

"He killed Ben, didn't he?"

"We don't know that for sure."

"Get your head out of your ass, Mitch. He broke Ben's finger. Any fool can figure that out. What do you think he'd do after finding out Ben was setting himself up as a rival drug dealer, welcome him to the club?"

"He might not have found out about that."

"Yeah, right. Ben wasn't the type to turn the other cheek, especially after he got caught up in the substances. It was just a matter of time before he retaliated for that broken finger. What better way than refuse to pay Tharp and then tell the bastard he's using the money to start his own drug business? Remember what Ben said about having something in his pocket to protect him? It was probably his father's note."

"Wasn't much of an insurance policy, was it?"

"You can't intimidate people like Tharp. They're always going to have the last word."

Mitch leaned his head back against the sofa. "Well, maybe he did kill Ben, but that's not good enough, at least not for me. I'm surprised it is for you. If you're going to kill somebody, shouldn't you be a hundred percent sure they're guilty?"

Shannon sighed in frustration. "I'm ninety-nine and a half percent sure Wardell Tharp murdered Ben."

"Then there's a chance he didn't, even in your own mind. What if you kill the guy and it turns out somebody else killed Ben?"

Shannon got up from the sofa and clomped over to the window. The wooden stockade surrounding the dumpster area reminded her of a fort in a western movie. She envisioned settlers inside and a small group of cavalry protecting them. When she pictured herself as an Indian scout trying to figure out the best way to attack the palefaces, she gave herself a mental slap and re-focused her attention on Mitch.

"You'd rather I leave everything to the sheriff, wouldn't you? How ridiculous is that? Grice didn't have a clue who killed Ben's dad until Ned Copeland confessed. What makes you think he's capable of solving Ben's murder?"

"You might wait and see what Mr. Ramsdell's friends come up with. They seem like pretty sharp cookies to me."

"They weren't all that interested in Ben. Besides, they're not even law officers."

Mitch fingered the stubble on his chin. "How about at least holding off a while, give yourself a chance to see things clearer. What happened to Ben really did a job on you, Shannon. Right now you're not capable of making important decisions like this."

"How long do you expect me to wait, Mitch?"

"I don't know. Long enough to let some of the anger out of your system."

"That's easy for you to say. More than anything in the world, I want Tharp to pay. If I just sit back and wait for time to ease my pain like you seem to think it will, I'll go stark raving mad. I've got to do something now. And I'm going to, with or without your help."

Mitch went over and stood next to her, and for a while they both gazed toward the dumpsters.

"I'll help you on two conditions."

Shannon looked at him. "Yeah? What are they?"

"First we find out for sure that Wardell Tharp killed Ben. I don't know how we do that, but unless we do, you can count me out."

"What's your other condition?"

"Whatever we end up doing has to stop short of murder. I won't go that far even for Ben."

Shannon went over to the recliner and stared at it. As she traced the fingers of her right hand across the leather top, tears welled up in her eyes. She fished a Kleenex from the pocket of her jeans. "If I agree to your conditions, I expect you to get sober and stay that way until we accomplish our mission."

Mitch nodded. "I'm sober now. I didn't want to be under the influence at Ben's funeral. Believe it or not, I haven't used since."

"I thought you seemed more with it than usual. How do you feel?"

"Like a lump of cow shit that's been trampled on by the entire herd."

"You seem bright enough when you want to be, Mitch. Got any ideas how we can find out for sure that Tharp is guilty?"

The young man shook his head. "How about you?"

"Not really. It would be a lot easier if we just skip that part and do what I originally planned, which is follow him some morning and serve him up a buckshot omelet. You know where Sugar 'N Spice is?"

"That little restaurant near the airport?"

"Yeah. Tharp usually goes there for breakfast. There's a crossroads nearby where we could wait for him, maybe on a Sunday when there's not much traffic. After he drives by, we'll follow him. When it's clear nobody's coming in either direction, you pull alongside, and I'll take care of the rest. That's why I need you in the first place, Mitch. I can't drive and shoot too."

"Sounds like a good recipe for spending the rest of our lives in jail, assuming we avoid the death penalty."

"I think we can pull it off. Everybody'll figure a dis-gruntled customer or a rival drug dealer did it. But I won't insist. We've got an agreement and I'll abide by it—at least the first part anyway. Once we know for sure Tharp murdered Ben, I reserve the right to kill the son-of-a-bitch. But I won't expect you to help me."

"And I won't. I meant what I said about that."

"Understood." Shannon plunked herself down on one end of the sofa and patted the middle cushion. "Have a seat. We've got some serious planning to do."

The young man sat down at the opposite end of the sofa. "I might be sober, but I'm not going to be much help, at least in the planning department."

"Stop selling yourself short, Mitch. Tell me some-thing—how do you think I'd look as a blond?"

"What's that got to do with Wardell Tharp?"

"Well, if you're not going to let me kill him, I want to

make sure he doesn't recognize me when I get up close and personal."

"You do have something in mind, don't you?"

Shannon gazed at Ben's recliner. "Considering the limitations you've put on me, I think the best approach might be to pretend the bastard owes me money."

Chapter 33

Hogback Road coiled into the hills above Haw-thorne like a massive black snake with two yellow stripes down its back. Even if passing were permissible, Abby would have been reluctant to attempt it because of the road's many twists and turns. Each house had a roadside mailbox with ascending three-digit numbers. Two miles past the city limits, she was only in the four hundreds, well shy of her intended destination. In the five hundreds she got behind a school bus and had to stop twice before it turned onto a dirt road and disappeared in a cloud of dust. Finally, in the middle of a sweeping S-shaped curve, she came to the number she was looking for and turned into the asphalt driveway directly across from the mailbox.

Set farther back than most of the houses on the road, the two-story raised ranch was surrounded by trees. An older woman dressed in jeans and a sweatshirt was raking leaves in the front yard, and a white-haired man wearing a flannel shirt and khaki pants sat in a folding chair on the nearby porch. He eyed Abby as she pulled in behind the only other vehicle in the driveway, an aging mini-van with a faded Hawthorne College sticker attached to its rear window.

"Mr. Andrews?" she called as she got out of her car.

"Dr. Andrews," he corrected. "I have a doctorate, young lady. Earned it in nineteen seventy-five, I did." He paused, his eyes no longer focused on Abby but on the woman who had put down her rake and was walking toward them. "Seventy-five was a good year, but sixty-eight was even better. That was the year I married Rachel."

Abby noticed a slur in the man's speech, and she thought his eyes looked glazed, almost out of focus. She started to introduce herself but decided to wait until the woman reached the porch.

"She would've preferred a church wedding," the man continued. "But she was gracious enough to defer to my wishes. I was a dyed-in-the-wool atheist in those days. Thought I knew everything there was to know." He chuckled ruefully. "I don't know diddly squat now. Ask Rachel. She has to put up with me—at least for the time being." He gave his wife a wary look as she climbed the porch steps. "But we can both hear the nursing home calling my name, can't we, Rachel?"

"Not true," the woman said, placing a hand on his shoulder. "This is our home, Paul. We're both going to stay here as long as we can."

"What then?" he asked in a plaintive tone. "What happens when the foreseeable future becomes the intolerable present? It's bound to sooner or later, you know."

"I don't know any such thing. But if it does…well, as a young instructor once said to his anxious wife after she asked what they would do if he were denied tenure, we'll jump off that bridge when we get to it." The woman turned to Abby. "I don't believe we've met, Ms…"

"Burlew. Abby Burlew. The reason I'm here—"

"I remember that," Dr. Andrews said. "Teaching jobs were hard to come by then. I hadn't published a thing and was struggling with my dissertation."

"Things turned out all right, though, didn't they?" his wife said.

"They did, and they didn't." The man began rocking back and forth, bending at the waist, his upper body moving slowly and not quite rhythmically, like the pendulum of a worn-out clock.

"The reason I'm here concerns your adopted daughter," Abby said to his wife.

"Is something wrong?"

"No, nothing like that. I'd just like to talk to her."

"'Do not go gentle into that good night,'" the man intoned in a deep, sonorous voice. "'Old age should rage and burn at close of day. Rage, rage against the dying of the light...'" His lips quivered. "Forgotten the rest," he said in a sheepish voice. "Can't even remember who wrote that poem. All I can think of is Bob Dylan. I'm not worth a damn anymore, Rachel. I'm not worth a tinker's damn...whatever the hell that is."

"You're just overtired, Paul. You'll feel better after your nap. In the meantime, I'll fix you a nice dinner. Things won't seem so bleak when you wake up. Remember the old saying: 'Sleep knits the raveled sleeve of care.'"

"Clichés are for the small minded," Dr. Andrews said as he stood up. "But you're right. I am tired. I'm so tired I feel like...like whatshisname in that Kesey book. Not McMurphy or the big Indian. Who am I trying to think of, Rachel?"

"Billy Bibbit," Abby offered. "*One Flew Over the Cuckoo's Nest* is my all-time favorite novel."

Dr. Andrews looked at Abby as though seeing her for the first time. "Who're you?"

"My name is Abby. I'm—"

"Oh, I know who you are. You teach at the local high school and you're in my night class. You want me to raise your grade, don't you? I don't change grades, Abby. The mark I give a student is what he or she deserves. You'll just have to live with yours, maybe work a little harder next time."

"It's time for your nap," Rachel said and gently took her husband by the hand. "Wait here," she told Abby. "I'll be out as soon as I get Paul to bed."

As the front door closed behind Rachel and Paul Andrews, Abby zipped up her jacket and sat down on the porch steps. A gust of wind ruffled the pile of leaves Rachel had raked, threatening to scatter them. Two grey squirrels, one with whitish ears, chased each other through the branches of a nearby maple tree, amazing Abby with their acrobatics. The squawking of crows caught her attention, and she watched as six of them lifted, one by one, from a cluster of pine trees across the road and flapped toward a distant field.

A moment later, Abby noticed a large brown creature standing on its hind legs near one of the pine trees the crows had vacated. A bear? It must be, she thought, though it had a vaguely human look that made her envision a man in a bear suit. Whatever the creature was, it was staring at Abby. Suddenly it let out a growl, dropped down on all fours, and headed in her direction, picking up speed as it approached the road.

Abby stood up and was about to retreat into the Andrews' house when the animal seemed to disappear. She kept staring at the spot where it had been, seeing nothing out of the ordinary, no bear or whatever it was, no tree or bush large enough to hide it. Whatever she had seen—or thought she had seen—had vanished.

Easing herself back down on the steps, Abby thought of the time she was picking tomatoes in her mother's vegetable garden and the neighbor's rotund tabby cat sauntered up to the fence separating the two yards. "Hello there,

fatso," Abby had said. "Don't you think it's time somebody put you on a diet?"

The cat looked at her. "Mind your own business, bitch.
Or I'll come over there and kick your scrawny ass."

Abby had heard the words just as clearly as if a man
with a deep voice had uttered them. She had stared at the
cat, more in amazement than fear. For a moment they had
locked eyes, and then the cat had turned and waddled back
to the house next door but not before saying, in the same
masculine voice, "Have a nice day, Toots."

At the time of the incident, Abby had been in the throes
of mania, and in retrospect she had reluctantly acknowl-
edged that the voice she heard had been in her own head.

"Sorry to keep you waiting."

Startled by the woman's voice, Abby stood up. "Not a
problem. Are there bears around here, Mrs. Andrews?"

"Bears? I don't think so. I've never seen one anyway,
and neither has my husband. Why do you ask?"

"I thought I saw one across the road, but my eyes might
have been playing a trick on me." Forcing herself to focus
on her immediate objective, Abby explained that she had
been a friend of Will Ramsdell's and was investigating his
murder.

"I thought his murder had been solved."

"The sheriff seems to think so. But I know for a fact
that Ned Copeland was nowhere near the scene of the
crime on the morning Will was killed."

"Did you tell that to the sheriff?"

"It's rather complicated, Mrs. Andrews. Do you mind if
we sit down?"

After a brief hesitation the woman motioned to the
chair vacated by her husband. She took the one adjacent,
turning it so she and Abby could face each other.

"So why exactly are you here?"

"I wanted to ask if you'd put me in touch with your

adopted daughter. She might have information that could help identify the real murderer."

"I'm afraid I don't understand."

"Will was conducting an investigation shortly before he was murdered. He was looking into your adopted daughter's past, Mrs. Andrews. I think he uncovered, or was about to uncover, something that someone didn't want known."

A troubled look replaced the skepticism on Rachel's face. "How did you find out about my husband and me? The adoption was closed. Our identity was supposed to be confidential."

"I know, and I apologize for intruding on your privacy. I wouldn't have done it if I knew of any other way to contact your daughter."

"I don't see what she has to do with any of this."

"I'd like to find out what—"

The roaring of a motorcycle interrupted Abby, its rider leaning far to his left as he entered the first part of the curve fronting the Andrews' property. The vehicle sped past, the rider leaning just as far to his right as he began negotiating the remainder of the curve.

"I'd like to find out what your daughter knows about her biological parents," Abby said as the sound of the motorcycle faded.

"She knows absolutely nothing about them," Rachel said and got up from her chair. "Neither do I. I'm sorry, but that's all I'm going to say on this subject."

"I can understand your wanting to keep your daughter out of this, Mrs. Andrews, but I really need to talk to her. She could be the key to solving Will's murder."

"I've told you all I'm going to, Abby. I'd like you to leave now."

Abby started to object but decided not to press the issue. "I'm sorry to have bothered you," she said as she stood up. "I know you don't have an easy time of it."

The woman's expression softened. "I didn't mean to be nasty, or imply that you're engaged in something unsavory. That's not it at all. It's just that we've always guarded our daughter's privacy."

"I understand. Before I go, I'd like to ask you one last question. It's not about your daughter."

"All right."

"Did Will Ramsdell ever try to contact you or your husband?"

"No. I'd never heard of the man until I read about his death in the paper."

Abby thanked Rachel Andrews for her time, shook her hand, and headed for the Corolla. After backing out of the driveway and onto the road, she took a moment to scan the terrain behind the Andrews' mailbox, the area where she thought she had seen a bear. Seeing nothing but pine trees and bushes, she headed south toward Hawthorne.

She had driven less than a hundred yards when she noticed a sports car heading toward her, a bright red Corvette with the top down and a woman at the wheel. The car slowed as it passed, as though the driver intended to stop. Thinking the woman looked familiar, Abby glanced in the rearview mirror and saw the Corvette pull into the Andrews' driveway, saw it continue on toward the house.

By the time Abby reached the next S-shaped curve, she knew why the driver had looked familiar. She was the spitting image of Maggie Calahan.

Chapter 34

Wearing the blonde wig she had purchased earlier at Maltby's, Shannon Pfeiffer approached the white-columned portico of Orchard Knoll Apartments with trepidation. Other than a denial, she didn't know what to expect from Wardell Tharp. If she did her job properly, she believed, at some point he would let down his guard enough to provide the evidence she required. Not the smoking-gun kind that could be used in court—she didn't need that. She would settle for something less dramatic: a snide off-the-cuff comment, a self-incriminating smirk, an obvious falsehood, any lapse that would confirm her suspicion that Tharp had killed Ben Ramsdell. Shannon didn't really know what she was looking for, but she was confident she would recognize it when she saw it.

She adjusted the wig as she scanned the names of resident listed next to the call box. She pressed the button next to *Tharp,* released it, and pressed it again, holding it down until she heard the intercom crackle.

"Yeah?" a gruff male voice cut through the static.

"You owe me money," Shannon said, hoping her anxiety didn't betray the confident tone she tried to project. "My name is Amber and—"

"Say that again. I don't think I heard you right."

"I said my name is Amber and I'm here to collect the money you owe me."

"You got the wrong apartment, girl. Definitely the wrong guy."

"You're Wardell Tharp, aren't you?"

"I don't owe you or anybody else money."

"We have a difference of opinion about that. How about letting me in so we can discuss it. Otherwise, I'll take what I know to the cops."

There was a pause. "What's your last name, Amber?"

"I'll tell you after I get inside. What's important right now is what I know and what you owe." *Need to do better than that*, Shannon told herself. *You sound more like a bad rapper than an angry business partner*. "Are you letting me in or not?"

There was a click followed by a prolonged buzz. Shannon tugged at the brass handle and the door opened easily. "Third floor, apartment nine," the voice on the intercom growled.

The building's interior was even more upscale than its exterior. An attractive light brown carpet, clearly of good quality, covered the hallway floor, and the walls were painted a creamy ivory. Large framed prints hung here and there, mostly landscapes. One of them reminded Shannon of the view from the Skyline Drive overlook where she and Ben had once shared a bottle of scuppernong wine he stole from a Hawthorne liquor store.

She had to wait nearly a minute for the elevator. After a young white couple and their towheaded toddler stepped off, she rode the elevator uninterrupted to the third floor. Apartment nine was to the right. She was about to knock when the door opened, revealing a large muscular black man wearing flip flops, cut-off jeans, and a Dallas Cowboys' tee shirt.

"You look like a hooker to me. You con me into letting

you in so you could strut your stuff? Not that you've got much to strut."

"Thanks. My name is Amber Higgins, and—"

"Got a nice ring to it," Wardell interrupted, continuing to give her the once over. "Well, come on in, Amber Higgins. Let's see if we can clear up this little misunderstanding."

Shannon entered a spacious living room with shiny hardwood floors and a high coved ceiling. Directly in front of her on a multi-color area rug sat a white leather sofa flanked by black leather recliners and fronted by a slate tile coffee table. To her left stood an entertainment center replete with stereo, a flat-screen TV, and several speakers. To her right loomed a metal and glass display case packed with sports memorabilia: trophies, footballs with signatures scrawled on the leather, photographs of various teams and players. The centerpiece of the display was a blown-up, framed newspaper clipping of a younger Wardell Tharp in a menacing three-point stance, its caption reading "Panthers' Punishing Lineman." Straight ahead, on the far side of the room, a picture window provided a panoramic view of the Blue Ridge Mountains.

With a flick of the remote, Wardell turned off the television. He nodded toward the sofa. "Take a load off, Amber," he said and eased himself into the adjacent recliner. "Now what's this bullshit about owing you money?"

Shannon sat down on the sofa. "It's not bullshit," she replied, careful not to rush her words. "Ben Ramsdell was my business partner. The money he took to Richmond the day he got murdered was mostly mine, four hundred dollars of it to be exact."

"What's that got to do with me?"

"I think you know the answer to that as well as I do. Ben wanted to get into the same business you're in, and against my better judgment I agreed to back him. Our deal was he'd have six months to repay my loan. Every month thereafter, I'd get a percentage of his profits. To make a short story even shorter, you ended Ben's career before it got started."

"You're barking up the wrong tree, girl. I had no reason to kill Ramsdale. I didn't know squat about his career goals."

"I don't believe that. But even if you didn't, that's not why you killed him, at least not the main reason. You killed him because he wouldn't pay his drug debt and threatened to go to the cops if you did anything about it."

Wardell shook his head. "You're right about some of that stuff. Ben did owe me money. He kept on putting me off, and finally he refused to pay me altogether. And he did threaten to tell the cops what he knew—or thought he knew—about me. I don't deny any of that. In fact, he showed me a copy of a letter he wrote to the state police, saying if anything happened to him, I was the guy responsible." Wardell held out his hands palms up in a gesture of innocence. "You've got a mighty low opinion of me if you think I'd kill somebody under those circumstances."

Shannon was momentarily at a loss for words. Ben's letter had been her ace in the hole, to be played if and when the situation dictated. "Apparently, you thought you could get away with it," she finally said, less than pleased with her response.

"There's nothing to get away with. If the cops question me, I'll tell 'em the same thing I'm telling you—the truth. They try to pin Ramsdale's murder on me, all I can say is they're leaning on the wrong guy."

Discouraged by the calm, easy way Tharp responded to her accusations, Shannon decided to ratchet up the pressure. But how? He seemed prepared for anything she might say. Finally, an idea occurred to her, and she got up and walked over to the window.

"Nice view. This pad must cost you plenty."

"It's not cheap, that's for sure."

"Not quite an arm and a leg?"

"Not quite."

"How about a finger?"

"A what?"

Shannon swung around and glared at the big man. "Was Ben already dead when you cut off his finger and stuffed it in his mouth?" she asked, her voice trembling from a combination of anxiety and anger.

Wardell got up and went over to the window. "I heard about that," he said as unruffled as ever. "I hope whoever did it gets what he deserves."

"It was you who broke Ben's little finger, though, wasn't it? You're not denying that too, are you?"

"No, that was my doing. I wanted to teach him there's consequences when you keep falling behind in your payments. I'm a businessman, Shannon. I wouldn't stay in business long if I tolerated that kind of thing."

It took her a few beats for the word to register. "What did you call me?"

"Your name is Amber, right?"

"You just called me Shannon."

Wardell's puzzled expression turned sheepish. "Well, what do you expect when you tail somebody like you've been doing me lately? You look better without that wig, you know."

"But my name? How'd you know my name?"

"Not many people drive a Totem Taxi. Just two I'm aware of. Is your mother in on this con too?"

"No. And it's not a con. You owe me four hundred dollars, and I expect you to pay it."

Moving a step closer, Wardell reached out as though to

touch Shannon's shoulder. Apparently reconsidering, he let his arm fall back to his side. "I can understand you feeling that way. In your position, I'd probably feel the same. I'm tempted to give you the money just to put the whole thing behind us."

"Then do it."

"Can't. It would set a bad example. Word got around, folks would start thinking I'm soft."

Shannon took a deep breath and slowly let it out. "Is that the only reason?" she asked, looking the black man straight in the eye. "I mean it's obvious you killed Ben, whether you pay me or not."

"You couldn't be more wrong," Wardell said in his usual calm voice. Then he went over and opened the door to the hallway. "I think we've both said all there is to say on the subject. It wasn't exactly a pleasure meeting you, Shannon, but under different circumstances I think we'd get along fine. I hope you won't hold a grudge against me. I'm guilty of a lot of things, but killing Ben Ramsdale isn't one of 'em."

Wardell stepped to the side and waited for Shannon to leave. For a moment she continued to stand near the window, searching for something more to say, anything to let Tharp know he hadn't won. Then she shook her head and, without looking his way, walked past him into the hall. The door quietly closed behind her.

Chapter 35

On her way back from Hawthorne, Abby stopped at an Arby's and ordered a roast beef sandwich and a vanilla milkshake. After the day she had put in, she felt she owed herself a hyacinth, a term her mother used to describe a special treat someone normally wouldn't allow herself, so she added two triple chocolate cookies to her order. She took the meal back to her motel room and ate every bit of it. Then she turned on the television.

The only program even remotely interesting featured a young couple in the process of selling their first home and buying another, and Abby soon tired of watching that. She considered calling her mother and Kevin but decided to give them a rest.

The person she really wanted to talk to was Luke Dawson, not just as a sounding board for what she had learned today but because she actually missed him. She wished she hadn't acted so nasty to him earlier in the day.

Swallowing her pride, Abby dialed his cell phone number.

After three rings, she was about to resign herself to spending the evening alone when the familiar voice answered, "Luke Dawson."

"I didn't think you went by that name around here."

"People with my cell phone number know my real name, Abby."

"I see. Well, I've had a very busy and productive day. I was wondering if you'd be interested in hearing about it."

"Sure. What did you find out?"

"I don't think we should discuss it on the phone. It involves some sensitive information."

"Want me to meet you somewhere?"

Abby hesitated, hoping she wasn't about to do something foolish. "Actually I'm kind of weary, too tired to go out again. How about coming over to my place?"

"Got anything to drink over there?"

"There's a pop machine down the way."

"Are you sure about this, Abby? Earlier today I got the impression that you didn't want anything more to do with me."

"Well, I've mellowed some since then."

"Ah. Kind of lonely over there at the Shenandoah without old Mulder to talk to—is that it?"

"Something like that. Now stop rubbing my nose in it and get your butt over here so we can compare notes."

"Yes, ma'am. I'll be right over."

"And bring some ID. I want to make sure you're who you say you are."

"No problem. By the way, do you happen to like licorice?"

"I do. Why do you ask?"

"Just curious. See you in a bit, Ms. Scully."

A half hour later Abby opened the door for a smiling Luke Dawson. He was holding a brown paper bag, and as soon as Abby closed the door behind him, he opened the bag, took out a bottle of Hiram Walker Anisette Liqueur, and handed it to her.

"Oh, my God!" she said, not knowing whether to laugh or cry. "My ex and I used to drink that stuff." She decided not to mention the fact that they usually ended up in bed—and not for the purpose of sleeping. "It tastes so good, it's almost impossible not to drink too much."

"I guess we'll just have to take it slow."

"We will indeed." Abby set the bottle on the counter next to the sink. "Now, how about showing me some ID."

Luke reached for his wallet. He took out his badge and held it up so Abby could see it. She studied it long enough to satisfy herself that he was, in fact, Lucas Benjamin Dawson, a special agent for the Federal Bureau of Investigation.

"You can call the field office and give them the ID number next to my picture. They'll verify I'm legit."

"No need. I'm satisfied."

Luke put the badge back in his wallet and returned the wallet to his hip pocket. "Now that we've got that out of the way, have you got something we can drink out of?"

"I do, but they're not exactly fine crystal."

While Luke uncapped the anisette, Abby unwrapped the two Styrofoam cups the maid had left on the counter next to an electric coffee maker, the only upgrade to her room since the previous year. She handed a cup to Luke, and he poured it nearly half full.

"Keep that for yourself," she said. "I'm going to hold off until I've told you what I learned today." And hopefully even after that, Abby said to herself as she sat down on the foot of the bed, an empty cup in her hand.

Luke eased himself into the cushioned chair next to the chest of drawers. "So what have you learned that's too sensitive to talk about on the phone?" he asked and took a sip of anisette.

"Quite a lot actually. I followed a hunch and checked into Jamie Lang's background."

Luke shook his head. "You can't help barking up that same old tree, can you?"

"Not as long as I think there's something up there. The daughter Jamie had in high school was adopted by an old couple named Andrews who live a few miles north of Hawthorne. The husband has Alzheimer's now and wasn't any help. His wife was nice, but she wouldn't talk about their adopted daughter. Right after I left, I passed a woman in a Corvette. Luke, I'm almost certain it was Maggie Calahan. She pulled into the Andrews' driveway and drove right up to their house. I know that doesn't prove anything, but—"

"If she really is their adopted daughter, she's having an affair with her birth mother's husband."

"I know. And that's not all I learned today. Shortly before Will was murdered, he was checking into Jamie Lang's past."

On the verge of drinking more anisette, Luke lowered his cup. "Are you sure about that?"

"I'm positive. Earlier this afternoon I talked to Jamie's high school boyfriend, a guy named Rudy Teague. He's an insurance agent in Hawthorne. Most people thought he was the father, including Rudy until he found out he's sterile. And guess what? Not long before he was murdered, Will paid Rudy a visit. He wanted to find out if Rudy really is the father of Jamie's daughter. He said he represented someone with an interest in the matter but wouldn't say who. Luke, I've got a feeling that person was Maggie. I think she asked Will to find out who her real parents are."

"She wouldn't have needed his help for that. There are procedures that make it easy for an adopted person to access that kind of information."

"Maybe she didn't know that. Whether she did or not, the fact remains that Will was digging around in somebody's past, either Maggie's or Jamie's. He must have learned something that whoever hired him didn't want people knowing."

Luke took another sip of anisette. "If that really was Maggie you saw, the reason she turned into the Andrews' driveway might not have had a thing to do with being their adopted daughter."

"We'll know the answer to that soon enough. First thing tomorrow I plan to ask her about her relationship with the Andrews. I'd like to talk to Jamie Lang too. Any idea when she's getting out of the hospital?"

"Ten o'clock tomorrow morning, according to Nelson." Luke stood up and, liqueur bottle in hand, went over to Abby. "Hold out your cup. It's no fun drinking alone."

"Just a small one," she said, extending her cup. "No more than a quarter full. So what do you think? Am I still barking up the wrong tree?"

Luke poured Abby's cup about a third full. "Right now I don't know what to think," he said as he returned to the chair. "Tell me more about this high school sweetheart of Jamie's."

After taking a sip of the liqueur and finding it even tastier than she remembered, Abby explained that Rudy Teague and his wife had adopted two children after a doctor told Rudy that he couldn't have children of his own. "You don't think Rudy could have killed Will, do you?"

Luke shrugged. "He could be lying about being sterile. Maybe he's the father of Jamie's daughter and doesn't want people knowing it, especially his wife."

Abby took another sip of anisette. "He didn't strike me as the kind of person who'd lie about something like that—or commit murder."

"That's the way I feel about Jamie. And I've known her a lot longer than you have this guy."

"Point taken. Maybe we both should set aside our prejudices for and against potential suspects and not rule out anybody just yet."

"Agreed. Anything else to report about your day?"

Abby started to drink more anisette, then reminded herself that this wasn't like drinking beer. She needed to watch herself. "I spent quite a while in Quentin Grice's office," she said, lowering her cup. "I was alone part of that time, so planting a listening device would have been easy. By the way, Grice asked the handwriting expert in your Charlottesville office to verify that Ned Copeland's suicide note is actually in Copeland's handwriting."

"Grice told you that?"

"Maybe he's more competent and responsible than you think."

"There are only two FBI handwriting experts in the state of Virginia, Abby. One is in the Richmond office and the other in Roanoke."

"Maybe Grice assumed the note would be forwarded to the appropriate office," Abby said and took another sip of anisette.

"What were you doing in his office anyway?"

"I needed a point of contact at the Department of Social Services, someone who might tell me who adopted Jamie's daughter. It turned out that whatever Quentin Grice's deficiencies, he knows how to get things done."

"Both inside and outside the law. If he's indicted for Copeland's murder, you might need to testify about the lie he told you."

"Assuming it was a lie. Maybe he said that just to get me off his back."

"Maybe. We're still a long way from solving Will's murder, Abby, whoever the killer turns out to be."

As their conversation began winding down, Luke finished his cup of liqueur. Abby, who had almost finished hers, sensed that he might be on the verge of leaving. What the hell, she told herself. Raising her cup to her lips, she drained it. "There's no reason to keep sitting in that uncomfortable chair," she said. "You can sit over here next to me if you're so inclined."

Luke's quizzical expression slowly turned into a smile. "Are you the woman with the rule about never mixing her professional and personal lives?"

Abby set the empty cup on the bedside table. "One and the same. I figure we've pretty much taken care of all the professional stuff we're going to for one night. Correct me if I'm wrong, Special Agent Dawson."

Chapter 36

Graham Calahan stood in the doorway of their up-stairs bathroom watching his wife color her hair. "How did your dad like your new wheels?"

Maggie glanced at him in the mirror. "He loved it," she said and continued squeezing the reddish-brown liquid onto her scalp. "I took him for a ride, and when we got back, I let him sit in the driver's seat. Mom and I had a heck of a time getting him to come back in the house."

"How did she like the car?"

"She thinks it's too dangerous." Maggie applied some of the bottle's contents to the back of her head. "Is that why you bought it for me?"

"I bought it for you because I thought you'd like it. You've wanted a sports car for a long time."

"How come you chose now to get me one?"

"No particular reason."

Maggie gave him a suspicious look, this time staring at him instead of at his reflection in the mirror. "You always do things for a reason, Graham. You're the most calcu-lating man I've ever met."

"Is that so? Well, you're the best-looking woman I've ever slept with, but right now you look like hell. If we ever split up, and you decide to re-marry, I suggest you keep the prospective groom from seeing you in that get-up until after the wedding."

Maggie peeled off the thin rubber gloves and placed them on a paper towel next to the hair dryer. "I'll be sure to remember that."

"I wasn't being nasty. I like seeing you that way. Makes me think there's hope for us yet."

"Us?"

"Our marriage." Graham gazed at his wife's breasts, which hung loose and full inside the drip-stained nightgown she always wore when coloring her hair. "In spite of the obvious contrasts—your youth and good looks and my sinus problem and middle-age bulge—we still might be a viable match. Whether we are or not, I'd appreciate it if you acted like we are."

Maggie reached for the first of two towels that lay folded on the countertop. "I assume you're trying to make a point. Mind connecting the dots for me?"

Graham continued to stare at her breasts, impressed by the way they held their shape with no support. "I know you and Nelson Lang have been doing a lot more than playing bridge, Maggie."

She unfolded the towel and wrapped it around her shoulders. "Couldn't you have picked a better time to bring that up? I'm pretty well occupied at the moment, don't you think?"

"Maybe you'd rather I broached the subject at Motel Six. I could have knocked on the door and invited myself in for a little three-way chat. Or I could have tapped on the car window while you two were necking in the high school parking lot. Or maybe you'd rather I interrupted one of the bridge games at the YMCA. When exactly would have been a good time, Maggie?"

"Most any time other than now."

"I brought it up now because you look so pitiful with all

that gunk on your head. Must be my legal training. If conflict is inevitable, pick the time and place that puts your adversary at a disadvantage. I can't imagine you being at more of a disadvantage than you are right now."

Maggie attempted to close the bathroom door, but Graham grabbed it with both hands and pushed back until she was forced to let go.

"Bastard," she muttered. "What are you going to do about it, divorce me?"

"That's out of the question, at least for the time being. The election is just around the corner. I need your support now more than ever."

"You're not up for re-election this year."

"A third of the Virginia supreme court is. Being mayor doesn't interest me anymore, Maggie." Graham paused, watching the change in his wife's expression. "George Blevins is retiring in a few weeks. I think I have a good chance of winning his seat. But I'll need a supportive wife—or at least one who gives the appearance of being supportive. Going through divorce proceedings in the middle of a campaign won't cut it. Neither will voters finding out you're cheating on me."

"I hate to sound crass, but what's in it for me?"

"A generous settlement, assuming you decide you really do want a divorce. On the other hand, if I win George's seat, you might want to experience what it's like living in Richmond as the wife of a supreme court justice. Unlike you, I haven't grown tired of our marriage. But I am tired of being a cuckold. That gets old fast, Maggie. It has to stop, regardless of where we happen to be living at the time."

"And if it doesn't?"

"Let's just say I have options, none of which are pleasant to think about."

"That sounds downright threatening, Graham. You're

not suggesting you'd go so far as to kill me, are you?"

"I'm not suggesting anything. I'd like you to remain my wife, but there's a limit to my patience. I won't tolerate any more unfaithfulness."

"What if I do want a divorce?"

"If you wait until after the election, that won't be a problem. But if you file before then, or go public with your intentions, I'll make things as difficult for you as I can. You'll get your divorce, but you won't get much of a settlement. Instead of having an antique shop to occupy your time, you'll have to find yourself a real job."

"Assuming I'm still alive to find one, right?"

"I didn't say that."

"I think I know where you're coming from, Graham. You really believe you've got a chance at the supreme court?"

"With my legal background and all the pro bono work I've done for the Republican Party over the years, I've got a damn good chance. I'm well respected in the district, and a lot of influential people owe me a favor."

Adjusting the towel to better catch the drips from her hair, Maggie focused her attention on her husband. "Exactly how much does a member of the Virginia supreme court make?"

"A little over two hundred thousand dollars a year, plus perks."

"You make that much now."

"As Justice and Mrs. Graham Calahan, we'll be playing in the big leagues, Maggie. Wouldn't you rather swim in the heady waters of Richmond society than keep slogging around in the stagnant backwaters of Augusta County?"

"What about my antique shop?"

"No reason you can't have one in Richmond, a nicer one than you've got now."

The corners of Maggie's mouth lifted in the beginning

of a smile. "That does sound tempting, Graham. When do you plan to announce your candidacy?"

"Early January, assuming you've stopped seeing Nelson Lang in the meantime and you've given your word you won't do anything else to embarrass me."

Maggie tore two paper towels from the roll next to the hair dryer and began cleaning up the mess. "Nelson and I have already stopped seeing each other," she said, dropping the wet towels into the wastebasket. She tore off two more sheets.

"I know for a fact that you're lying."

Maggie shook her head. "Nelson's wife is in the hospital with a nervous breakdown. He thought it best that we stop seeing each other, at least until Jamie gets back on her feet. I agreed."

"Then the affair isn't over. It's in hiatus."

"It's over," Maggie said and began swabbing the inside of the sink. "That's a unilateral decision I just made for the good of all concerned—Nelson, his emotionally disturbed wife, and—" She paused, giving Graham a knowing look. "And Justice and Mrs. Calahan."

Graham's face brightened. "Do you really mean that?"

"I'd like your assurance that if, at some point after the election, I decided I want a divorce, you won't fight me and you'll make good on your promise to give me a generous settlement."

"You have my word." Moving up behind his wife, Graham put his arms around her nearly flat belly, pulling her close. "God, that stuff smells awful."

"Nobody's forcing you to be around it," Maggie said, making no attempt to remove Graham's hands, even after they cupped her breasts. "I have a question."

"Shoot."

"Virginia's supreme court has a chief justice, right?"

"That's correct."

"How much does he make a year?"

"Last I checked, his annual salary was well over a quarter of a million dollars."

"Any chance you might end up in that job?"

"Actually, that's my long-term goal. It might take a while to get there, but I don't think the chief justice's job is unreachable. Any further questions, Mrs. Calahan?"

"Just one. Are there any Tic Tacs left?"

Graham's smile crumpled. "Is my breath a problem?"

"Not at the moment. I'm thinking about later. After I finish my hair, we can meet in the bedroom for a little pre-election caucus if you're so inclined."

For the first time since he could remember, Graham was at a loss for words. "We're out of Tic Tacs," he finally said. "Will a stick of gum do?"

"Don't worry about it, Judge Calahan. This one's on me." Then, realizing what she had just said, Maggie howled with laugher.

Chapter 37

Abby had just nestled into Luke Dawson's arms when there was a knock at the motel room door. She disentangled herself and sat up in the bed.

"Don't answer it," Luke said. "They'll go away, whoever it is." He reached out for Abby, but she was already putting on her nightgown.

There was more knocking. "It's me—Shannon. We gotta talk. It's important."

"Just a minute."

"I knew this was too good to be true," Luke groaned. "I just knew it."

"The night's still young," Abby said in a low voice. "Simmer down, Special Agent, and put on some clothes."

She switched on the bedside lamp, located her housecoat, and padded over to the sink where she flicked on the fluorescent lights that bordered the mirror.

After brushing her hair into a semblance of calm, she waited for Luke to zip up his pants, and then she opened the door on an obviously troubled Shannon Pfeiffer.

"I really need to talk to somebody about this," she said, noticing Luke standing next to the bed. "Oh, shit. I couldn't have picked a worse time, could I?"

"Not in a million years," Luke said. "If you two will

excuse me, I think I'll go for a walk while you discuss whatever the hell is so important."

"It's about Ben Ramsdell. I think I know who killed him."

The disappointment on Luke's face quickly turned to rapt attention. "In that case I'll stay." He pointed at the upholstered chair. "Have a seat, Shannon."

"I'll take your coat," Abby said. "Luke, bring over one of those straight-backed chairs if you don't mind."

"Luke?" Shannon said, handing Abby her coat. "I thought his name is Marty."

"Oh…it is. Luke is his middle name. Marty sounds too wimpy for my taste."

Shannon shrugged. "Whatever. I'm really sorry to bother you guys. I'll try not to take up too much of your time."

Once they were seated—Shannon in the upholstered chair next to the dresser, Luke in a small wooden chair he brought from the far side of the room, and Abby on the foot of the bed—Shannon told them about her failed attempt to get Wardell Tharp to incriminate himself.

"I really don't know what to believe now," she said. "I still think he killed Ben, but I'm not absolutely sure. If he did do it, he's a shrewd son of a bitch. He handled everything I threw at him like he knew ahead of time it was coming."

"Maybe he did," Luke suggested. "Maybe somebody tipped him off."

"I don't see how. Mitch Folby is the only person who knew about my plan."

"Did Mitch have something to gain by sharing that information with Tharp?"

"Money, I guess, assuming Tharp was willing to pay him. Mitch has been freeloading off Ben for a long time. Now he'll have to find some other means of support—or some other person to support him. Maybe he thought Tharp would be that person. Yeah, maybe the bastard already *is* that person."

Luke leaned forward in the chair. "What do you mean?"

"If Mitch warned Tharp about my plan, maybe he tipped him off earlier about Ben's plans too, including the Richmond trip."

Abby shook her head. "That would be like killing the goose that laid the golden egg."

"Not really. It was just a matter of time before Ben got himself in real trouble selling drugs. Mitch probably realized that, and the rat saw an opportunity to jump on board somebody else's ship—Tharp's. Yeah, that's probably what did happen. I just don't know what to do about it."

Luke got up from the chair and reached for his wallet. "I think you've already done all you needed to."

"I have? What?"

"You've shared your suspicions with the right people. My name really is Luke. Luke Dawson." He took out his wallet and showed Shannon his badge. "I'm an FBI agent."

Shannon stared wide-eyed at the card, then at Luke, finally at Abby. "Do you work for the FBI too?"

"No, I'm a reporter just like I said. He had me fooled for quite a while too."

"I needed a cover for the assignment I've been working on," Luke said. "I still do, so it's important you don't mention a word of this to anyone, Shannon."

"Oh, I won't. Is investigating Ben's murder part of your assignment?"

"It is now. I'll have a talk with Mitch Folby tomorrow and see what I can find out. If he denies being Tharp's informant, at least I should get a sense of whether he's telling the truth or not. Don't let him know you suspect anything. And definitely stay away from Tharp. If he did kill Ben, he probably wouldn't hesitate killing you if he thinks you're a threat."

Shannon nodded. "It's really important to me that Tharp gets what's coming to him. Will you keep me up to speed with what's going on?"

"Is there a way to contact you without arousing anyone's suspicion?"

Shannon fished a pen and a Totem Taxi business card from her purse and wrote a number on the back of the card. "That's my cell phone," she said, handing the card to Luke.

"Either Abby or I will call if there's any news. If you think of anything else we need to know, give Abby a call."

"Will do." After thanking them both for hearing her out, Shannon got up to leave. "Hope I didn't ruin your evening."

Abby retrieved Shannon's coat and accompanied her to the door. "Good night," she said then shut and locked the door. "Do you really think Mitch sold out Ben?" she asked Luke.

"It wouldn't surprise me. Ben might have already made a mess of things *before* he decided to become a drug dealer. Maybe he screwed up so bad that Mitch had already decided it was time to abandon ship."

Abby nodded. "A plan that went horribly awry?"

"Right. A scheme the two of them probably cooked up together. Mitch would have been counting on that scheme to elevate his life to a new level. Ben was counting on the same thing for himself."

"And the whole thing turned to shit when Ben wasn't even mentioned in his father's will."

"Exactly."

Abby mulled over the idea. "So what do you

think—Mitch Folby jumps to the top of our suspect list?"

"Not necessarily the top, but he should definitely be on it. I still think Quentin Grice killed Will or had him killed, but we can't discount what Shannon told us." Luke gave Abby a sideways glance. "Now the big question, at least in my mind, is whether she also managed to ruin the evening."

Abby turned off the fluorescent lights and went over to the bed where she slipped out of her housecoat. "I don't think so, Special Agent Dawson," she said and began removing her nightgown. "Would you like a spot of anisette first, or shall we cut directly to the chase?"

Chapter 38

Jamie Lang had trouble sleeping, even after Dr. Baxter had increased the dosage of her nightly medication. Her psychiatrist seemed like a nice man, low key in his approach yet genuinely interested in helping her "get back to normal," as he called it. In spite of the fact that she had given him little to work with, he hadn't chided her or acted put out. She had been pleasantly surprised when he set tomorrow as her release date.

"Why did you decide to kill your father?" he had asked during their only individual session of significant length. She had met with him briefly at other times, usually after supper when he touched base with patients to see if their medication needed adjusting, but during those shorter sessions, he hadn't attempted to delve into her psyche.

"I don't really know," she had replied. "I must have just snapped."

"When was the last time you saw him—prior to the night he hung himself, I mean?"

They were sitting across the table from each other in the room used for individual as well as group sessions. Dr. Baxter held a pen in one hand. A small notebook lay open in front of him on the table.

"About three years ago I ran into him at the mall."

"Did you speak?"

"He did. I ignored him."

"Why?"

"I loathed the man. Still do."

"Can you tell me why?"

Jamie sighed. "I'd rather not go into that, Dr. Baxter. Maybe at some point down the road I'll feel different. Right now I just don't feel up to talking about it."

"Getting things off your chest can be therapeutic, Ms. Lang. It's often the first step to recovery."

Jamie nodded but didn't reply. She gazed at the patients' artwork posted on the far wall. A picture of a large tree caught her eye, reminding her of the willow in the front yard of her girlhood home.

"Other than the chance meeting at the mall, how long has it been since you had any real contact with your father?"

"It's been ten years," Jamie said, closing her eyes as she recalled the brief interchange at the cemetery between herself and her father. "It was right after my mother's funeral. I told him he should be the one in the casket, not her."

Raising an eyebrow, the psychiatrist waited for Jamie to elaborate.

"My mother had lung cancer," she offered as explanation. "Mom didn't even smoke until after she married him."

"I take it your father was abusive."

Jamie nodded. "I never actually saw him hit Mom, but every now and then she had bruises that couldn't have come from anything else. My father's emotional abuse was more obvious than his physical abuse."

"Oh?"

Ward policy required Jamie to wear cloth slippers issued by the hospital. The tile floor had made her feet cold, and she covered her left foot with her right one. "There was no give and take in their relationship," she said, not sure why she was doing exactly what she had told Dr. Baxter she didn't want to do: discuss Ned Copeland. She supposed that, having been denied the pleasure of killing the man, revealing the specific nature of some of his abuses was the next best thing. "Absolutely everything had to be done his way," she continued. "When and where Mom did her shopping, the church they attended, what friends she could have. He even told her what to fix for our meals. For a long time, Mom pretended there wasn't a problem. But after she got sick, she told me she didn't realize how controlling the man was until after they were married. She said she had wanted to leave him almost from the start but was afraid he'd kill her if she tried."

Dr. Baxter nodded and jotted something in his notebook. "How did your father respond when you told him he should be the one in the casket?"

Jamie hesitated, deciding that no harm could come from answering the question. "He just smiled and told me how pretty I looked."

"I can see why you might have wanted to kill this man, Ms. Lang. What I don't understand is why you waited so long after your mother's death to make the attempt. How do you explain that?"

Jamie shrugged. "I can't really. Like I said, I must have snapped."

"But something causes a person to snap. An episode like this always has a trigger. A series of stressful events can bring it on. So can a single catastrophic event. Either way, a person tends to lose his or her inhibitions and becomes capable of things that normally would be totally out of character. What do you think brought about your episode? Why decide to kill your father now instead of ten years ago when his transgressions would have been fresh in your mind?"

Placing her left foot on top of her right one, Jamie reminded herself not to let Dr. Baxter lead her any further than she wanted to go. "I have been under a lot of stress lately," she said, leaning back in her chair.

"What kind of stress?"

"Pinecroft mainly."

"The golf course you and your husband own?"

"Yes."

"What exactly was the problem there?"

Jamie explained that she and Nelson had overextended themselves financially. "When the bank wouldn't lend us money to landscape the new holes, we found ourselves in a *Catch Twenty-Two* situation. To pay off what we already owed, we had to attract new customers. But to do that, we needed additional funding to make the new holes playable."

"I was under the impression that Pinecroft's monetary problems were solved. Won't your inheritance go a long way toward easing your financial burden?"

Regretting that she had allowed herself to be drawn into this line of questioning, Jamie again gazed at the pictures on the wall. "It'll definitely help," she said. "But we're not out of the woods yet."

"But the stress Pinecroft caused prior to your learning about the inheritance—that's not really an issue any longer, is it?"

"No, I guess not."

"Then something else must have triggered your decision to kill your father. I'd like to try to pin that down, whatever it is. I think it would be helpful in the long run if we identified it now."

After a momentary silence, Jamie re-established eye contact with the psychiatrist. "With all due respect, Dr. Baxter, I'd rather not go into my personal life any more than I already have," she said as calmly as she could. "I don't mean to be difficult. I know I have issues, but I'd like to deal with them on my own."

"According to the staff, that's the same position you've taken during your group sessions. I was hoping our individual session would be different."

"I've never been one to bare my soul, Dr. Baxter. I don't think it would be productive for either of us if I started now."

The psychiatrist nodded. He adjusted his glasses and jotted something else in the notebook. "Eventually, I hope you'll change your mind and get some professional help for your issues, Ms. Lang. We're not in the business of blaming people or trying to shame them. But we can't provide meaningful or lasting assistance if our clients don't help us identify what's troubling them."

"I understand. If my problems turn out to be more than I can handle, I'll make an appointment to see you."

Dr. Baxter handed her a business card. "You won't need to wait for an appointment. Just call that number any time day or night."

Jamie slipped the card in her gown pocket. "I don't think it'll come to that," she said and stood up. "But thank you anyway."

"Before you go, Ms. Lang, there's something else I'd like to ask. Suppose your father hadn't been dead when you arrived at Holly Oak? What were you planning to do after you killed him?"

Again Jamie gazed at the pictures on the wall, focusing momentarily on the willow tree. "I wouldn't have tried to get away with it, if that's what you mean."

"You were prepared to spend the rest of your life in jail?"

"If necessary."

Dr. Baxter distractedly ran his fingers through his hair. "One final question, Mrs. Lang. Did you ever consider suicide as an option to turning yourself over to the authorities?"

Deciding an honest answer to that question was definitely not in her best interests, Jamie shook her head. "Whatever else I might be, I'm not suicidal."

⌘

The night before her scheduled release from the hospital, Jamie slept fitfully, slipping in and out of unpleasant dreams. During the most painful of them, she was the defendant in a trial in which her daughter, Rudy Teague, and Nelson Lang all took the witness stand to attest to her failures as a mother, lover, and wife. At the conclusion of Nelson's testimony, Jamie turned to her attorney, who, she suddenly realized, was Dr. Baxter.

"What exactly am I being charged with?" she asked.

"Betrayal of the people who cared for you the most."

"Are there any more witnesses?"

"Just one. If his testimony isn't any more damaging than what we've heard so far, I'm confident you'll be found innocent."

The brief surge of hope Jamie felt was dashed when she heard the prosecuting attorney call the name of the final witness. "I'm changing my plea," she said. "I want to plead guilty. And I want to do it now, before there's any more testimony."

"Why would you do that?"

"Because I am guilty, Dr. Baxter. Please tell the judge to stop the trial. For God's sake, have him stop it now!"

Chapter 39

How could she have been such an idiot? Abby asked herself as she picked at her breakfast. What the hell had she been thinking? She knew, of course, that the answer to both questions was the same—she hadn't been thinking at all.

The words had just come tumbling out: *Bet that's the first time you ever fucked* a *bipolar chick!* More of a celebratory response than anything else, it was the equivalent of a golfer letting out a wild, joyous whoop after curling in a sixty-foot putt on an undulating green or smacking a monster drive down the middle of a narrow, tree-lined fairway.

She had cringed as soon as she said it, wishing she could take back the words and say something sensible. Or better yet, say nothing at all.

Revealing that she had bipolar disorder was not what troubled Abby. Eventually, she would have done that anyway, feeling she owed it to any man who might contemplate a serious relationship with her. But to do it in such a way—blurting out the first thing that popped in her head. That was…well, it was what people with bipolar disorder were noted for, wasn't it?…leaping before they looked.

"Yeah, I guess it is," Luke had replied after the awkward silence that followed. Then he had started in with his questions. When was she diagnosed? What kind of medication did she take? Did she have a psychiatrist? One question had led to another until it was long after midnight and Luke finally drifted off to sleep.

Abby had hoped they would make love again in the morning, vowing this time to keep her big mouth shut. But when she woke up, Luke was already dressed. He kissed her on the forehead, said he'd touch base with her later, and was out the door.

I did it again, she said to herself. *I had something really nice and I threw it the hell away. What an idiot!*

Don't expect perfection, she heard Dorene Milsap's voice say. *When you make mistakes—and you will whether you have bipolar disorder or not—don't beat yourself up. Just learn from your mistakes and try not to repeat them. One foot in front of the other, Abby. One step and then another—*

She heard another voice, one that wasn't in her head. Looking up, she saw the waiter standing next to her table. "I'm sorry," she said. "I didn't hear you."

"I asked what happened. Your appetite isn't the same since you found my wife's sausages not to your liking. Were they overcooked?"

It took Abby a moment to realize what he meant. "No, they just…well, they reminded me of something."

"A severed finger?"

"How did you know?"

"You weren't the only customer to have such a reaction."

∽∾∽

Abby's spirits lifted a bit when she spotted a red Corvette parked in front of Bygone Daze. Pulling into the first available space, she felt a surge of anticipation as she exited her car. According to the sign on the front door, the shop wouldn't open for another ten minutes. Abby knocked anyway and then tried the door, which was locked. A moment later the door swung open and Maggie appeared, a coffee mug in her right hand.

"I thought you might be stopping by today. Come on in."

"You were expecting me?"

"I was pretty sure you recognized me when we passed on the Hogback yesterday. After Mom told me you'd been to the house, I figured you'd put two and two together."

"So the Andrews really are your adoptive parents."

Maggie nodded. She held the door for Abby and then closed it behind her. "And Jamie Lang is my biological mother, as you apparently surmised. Care for some coffee?"

"No thanks."

Maggie took a sip and set her cup on the counter next to the cash register. "What makes you think Jamie killed Will?"

"Well, she's definitely gone out of her way to avoid me. Plus she stood to gain from Will's death."

"The Pinecroft inheritance?"

"That's right. If you know anything about Jamie that might be helpful to me, I hope you'll tell me."

"I know she turned her back on me when I was a toddler. Whether she's capable of murder, I have no idea. What makes you think Ned Copeland didn't kill Will?"

"He was in Blacksburg at the time of the murder. I'm not at liberty to say how I know that, but my source is impeccable. I also know Will was looking into your background shortly before he died."

"And you think there's a connection?"

"I'd be surprised if there isn't. Somebody must have

known what he was looking for and didn't want him to find it."

Maggie snorted. "I can't imagine anybody other than me giving a rat's ass about the identity of my birth parents," she said and stepped behind the counter. "And I already knew about Jamie."

"How?"

"When I was in college, I decided to find out who had the gall to dump me, so I hired a private detective. He was able to track Jamie down."

"Was he able to find out about your biological father too?"

Maggie reached for her coffee cup. "Nope," she said and took another sip. "Dear old dad remains a mystery."

Abby wondered if Rudy Teague's name had surfaced during the investigation, but she decided that question, as well as whatever answer Maggie might provide, would be irrelevant. "Does Jamie know you're her daughter?" she asked instead.

Maggie shrugged. "Supposedly the adoption process was closed. What difference does it make anyway?"

"None, unless she asked Will to find you. I know if I had a daughter out there somewhere, I'd want to know about her. Whether Jamie felt that way or not, someone must have asked Will to check into your background."

For a moment Maggie seemed lost in thought. Suddenly she rolled her eyes and chuckled. "You might ask my ever-loving husband what he knows about this."

"Your husband?"

"Graham Calahan, Wisteria's current mayor and aspiring state Supreme Court justice. He'll have a shit fit if he finds out I let that cat out of the bag. But so what? That man's life would be dull as a Baptist picnic if it wasn't for me."

છ૭છ૭

Graham's secretary told Abby that he had gone to lunch and that his next available appointment was at two.

"I'll take it."

"And the reason you want to see Mr. Calahan?"

"I…uh…I'd like to know what my rights are in a divorce case."

Back in her car Abby called Luke Dawson on her cell phone, almost hoping he wouldn't answer. When he did, she told him that Maggie had readily admitted being the Andrews' adopted daughter and Jamie Lang's biological daughter. "That's not all I learned either. It sounds like Will was trying to track down Maggie's biological parents for Graham Calahan. Graham plans to run for Virginia's Supreme Court, and apparently he wanted to make sure there isn't anything in Maggie's family tree that might jump out and bite him during the campaign. I've got an appointment this afternoon to see what he has to say about all this. In the meantime I'd like to talk to Jamie if that's possible. Is Nelson still picking her up this morning?"

"That's the plan. I really don't think this is a good time to question her, Abby. If she doesn't know Maggie is her daughter, finding out will come as a shock. That's not the kind of thing Jamie needs right now."

"I won't mention Maggie, and I promise to be discreet. I'd appreciate it if you didn't tell her I'm coming out."

"I won't be here to tell her anything. I'm getting ready to head to Charlottesville for the meeting with my boss. I should be back sometime late this afternoon. Would you like to have dinner with me?"

Abby wondered if Luke really wanted to see her again or if he was just trying to let her down easy. "Let me check my social calendar," she said and paused for exactly two seconds. "It so happens I'm free this evening."

"Pick you up around six?"

"That'll work. In the meantime, no hanky panky with any female agents."

There was a pause at the other end, during which Abby thought she had once again put her foot in her mouth.

"Let me tell you something, Abby Burlew. Compared to the woman I was with last night, every female agent in the bureau, including Dana Scully herself, pales in comparison."

ⲉⲟⲉⲟ

For the next half hour, Abby basked in the glow of Luke's compliment. By the time she left for Pinecroft, however, she was wondering if Luke would have said the same thing to any woman he slept with. *Don't get too high and you won't have far to fall if things don't work out*, she told herself.

Unable to heed her own advice, she let out a whoop of joy as she sped toward the course.

The golfers' parking lot was empty. Although its surface had dried since Abby's initial visit, the ruts left behind resembled hardened concrete. Parking her car near the putting green, she went around to the back of the house to see if any cars were there, finding both Jamie's coupe and Nelson's sedan parked near the back steps. Bogie appeared, ambling toward her from under the deck.

"Haven't seen you in a while," Abby said. As she leaned down to pet the cat, he threw himself down at her feet, tucking his head first one way and then the other, exposing his belly in the process. Abby noticed a pink spot about the size of a quarter where his skin was hairless and smooth. "What happened there, little guy? Lose some fur defending your turf?"

"We think he was born that way," a male voice replied.

"At least he had that bald spot when we took him in as a kitten."

Abby looked up and saw Nelson Lang standing at the deck railing.

"What can I do for you?" he asked.

As Abby stood up, she noticed the outline of someone in the partially open kitchen doorway, a woman with blonde hair. "I'd like to talk to Jamie."

"Mind telling me what this is about?"

"I have some questions for her."

"What kind of questions?"

"It concerns Will Ramsdell."

Nelson shook his head. "I'm sorry, but she can't have visitors yet. Doctor's orders."

"It's all right," Jamie said, opening the door wider. "I'll talk to her."

Nelson turned toward his wife. "I don't think that's a good idea. Remember what Dr. Baxter said about avoiding stressful situations."

"Abby's not going to bite. I'll be fine, Nelson."

"Are you sure?"

"Yes."

After a brief hesitation, Nelson turned back to Abby. "All right, come on up. Be careful on those steps. They can be slippery."

Chapter 40

I apologize for not keeping our appointment," Jamie said as she sat down at the far end of the sofa from Abby. "I wasn't feeling well that morning. I'm not exactly at my best now either, so—"

"I'll try to be brief," Abby said, noticing that Jamie's face was pale and drawn and that there were dark crescents under her eyes. The eyes themselves reminded Abby of her father's during the final stage of his cancer.

"There's no need for you to stay, Nelson. I'd appreciate it if you'd get a wash going for me. My suitcase is full of dirty clothes. There's more in the bathroom hamper."

"Are you sure you're up to this, Jamie?"

"Yes." She waited until Nelson started down the stairs. "I'm ready when you are," she said in a subdued voice.

It's crunch time, Abby told herself, and she felt a rush of adrenaline similar to what she might have felt had she stepped to the line for an important pair of free throws in a crucial game. "I assume you know Marty Stith is actually Luke Dawson and that he was keeping your father under surveillance."

Jamie nodded. "Nelson explained all that to me, including the fact that my father had nothing to do with Will's death."

"So you realize we're back to square one as far as who killed Will is concerned."

"I do."

No need to pussyfoot, Abby told herself. *Just ask the right questions in a non-threatening way and see how she reacts.* "Do you have any idea who might have killed him?"

Jamie took a deep breath. "No," she said calmly. "Having been police chief, Will must have made enemies. I can't tell you who they are, but I'd be surprised if there aren't several out there."

Abby thought she detected sadness underlying Jamie's apparent tranquility. Or was it anxiety? Or a combination of the two? "Did you know Will was planning to leave his estate to Pinecroft?" she asked.

"No," Jamie said, shaking her head. "That came as a complete surprise."

"When did you find out about it?"

"The same day you came here. Nelson told me after I got home from work that afternoon. He'd learned about it from Will's attorney. "

"Could Nelson have learned of it earlier? Prior to Will's murder, I mean."

"I don't see how. If Will told anyone, it would have been me. And he didn't tell me."

Abby considered asking about Jamie's relationship with Will, but decided not to broach that subject, at least not yet. Clearly there was a limit to how long Jamie would be willing to talk, and that particular line of questioning might eat up valuable time without leading anywhere productive. "Did you see Will the day he was murdered?"

Jamie took a breath and slowly exhaled. "We talked for a few minutes. Nothing in particular—just the normal chit chat I'd have with any customer. Since it was opening day of deer season, I tried to discourage him from playing the back nine. Hunters tend to stray onto that part of the course."

"Did Will seem preoccupied or give any indication that he might be worried about something?"

"Just the opposite, actually. He seemed in good spirits and focused on his golf game."

"And that's the last you saw of him?"

"Yes."

Hearing the sound of running water, Abby assumed that Nelson had turned on the washing machine. She decided to make him the focus of her next question. "Did your husband talk to Will that morning?"

"No. Nelson left shortly after daybreak. One of our members had given him permission to hunt on his property. He didn't get back until late that afternoon, long after Will's body had been found."

"And it was Marty Stith who found him?"

"Yes."

Abby decided that if there was a chink in Jamie's armor, she would have to probe deeper to find it. To do so risked violating her promise to Luke that she would be discreet, but she owed Will something too, a lot more than she did Luke. She decided that now was as good a time as any to play her one and only trump card. "At some point recently did you ask Will to do some investigative work for you?"

Jamie's brow furrowed. "Investigative work? No. Why do you ask?"

"Shortly before he was murdered, Will conducted an investigation that involved the daughter you gave up for adoption."

Again Jamie paused, this time the look on her face telling Abby she had finally struck a nerve. "Involved? In what way?"

"Apparently he was trying to locate her biological

parents. I know for a fact that Will asked Rudy Teague if he was the girl's father. I also know what Rudy told him. I think you do too."

For a moment Jamie didn't respond at all, simply continued to stare straight ahead. Then, for the first time since she sat down on the sofa, she looked Abby in the eye. "Exactly what do you want from me?"

"To start with, I'd like to know if you asked Will to find your daughter."

"I did not."

"Did you already know who and where she is?"

There was a longer pause during which Abby thought she might have to repeat the question. "I've known that for a long time," Jamie finally said in a weary voice.

Abby hesitated, not wanting to mention Maggie in case Jamie really didn't know about her. "What's your daughter's name?" she asked.

"I don't think that's any of your business."

"Actually, I already know. I just want to make sure you're telling me the truth."

Jamie got up from the sofa. "You must think I'm a fool to fall for a trick like that. I'd like you to leave now. You have no right prying into my private life."

"It's Maggie, isn't it?" Abby said, not knowing what else she could do under the circumstances. She hoped she wasn't making a terrible mistake. "Maggie Calahan."

Looking defeated, Jamie slowly sat back down on the sofa. "So where are you going with this? Do you think I killed Will?"

"I don't know what to think. Did you kill him?"

Her face contorting with grief, Jamie shook her head. "I—I can't take any more of this."

Abby heard footsteps on the stairs. "If you didn't kill him, I think you have a good idea who did," she said, thinking this might be her last chance to get the truth from Jamie, whatever it might be.

By the time Nelson reached the living room, Jamie had covered her face with her hands and was sobbing.

"I never should've let you in," Nelson said, his words laced with anger. "Get out of this house! Right now, damn you, or I'll throw you out!"

Abby stood up and headed for the back door, more afraid that she had subjected a vulnerable and possibly innocent woman to an unnecessarily harsh interrogation than of Nelson's wrath. Still, had this been a high-stakes poker game, she would have bet most of her chips that Jamie Lang knew more about Will's murder than she was willing to let on.

೮�꩜ೱ

As she sat in Graham Calahan's waiting room, Abby could still hear Jamie's quavering voice: "I—I can't take any more of this." *Can't take any more of what? More talk about Will? More suspicion that Jamie might somehow be connected to Will's murder? More guilt?*

"Mr. Calahan will see you now."

Abby got up and made her way past the secretary to where Graham stood in the open doorway of his office. Pointing to the chair next to his desk, he told her to have a seat.

"Do you really want to talk about Virginia's divorce law, Ms. Burlew, or is there something else on your mind?"

"How did you know?"

Graham closed the door, went behind his desk, and sat down. "Wisteria is a small town. As mayor, I try to make it my business to keep up with what's going on. I know, for example, that you've been investigating Will Ramsdell's murder. I also know you live in North Carolina. If you're really interested in your divorce options, wouldn't you have contacted an attorney who practices law in that state?"

"Actually, I'm here to talk about Will," Abby said, pleased that she didn't feel the least bit intimidated by this lawyer. "I have reason to believe that shortly before he died, Will was looking into your wife's background. One of the things he was trying to find out was the identity of Maggie's biological parents."

The only change in Graham's expression was a slight furrowing of his brow. "That's a mighty strange thing to be investigating, don't you think?"

"Not necessarily, especially since you're the person who asked him to do it."

Graham snorted. "If I didn't care about Maggie's lineage when I married her, why would I care about it now?"

"Probably because you wanted to make sure there wasn't something in her background that would jeopardize your campaign for the Virginia Supreme Court."

Graham gave a mirthless chuckle. "Apparently, you've been talking to my loose cannon of a wife," he said and leaned forward in his chair. "You're meddling in something that's none of your business, Ms. Burlew."

"Listen, Mr. Calahan. I don't care about your political ambitions or when you plan to announce them. That's your business. Mine is to find out who killed Will Ramsdell. Contrary to popular belief, it was not Ned Copeland. I know that for a fact. I also know someone asked Will to look into your wife's background. Was that someone you?"

"How do you know Copeland didn't kill Will?"

"He was in Blacksburg at the time of the murder. I'm not at liberty to tell you how I know that, but it's indisputable. Now answer my question. Did you ask Will to check into your wife's background?"

Graham sat back in his chair, his demeanor no longer threatening, a lawyer who knew he'd just lost his case. "I'd appreciate it if you wouldn't mention anything about my running for the supreme court," he said. "I'd like to make that announcement myself."

"That's fine with me. In return for my keeping quiet about it, though, I'd like you to tell me what Will found out about your wife's birth parents."

"He didn't find out anything."

"I don't believe that."

"Frankly, neither did I. Not at first anyway. But that's exactly what Will told me. He said he'd run into a brick wall. I offered to double his fee if he located Maggie's parents, but he said he'd already exhausted every avenue. Will had always been a straight shooter, so I took him at his word. I couldn't imagine why he'd lie to me."

Abby was feeling in the zone now, the way she used to feel when her shots were dropping during a crucial basketball game. If she could discover that Maggie's birth mother was Jamie Lang, then Will would have been able to discover that too—and probably a whole lot more. So why would he withhold the information? Was it because he didn't want to reveal something that wasn't in Jamie's best interest?

"Is that all you wanted to talk to me about, Ms. Burlew?"

"No, it's not. When exactly did Will decide to leave his money to the Langs?"

"I don't know the answer to that. All I can tell you is shortly before his death he gave my secretary a sealed envelope with the word *Pinecroft* on the front and asked that it be put with the rest of his papers. I had no idea what was in that envelope, or I would have opened it as soon as I learned Will was dead. It took me several days to get around to reading it. It would have taken even longer if Ben Ramsdell hadn't asked me to go through his father's papers to see if there was anything about an inheritance."

Abby was reminded of another supposedly sealed envelope. She considered asking Graham when Will gave him the one with Marty Stith's name on it. Whatever the lawyer's response, however, it probably wouldn't justify having to explain how she knew of that envelope's existence. "Did Will ever discuss his estate with you?" she asked.

Graham shook his head. "I had no idea he was planning to leave a penny to Pinecroft."

Abby wondered if Will had found out something about Maggie so potentially damaging that someone—Graham or possibly Maggie—killed him in order to keep the information secret. Knowing there was no way Graham would ever admit to being part of such a scenario, Abby decided it was time to gather up her winnings and leave the table.

"Thanks for your time, Mr. Calahan," she said, standing up.

Graham went over to the door and opened it for her. "If you really do have information that Will was killed by someone other than Ned Copeland, I suggest you share it with the authorities."

"I already have," Abby said, confident that her response would make Graham think twice if he thought killing her was a good idea.

As she headed to her car, Abby was flush with pride. She had actually gone toe to toe with a hot shot lawyer on his home turf and bested him. She could almost hear the applause cascading from the bleachers.

Chapter 41

It was going on three-thirty when Abby got back to her motel room, time enough to do some jogging and still be ready for her dinner date with Luke. While changing into her sweats, she wondered what the next step in her investigation should be. Although Quentin Grice, Wardell Tharp, Nelson Lang, Ben Ramsdell, and even Mitch Folby remained legitimate suspects, Abby now believed that Will Ramsdell had been killed by one of three people: Jamie Lang, Maggie Calahan, or Graham Calahan. To determine which one committed the murder, she needed to find out what Will discovered while conducting his investigation into Maggie's background.

According to Graham, Will hadn't discovered anything. Abby didn't believe that for a second; he must have learned something. Either he told Graham about it and Graham killed him so nobody else would find out, or Jamie or Maggie learned about it and murdered him for the same reason. But what could Will possibly have discovered that was so potentially damaging or incriminating that it got him killed? Abby hoped the answer would come to her while she was jogging.

Just as she finished tying the laces of her running shoes, there was a knock at her motel room's door. Abby opened it, thinking Luke had returned from Charlottesville earlier than expected. Instead, she found Jamie Lang standing on the concrete stoop, her left hand clutching a satchel handbag.

"May I come in?"

"Of course." Abby stepped aside as Jamie entered the room. She was on the verge of offering to hang up Jamie's coat when the woman reached in the handbag and pulled out a small pistol.

"Don't do anything foolish or I'll kill you where you stand. I have nothing to lose, Abby. Do you understand what I'm telling you?"

Abby nodded, her heart pounding.

Jamie shrugged off her coat and tossed it on the bed. "Sit down. I want you to listen carefully to what I have to say."

Abby sat down in the cushioned chair, and Jamie sat on the bed next to her coat. Although her eyes were red and puffy, there was a purposefulness in her expression that Abby hadn't seen earlier.

"You were right to suspect me," Jamie said in a voice containing both sorrow and resignation. "I'd give anything to be able to go back and do things differently."

Abby remained silent, afraid whatever she might say would make the situation worse.

"A while ago Maggie's husband asked Will to check into her background. Will did as requested, and when he found out that I'm Maggie's mother, he came to me and asked if I'd object to the information being passed on to Graham Calahan. I told him I most certainly would. I didn't want Graham or anyone else knowing Maggie is my daughter. I made Will swear he'd never tell a soul."

A delivery truck rattled into the motel's parking lot, the noise causing Jamie to look toward the window. When she again focused on Abby, there were tears in her eyes.

"As Will was leaving the pro shop that morning, he said

something that took me completely by surprise. He said he had something important to discuss with Nelson and me and that he'd come back later to do it. I stood there like a ninny, like I was in shock, which in a real sense I was. I was absolutely certain Will was going to tell Nelson that Maggie is my daughter, hoping to get him to break off their affair." Jamie wiped at her eyes with her free hand. "I didn't realize what a horrible blunder I'd made," she continued, her voice cracking, "until I learned Will had left his estate to Pinecroft. It wasn't Maggie he wanted to talk to Nelson about. It was Pinecroft. There was a paragraph in his will that said if he should die before Nelson and I had paid back any money he might have lent us, the debt was to be forgiven. That's what Will wanted to talk to us about the day I killed him, Abby. He was going to offer to lend us the money we needed to landscape the new holes. What a fool I was not to see that. I killed a decent man who wanted nothing more than to help me and my husband out of a financial bind."

"Why are you telling me this?" Abby asked in a low voice.

"So you'll know the real reason I killed Will. I want the official reason to be different."

"I don't understand."

"I'm offering you a trade, Abby. Your life for a solemn promise. It's extremely important to me that neither Maggie nor anyone else know she's the bastard daughter of Jamie Copeland and…some guy I had sex with in high school. Your part of the bargain is to agree not to ever, under any circumstances, reveal to anyone that Maggie Calahan is my daughter. Do you understand?"

"Yes," Abby said, relief beginning to wash over her.

"When I gave Maggie up for adoption, we had already bonded. I loved her dearly, and she seemed to feel the same about me. No mother and child could have been closer. But I knew I couldn't keep her. My home life was intolerable, and yet I had no place to go. If I'd struck out on my own with Maggie, I would have been lucky to get a minimum-wage job. We would have had to live in some dumpy apartment, assuming I could have afforded one. And there would have been no one to take care of Maggie while I worked. I wanted her to have a good life, Abby, one a lot better than I could have provided her. Putting her up for adoption was the hardest thing I ever did. I didn't make that sacrifice to have it all ruined now. Can you promise me you'll never tell Maggie or anyone else that she's my daughter?"

Abby started to say that other people, including Maggie, already knew she was Jamie's daughter. Considering how desperate and unstable Jamie seemed, Abby decided that saying such a thing would be unwise, perhaps even fatal. "I promise."

"On your word of honor?"

"Yes."

"Will you also promise that if I confess to the authorities and am adequately punished for what I did, you'll stop digging into my background or Maggie's, regardless of what questions you might still have?"

Abby nodded.

"Say it!"

"I promise. On my word of honor."

A modicum of relief mingled with the sadness on Jamie's face. "There's a confession in my handbag, a signed note admitting I killed Will. I want you to know his murder was solely my doing. Nobody else had a thing to do with it. Not Nelson, not Maggie, nobody. I'm the one who decided to kill Will, and I'm the one who pulled the trigger. I used the shotgun Nelson bought me when we moved to Pinecroft. I want you to be completely clear on these things, Abby. Are you?"

"Yes."

"I say in the note that you suspected all along I had something to do with Will's death and that you were getting close to the truth. As for my motive, I say that when I learned Will would be playing the back nine that morning, something clicked in my brain, and I saw a way to rescue Pinecroft from bankruptcy. By the time he teed off on the tenth hole, I'd already chosen the location of his murder. The seventeenth tee can't be seen from the clubhouse or the road, and it's far enough from where Luke was cutting brush that he'd think the shotgun blast came from one of the hunters in the woods."

"I don't understand. That's different from what you just told me."

"My written confession is plausible, and it will let the police close the case without involving Maggie. Even though some of what I wrote isn't true, I want you to go along with it. In fact, if your promise to me means anything, you'll have to go along with it." Jamie paused, looking Abby directly in the eye. "Knowing what you do now, will you stand by your promise?"

"Yes," Abby said, her relief tempered by her growing fear that Jamie might be on the verge of killing herself.

"If the sheriff or Luke Dawson or any other law officer asks if you have any reason whatsoever to doubt my written confession, what will you tell them?"

"That—that I have no reason to doubt it."

Jamie studied Abby's face as though trying to decide whether to believe her. "I understand you're a mother."

Abby nodded. "I have a young son."

"Would you do whatever is in your power to protect him?"

"Of course."

"Then I'm begging you as one mother to another to

help me protect my child. Apparently, you're a decent person. Luke certainly feels that way."

Abby remained silent, unable to think of anything to say that wouldn't endanger her own life.

"Your reason for coming to Wisteria was to make sure Will's murderer was brought to justice. That's exactly what will be accomplished. As the good person I think you are, please just leave it at that." Jamie paused again, her face calmer now, almost serene. "Keep in mind that I could have killed you and didn't. You owe me something in return, don't you think?"

Before Abby could respond or make an attempt to stop her, Jamie raised the gun to her own temple and pulled the trigger. There was a loud popping sound similar to what Abby heard when she fired her mother's .22 caliber pistol. Jamie's head jerked to the side and the pistol recoiled slightly. Still clutching the handle, Jamie remained on the edge of the bed for a brief moment as though nothing had happened. Then slowly she pitched forward onto the floor. Blood trickled from her temple, turning a shade darker as it soaked into the carpeting. There was a momentary silence. Then Abby's cell phone began ringing.

Chapter 42

Ignoring her cell phone, Abby hurried to the bedside table and dialed 911 on her room phone. In a quavering voice she told the operator there had been a suicide attempt at the Shenandoah Inn and asked that an ambulance be sent immediately. Then she knelt beside Jamie to see if there was anything she could do, knowing there probably wasn't. She was encouraged when she detected a slight pulse, but she didn't like the vacant look in Jamie's eyes.

Abby considered pressing a damp washcloth against Jamie's temple to stanch the flow of blood but decided that might do more harm than good. Her cell phone, which had stopped ringing while she talked to the 911 operator, started ringing again. She reached for it, hoping the caller was Luke. It was her mother.

"I can't talk now, Mom. I'll call you back later." Abby disconnected the call and dialed Luke's number. The cheerfulness with which he answered turned to stunned disbelief when she told him that Jamie Lang had just tried to kill herself. "I'll explain everything when I see you. Tell Nelson what happened. I'll meet you at the hospital."

Hearing the faint wail of a siren, Abby decided there was time enough for one more call. She dialed her mother's number and briefly explained the situation. "I have to ring off now, Mom. The ambulance is here, and I need to make sure it comes to the right room."

As soon as the ambulance rumbled into the parking lot, Abby opened the motel room door and hurried outside, waving her arms. The vehicle lurched to a stop behind her car. Two EMTs got out, one running to the back for a stretcher.

After holding her room's door open for the men, Abby watched as they rolled Jamie onto her side, applied an oxygen mask to her face, and checked her vital signs.

She heard one of them say the wound had been made by a .22 caliber bullet; otherwise she'd be missing part of her head and her brains would be scattered all over the wall.

"What are her chances?" Abby asked as they began loading Jamie onto the stretcher.

"There's no exit wound, so the bullet must be lodged in her brain," the EMT closest to Abby said. "Depending on exactly where it is and how much damage it did getting there, she might make it. But don't count on it."

Abby held the door for the men as they wheeled Jamie outside, and then she hurried to her car. She was about to get in and follow the ambulance when a police cruiser pulled into the adjacent parking space and Mel Taggart got out. "You called in the suicide attempt?" he asked as the ambulance pulled away, its siren blaring.

"It's Jamie Lang. She shot herself."

"Show me where it happened. Then I'll need you to tell me the particulars."

಄಄಄

"That doesn't make sense," Luke told Abby as they sat next to each other in Hawthorne General's ER waiting room. "It would take a monster to kill a friend, especially to inherit his money. Jamie is not a monster."

"What she put in that note is her official version, Luke. It's what she wants the police and everybody else to think was her motive. Her real reason—at least what she claimed was her real reason—was to keep Will from revealing that Maggie is her daughter."

Luke looked more skeptical than ever. "Then there was no reason to kill him. If Will said he would have kept it a secret, that's what he would have done."

"Apparently, Jamie got it into her head that he was going to tell Nelson, hoping that would put an end to Nelson's affair with Maggie."

"That doesn't make any more sense than her official version. She must be covering up for somebody."

"Who?"

"I hate to say it, but Nelson comes to mind. Or maybe Maggie killed Will and Jamie is trying to protect her."

"Maggie doesn't strike me as the kind of person who needs protecting. I don't think she gives a rip who her birth parents are."

Abby saw the door to the emergency room swing open and a somber-looking Nelson Lang appear. She and Luke both got up and hurried toward him.

"She didn't make it," Nelson said in an almost inaudible voice. Then his eyes filled with tears, and he broke into sobs.

∽∂∽

Forty-five minutes later, the three of them sat in a room provided by the hospital for grieving relatives and friends. Nelson seemed beyond consoling and had said almost nothing, staring at the wall as though in a trance. Finally, he turned to Abby. "Did she say why she killed Will?" he asked in a voice that might have come from a sleepwalker.

Abby wasn't sure how to respond. The last thing she

wanted was to compound Nelson's grief by revealing that Jamie was Maggie's mother. Better if he found that out later in the grieving process, when the news might be a little less painful.

"She said there was a note in her pocketbook that would explain everything. I told Mel Taggart about it before I left for the hospital."

"You don't know what the note said?"

"No."

Nelson heaved a sigh. "I don't understand why she went to your motel room. Why confess to you when she'd already done it in a note?"

"I don't know. Maybe it was to punish me by making me witness her suicide, something that wouldn't have happened if it wasn't for my investigation. She did say she was afraid I was getting close to the truth, which I was."

"But why kill Will? What was her motive? You must have had one in mind to suspect her. What was it—the estate?"

Abby nodded. "I thought she might have known about the inheritance ahead of time. I had no evidence of that. It was just a hunch I wanted to follow up on."

Nelson shook his head in a sad, confused way. "No way would Jamie have killed Will Ramsdell for the inheritance. She wouldn't have done it period. They were friends for God's sake, maybe even lovers. I don't understand any of this."

Abby wanted to say something comforting but found herself at a loss for words. Finally, Luke went over and placed a hand on Nelson's shoulder. "Maybe we should go home now," he said in a quiet voice.

At first, Nelson didn't respond. When he finally looked up at Luke, his expression was almost childlike in its anguish. "I don't think I can stand being alone out there tonight."

"I'll stay with you," Luke said and patted Nelson gently on the shoulder. Then he turned to Abby. "How about following us out to Pinecroft. I'll fix something to eat when we get there."

Not wanting to be an unwelcome distraction so soon in Nelson's time of grief, Abby shook her head. "I'll stop for something on the way back to the motel. Give me a call later if you get a chance."

Chapter 43

On the way back to her car, Abby noticed an ambulance that had just arrived at the emergency room entrance. The same two EMTs who had brought in Jamie Lang were wheeling a large black man across the parapet. A police cruiser pulled into one of the nearby spaces designated for official business, and a harried-looking Mel Taggart got out.

"How's Jamie?" he asked.

Abby shook her head. "Unfortunately, she died."

"I'm sorry to hear that. For her sake and mine. First Jamie Lang and now Wardell Tharp. And there's not even a full moon tonight."

"Was that Tharp they just brought in?"

"Yeah. Somebody shot him as he was leaving his apartment complex."

"Damn," Abby said, wondering if Shannon Pfeiffer had decided to administer her own brand of justice. "Any idea who did it?"

"That's what I want to talk to Tharp about. I was hoping to speak with Jamie too. Something about her suicide note doesn't sound right. Gotta go, Abby. If Tharp's as bad off as I think he is, he won't last much longer."

Mel hurried across the parapet toward the emergency room entrance. The automatic doors parted and slowly closed behind him. Abby headed for her car. Just as she started to get in, she changed her mind, turned around, and retraced her steps to the sliding glass doors.

ତ୨ତ

Mel Taggart sat on a bench just outside the ICU, anxiously waiting for a report on Wardell Tharp's condition. Twenty minutes earlier, a slightly-built doctor of Asian descent had refused to let him question Tharp. Mel, therefore, was surprised when the same doctor hurried up to him and said Tharp wanted to see him.

"He's dying," the doctor explained. "You are the police chief, correct?"

"Acting chief," Mel said, the fact that he still hadn't been promoted nagging at him like a dull toothache.

"Close enough."

The doctor escorted Mel to an area divided into cubicles by curtains suspended on runners from the ceiling. The bed in the first cubicle had blood on it—probably Jamie Lang's, Mel thought. Wardell Tharp lay on his back in the second cubicle. Tubing ran from his nostrils to a nearby oxygen machine, and an IV was attached to his right arm. Mel's eyes focused on Tharp's naked torso, which was pockmarked with bullet holes.

"I'll check back in a few minutes," the doctor said.

Mel went over and stood next to the black man. "Who did this to you, Wardell?" he asked, hoping the queasiness he felt building in his stomach wouldn't erupt into full-blown nausea.

ତ୨ତ

From where she sat in the ER waiting room, Abby saw Mel Taggart making his way down the corridor from the

ICU, apparently too preoccupied to notice her. She got up and followed him into the alcove.

"Mel."

He swung around, clearly startled. "I thought you'd left."

"I wanted to find out if you learned anything from Tharp."

"I learned that he died," Mel said and headed for the double doors.

Abby caught up with him on the parapet. "Did you get to talk to him?"

"What business is that of yours?"

"Someone I know wanted him dead. I'm hoping somebody else beat that person to the punch."

Mel kept walking until he reached his cruiser. "You're working for Quentin Grice, aren't you?"

"Why would you think that?"

"Aren't you?"

"No, of course not."

"Do you swear to that—on everything that's holy?"

"Absolutely. I work for a newspaper in North Carolina just like I told you."

Mel glanced anxiously around as though afraid some-one might be eavesdropping. "If I level with you, what do you plan on doing with the information?" he asked in a voice that was little more than a whisper.

"Probably nothing. I'd just like to satisfy my own curiosity."

"Will you promise to do something for me in return?"

"I guess that depends on what it is."

"If I end up like Tharp, God forbid, I'd like you to pass on what I tell you to an appropriate law enforcement person. Somebody at the FBI or the State Bureau of In-vestigation would be best. Next best would be the state police. Under no circumstances should you tell Quentin

Grice or anybody connected to him. Can you do that for me, Abby?"

"Sure," she said, anxious to hear what Mel had to say. "That won't be a problem."

"And you won't mention a thing about this to Grice or anybody with ties to him?"

"Not if you don't want me to."

"I definitely don't." Mel sighed. "I hope I'm not making a big mistake trusting you."

"You're not. I won't do or say anything that might jeopardize you or your investigation. You have my word on that."

A car approached from behind, and Mel reached for his pistol, lifting it part way from its holster. The car slowed, turned into the lot where Abby's Toyota was parked, and pulled into one of the spaces reserved for doctors. Easing the pistol back into its holster, Mel stepped closer to Abby. Then he leaned closer still. "Before Tharp died, he told me he killed Ned Copeland *and* Ben Ramsdell."

Abby's jaw dropped. "You're kidding me."

"You have no idea how much I wish that was true. Tharp wouldn't go into specifics about Ben, but he wanted me to know exactly why he killed Copeland. He said Quentin Grice paid him to do it. Grice thinks Copeland killed Will Ramsdell but he can't prove it, so he got Tharp to take care of the problem and make it look like a suicide. That way, Grice will only have one unsolved murder to contend with—Ben's. I know it sounds crazy, Abby, but that's exactly what Tharp told me before he died. He also told me it was one of Grice's deputies who shot him."

A door of the recently-parked car opened and a tall middle-aged man got out and headed for the emergency room entrance. Mel didn't say anything more until after the doctor disappeared through the double doors.

"Unfortunately nobody else heard Tharp's confession.

It'll be my word against the sheriff's. He's got a lot more clout than I do, not to mention muscle, which he's obviously not afraid to use."

An idea began taking shape in Abby's mind. "What do you plan to do about this?" she asked.

"I don't know. If I arrest Grice, he'll be out on bail in no time. Then I'll have to worry about staying alive long enough to testify against him, assuming the DA even decides to prosecute." Mel shook his head, his face riddled with anxiety. "Another possibility is to pretend Tharp went to his maker without saying a word. That's tempting, Abby—real tempting."

"I think you're in luck, Mel. It just so happens I know an FBI agent who will be quite interested in what you learned tonight. His name is Luke Dawson. He should be more than happy to help you figure out what to do. I'll call him first thing in the morning. If for some reason he'd rather not get involved, I'll let you know. If Luke wants to get together to talk, which I'm ninety-nine-and-a-half-percent sure he will, I'll let him tell you that himself. Fair enough?"

"You're not bullshittin' me, are you, Abby?"

"Nope. Help is on the way, Mel. You're not in this alone."

Chapter 44

Abby stopped at Burger King's take-out window for a hamburger and a small order of French fries, a modest meal for her. By the time she unlocked the door of her new room at the Shenandoah Inn—her old one having been cordoned off by police tape—it was after ten o'clock. Not particularly hungry, she decided to make two phone calls before eating her supper.

The first was to her mother who, after hearing about Jamie Lang's suicide, wanted to know why the woman had killed Will.

"She said it was to keep him from revealing the identity of her illegitimate daughter. I'm not sure that was her real reason, Mom. I'm not even sure Jamie killed Will. Luke thinks somebody else did and Jamie took the fall."

"Luke?"

"That's Marty's real name. He's an FBI agent."

"There's a lot you haven't told me about, Abby."

"I'll explain everything when I see you, which will probably be tomorrow night. Can you take care of Kevin one more day?"

"Of course. You be careful, sweetheart. If Will's killer is still on the loose, he's not going to sit idly by and wait for you to nab him."

"Stop worrying, Mom. I'm a big girl now."

After ringing off with her mother, Abby left a message on Charlene Greer's voice mail explaining the latest developments and giving the day after tomorrow as her probable return date to the office. "However this turns out," she concluded the message, "the *Gazette* will have one hell of a story."

Abby sat down at the circular table at the far end of the room and began picking at her supper. The burger and fries were cold, but she was too wrought up from the day's happenings to really care.

Although she agreed with Luke that Jamie Lang's *real* reason for killing Will made little sense, she still believed Jamie committed the crime. Why kill yourself unless tormented by overwhelming feelings of guilt? The problem wasn't so much accepting that Jamie murdered Will as it was figuring out why she had done it.

The telephone rang, sending a jolt through Abby's already overcharged nervous system. Wondering why someone would call her room phone instead of her cell phone, she hurried to the bedside table, picked up the receiver, and barked a hello.

"This is Shannon Pfeiffer. Sorry to bother you again so soon, but I just heard that somebody shot Wardell Tharp. I wanted you to know it wasn't me."

"I was wondering about that. I was at the hospital when they brought him in." As soon as she said it, Abby wished she hadn't. The last thing she wanted was to get involved in a question-and-answer session about Jamie Lang.

"You were at the hospital? Why?"

"I thought I was having a panic attack," Abby said after only a brief hesitation. "It was just a precaution. Turns out I'm okay. In case you didn't know, Tharp is dead. A cop told me that as I was leaving the hospital."

"Well, I can't say I'm sorry. Do they know who did it?"

"No, but their focus isn't on you."

"Are you sure about that?"

"Your name wasn't even mentioned."

"Thank goodness. As long as I'm not blamed for the murder, I'm happy. The bastard had it coming. Abby, there's one other thing I wanted to tell you. Mitch Folby called me this afternoon. He's at the Salvation Army's halfway house in Hawthorne. I went over there to see him tonight, and I've changed my mind about him ratting out Ben. Mitch doesn't have an evil bone in his body. He's trying hard to kick his drug habit."

"Good for him," Abby said. Then she thanked Shannon for the news and ended the call.

Abby ate a little more of her burger and fries then dumped the rest in the waste basket. She brewed a pot of decaffeinated coffee, poured herself a cup, and once again attempted to make sense of Jamie Lang's story. Figuring out who really killed Will and why, she decided, was like trying to put together a puzzle with at least one major piece missing and some of the others so badly damaged she couldn't tell what they looked like or where they fit.

Taking her cup of coffee to the circular table, she sat down and propped her feet up on the adjacent chair. Why would Jamie give two different explanations for murdering Will when neither one of them made sense? Were both equally false? If so, why even give a second explanation?

Could it be, Abby wondered, that Jamie's *real* reason for killing Will was accurate as far as it went? Assuming her motive really was to keep Will from revealing her daughter's identity, was there something that went beyond Jamie's stated motive but didn't conflict with it? Was she afraid something catastrophic would happen if people found out about Maggie, a result so devastating, at least in Jamie's mind, that it justified killing a friend?

To help answer that question, Abby asked herself another one. What was the worst thing that could happen, from Jamie's perspective, if people found out that Maggie Calahan was her daughter? What would they do that could be so damaging? The answer, Abby decided, was to start speculating about the identity of Maggie's father.

Conventional wisdom would suggest Rudy Teague as the likely candidate, but Rudy had proof he wasn't anyone's biological father and would have no trouble diverting suspicion elsewhere. Was that what Jamie feared? Did she kill Will to prevent the finger of suspicion from pointing at someone other than Rudy? But even if Maggie's father were the devil himself, would that be reason enough for Jamie to kill Will Ramsdell, a man who cared enough for her to leave his estate to Pinecroft?

Abby recalled what Jamie had said shortly before turning the pistol on herself: *It's very important to me that neither Maggie nor anyone else know she's the bastard daughter of Jamie Copeland and...some guy I had sex with in high school.* Why did Jamie pause in mid-sentence? Was she going to say something other than '*some guy I had sex with in high school*'? If so, what?

Abby's cell phone rang, a muffled jangling that once again set her nerves on edge. She got up to answer it but couldn't remember where she had put the damn thing after leaving the message on Charlene Greer's voice mail. Finally realizing it was in her handbag, she fished it out, punched the talk button, and growled a hello.

"I thought you wanted me to give you a call."

Abby's anger faded. "I did," she said and explained that she had been frustrated at not being able to locate her cell phone.

"You're forgiven," Luke said. "How about meeting me at Sullivan's Diner for breakfast tomorrow morning?"

"What time have you got in mind?"

"Eight o'clock?"

"Sounds good to me. Will Nelson be coming?"

"He said he'd rather not. By the way, I've pretty much come around to your way of thinking. Jamie probably did kill Will. I think I know why but it's just a theory. I doubt we'll ever know for sure."

"Why did she do it, Luke?" Abby asked, anxious to hear his theory.

"I'd like to give it more thought. Assuming I'm of the same opinion in the morning, I'll tell you at breakfast. Ideas like this tend to lose their luster overnight. Sleep tight, Scully. I'll see you at eight."

Abby started to tell him about Wardell Tharp's murder and Mel Taggart's dilemma but decided that too should wait until tomorrow. "Good night, Mulder," she said and turned off her cell phone, pleased that Luke had called her. Returning the phone to her handbag, she sat back down at the table, propped up her feet, and focused on Jamie Lang's exact words that supposedly explained why she killed Will.

Eventually, the germ of an idea formed in Abby's mind, a notion so radical and bizarre that her initial impulse was to discount it. The idea grew clearer, took shape, finally blossoming into a theory so chillingly credible that the coffee cup nearly slipped from her hand.

"If that's what happened," Abby muttered, "you were one sorry, low-life son of a bitch."

It was all Abby could do not to call Luke back and see if their theories jibed. She decided to wait, knowing Luke was right about ideas that seemed so insightful when a person first thought of them tending to lack credibility when re-examined later. *Nobody knows that better than a person with bipolar disorder*, she mused. *Assuming we happen to be thinking straight at the time.*

Taking a final sip of coffee, Abby crushed the cup in her hand. She got up from the table and tossed the crumpled cup at the wastebasket in the corner, fully expecting to have to go pick it up off the floor. Like her winning shot at the buzzer against New Bern's Lady Bears almost fifteen years earlier, the sphere dropped straight through the cylinder.

"Yeah!" she yelled and started a little victory dance, stomping her feet and pumping her fist. "Nothing but net!"

Abby's gyrations continued—until the image of Will Ramsdell filled her consciousness, forcing her to sit down in the chair. Visualizing the man lying dead on Pinecroft's seventeenth tee, she began to weep.

"She screwed up big time, Will," she said and slammed her fist against the table top. "There was no reason whatsoever for Jamie to kill you." She buried her face in her hands and gave herself over to sobbing.

When she opened her eyes a few minutes later, Abby sensed that she wasn't alone. Slowly turning her head, she saw someone standing beside her, a tall middle-aged man with a craggy, weathered face. He was regarding her with a melancholy expression, one almost as somber as her own.

"Will?"

Seeing him nod, she waited for him to speak.

"She had her reasons," he finally said, reaching out and gently patting Abby's shoulder. "They just weren't based on reality."

Chapter 45

The fog was so thick Jamie Copeland could barely see the sagging back porch or the tin roof that sloped down over it. Beyond the house, the fog hid everything—the willow tree in the front yard, the telephone poles dotting the road, even the road itself. Visibility was so poor, Jamie felt a shiver of anxiety about the safety of her mother and little brother, who had left a half hour earlier to spend the day with Aunt Sallie, a short drive from Blue Ridge Prison Farm.

Oh, they'll be fine, *she told herself as she pinned a wet towel to the clothesline.* God looks after saints and the innocent, and goodness knows Mama's a saint to put up with that man. *Jamie reached into the clothes basket for another item, a flannel shirt that belonged to her father. She resisted an impulse to spit on it as she hung it on the line.*

As she pinned up one of her nursing bras, Jamie thought of Rudy Teague, imagined he was standing next to the clothesline admiring her breasts, still swollen with milk. As if for his benefit, she arched her back and thrust out her chest, pleased to have regained her figure so soon after childbirth. She could almost feel Rudy's hands, taste his kisses.

"Free at last!" she cried, knowing they'd have the

place all to themselves until tomorrow afternoon at the earliest. She smiled as her voice came echoing back across the yard.

After hanging up the clothes, Jamie sprinted toward the house, dancing past a ceramic statue of a bearded holy man doing battle with Satan, then sidestepping a bullet-riddled tree stump surrounded by tin cans and broken glass. The thought that Ned Copeland would once again be using that stump for target practice, as unpleasant as it was, didn't dampen her spirits.

She bounded up the sagging steps and hurried across the porch. The screen door slammed behind her, echoing like the sound of her father's Glock. The fog whirled for a moment around the steps before settling into a white stillness.

෴

Half an hour later, Jamie was on her way to Wisteria, walking as fast as she dared, her baby daughter cradled against her neck. The fog was so dense she could hardly distinguish the road from the fields on either side. A few random corn stalks poked through the whiteness, but all signs of the cotton field and the river had disappeared.

"Whole island looks like a big eraser swept over it, Maggie. Left a bunch of chalk dust on everything."

The simile reminded Jamie of English class, which was where she had been when she finally decided what to do about her predicament. After the bell, she had walked with Rudy to his locker and told him the news.

"You don't have to look go glum," she'd said. "It's not the end of the world."

"Might as well be. Soon as your old man finds out, I'm dead meat."

"He won't find out. I'm not going to tell him or any-body else who the father is."

"It'll be obvious, Jamie."

"Not if we stop seeing each other while nobody's the wiser. Right now you're the only one who knows I'm pregnant. I can keep it a secret until after graduation. People might talk during the summer, but you can say we were just friends. They won't have any reason not to be-lieve you."

"Wouldn't it be a lot simpler if you just get an abor-tion?"

"Are you kidding! Daddy would kill me. You know how fanatical he is about that."

"Yeah. That man really scares me."

"He won't be a problem. He doesn't know you from Adam. I plan to keep it that way."

Rudy gave her a quizzical look. "Why're you doing this, Jamie?"

Though she hadn't told him everything, what she said now was the absolute truth. "If we end up getting married someday, I'd like it to be because you want to, not because you have to."

A look of relief spread over the young man's face. "You're really going to take all the heat yourself?"

"You're a free man, Rudy Teague. I won't stand be-tween you and your future."

"You're incredible, Jamie—one in a million."

"Finish high school and then do whatever you want—go to college, join the army, anything that suits your fancy. If along the way you decide you'd like me and the little one to be part of your life...well, you'll know where to find us."

"What're you going to do? After you have the baby, I mean."

"I don't know. I'd like to finish high school and go to

college, but that's probably out of the question now. At least the college part. Are you still planning to work at your father's store this summer?"

"Yeah, I guess so."

"Mind if I stop by and see you sometime? I don't want us to lose touch. We'll just have to be...you know, discreet."

"Sure, I understand. Yeah, stop by, Jamie. Listen, I gotta go. I'm late for math class."

That was the last real conversation she'd had with Rudy. Once school was out and she could no longer hide her pregnancy, things had gotten so crazy—her mother's constant barrage of questions concerning the baby's paternity, her father's third arrest for poaching and the resulting trial, Maggie's birth—that she hadn't had a chance to see Rudy.

A series of staccato shrieks gave Jamie a start. Her daughter began to squirm.

"Don't be scared, honey. That's just a crow. They don't mess with folks, even little ones like you."

Again Jamie thought of Rudy. He'd be at the hardware store now, waiting on customers. She'd buy something from him, a pack of mousetraps maybe, or a fishing lure for her brother's birthday. And then, since Mr. Teague or a customer would probably be within earshot, she would slip Rudy the note.

A soft padding sound intruded on Jamie's thoughts. She swung around, staring into the whiteness. After a moment the corners of her mouth lifted in a smile.

"Who you think you're fooling back there, Elvis?" She waited for the hound to materialize out of the mist. "Yeah, I see you now." She watched the lean body push through the fog. "Had no intention of letting us slip away, did you?"

The dog, mottled with splotches of brown over white,

flopped down on his haunches and began to pant, his head moving up and down in rhythm with his lolling tongue. As though she just remembered it belonged there, a harshness came over Jamie's face. "Go back to the house," she said, keeping her voice low so it wouldn't disturb Maggie. "I don't want any more company this morning."

The dog stayed put, slapping the road with his tail.

"It'll look silly, an old hound traipsing along behind like we're hillbillies. Go on, Elvis, git." Giving the dog a final leer, Jamie turned away.

When she realized she was still being followed, Jamie whirled around. "Just like a male," she said, glaring at the animal. "Do any way you please and never mind me. I've got rights too, you know. I've got a right to decide who'll leave me alone and—" She hesitated, as though not wholly confident in her pronouncement. "And who'll take an interest."

Her expression softened, and she leaned down and patted the dog's head. "Soon as we get to the gut, you go back to the house. I mean it." She started walking again, the hound following gingerly at her heels.

Up ahead was a thick bank of fog where the road was barely visible. Jamie slowed her pace, squinting into the haze as if trying to locate a familiar object. A crow shrieked from somewhere in the whiteness, the sound resonating in the stillness.

"If I didn't know different," Jamie said to her two companions, glad, for the moment at least, to have the dog nearby, "I'd think something happened to the world. Seems like nothing's left but us three and the fog." Then she noticed a clear spot in the road ahead and, relieved, hurried toward it.

When she reached the bridge that spanned the gut, Jamie stopped to rest, leaning against the wooden railing. The sun had burned the fog into a thin sparkling mist, except in the ravine where it still nestled thick, twining against the tree trunks like giant cobwebs, thinning to smoky swirls in the upper branches.

"Mush Island ends and the world begins," she said to her daughter, who snuggled against her shoulder, making cooing noises. Jamie gazed at the water, deep enough for fish but too shallow for swimming.

"This old gut's a funny creek. Flows out of the Shenandoah down there in the fog and circles right back in behind our house. Like its sole purpose is to slice off an island."

Jamie gazed at the bend in the creek beyond which she and Rudy had spread their blanket for a picnic. "Over there's where your father and I made love," she said and gave Maggie a hug. "No highway marker here to commemorate the occasion, but I bet someday you'll agree it was a mighty significant event." She rocked the baby back and forth. "Rudy's going to love you. No way he'll be able to help himself."

Jamie noticed a school of minnows near the base of the bridge. Then she spotted a sweetening bug darting about like a tiny boat without a rudder. "Good thing there's no bass around. You guys would be somebody's breakfast by now."

Shifting Maggie higher on her shoulder, Jamie continued across the bridge, careful not to trip over loose planks.

When she reached the other side, the howling made her stop. Glancing around, she saw the hound sitting in the middle of the bridge, head cocked to one side. Bending her knees, Jamie leaned down to pick up a rock, sighed, and stood up again.

"You aren't worth the effort, Elvis. Come on. The sooner Rudy knows we'll be home by ourselves tonight, the sooner he can make plans to come out and see us."

ℰ᷾ᴑℰ᷾

Dressed in freshly laundered jeans and her best blouse, Jamie sat on the edge of the front porch and watched the evening fade into twilight. Her right hand pushed up and down on the handle of a dilapidated buggy, gently rocking it. Maggie made soft contented noises in her throat.

"Probably had to work late," Jamie said with little conviction after all the color had drained from the sky.

For a long time she watched the darkening road that lay like a strip of dull yellow tape a shade lighter than the fields it pieced together. A cicada began to shrill from the nearby willow, the sound rising and falling like a miniature version of the fire alarm in Wisteria. A vague heel print of moon appeared over the river trees, coming and going with the drifting clouds. Jamie sat as though in a trance, her hand still on the buggy. Heat lightning flickered in the west, bringing no thunder.

Suddenly, Jamie shoved the buggy against the side of the house and slammed her fist against the porch floor. In an instant she was running through the yard toward the willow. As she neared the tree, she tripped and fell, scrambled to her feet, and scurried under the dangling foliage. She began unbuttoning her blouse with stiff, jerky movements. The last button refused and she ripped open the blouse. Clutching her right breast with both hands, she squeezed until milk dribbled out, welcoming the pain, hoping it would dull the memory...

It was past midnight, just two days after she and Rudy had made love, and she was lying in bed. She'd been sleeping—Jamie knew that much—but whether she was still asleep and having a dream she wasn't sure. Her body felt alive with desire, the way it did when she was with Rudy. Either she was dreaming that he was stroking her in places only he would be allowed to touch, or he was ac-

tually there, having slipped in through the open window. She felt her nipples being kissed and a hand moving between her thighs. Unable to resist any longer, she reached out and drew him close.

When she realized it wasn't Rudy, Jamie tried to pull away, but the man had already entered her. He covered her mouth with his mouth and pinned her body to the mattress with his body, thrusting up and down until finally he was spent. Then he sat on the edge of the bed and apologized.

"You've gotten so pretty I couldn't help myself," he said. "I wanted to touch those curves and sweet places just once before you grew up and left the nest. I never intended to do more—I swear as God is my witness. I wouldn't have if you hadn't encouraged me."

"I was half asleep," Jamie sobbed. "I thought you were—"

"Shhh, it's all right, honey. You didn't do anything wrong and neither did I. These things happen. Just make sure you keep it to yourself. We wouldn't want your mother finding out, now would we? It would hurt her feelings something terrible—"

Jamie screamed and wrung herself again. When the milk would no longer flow, she wrenched her other breast, shaking her head wildly and sobbing. Finally, her legs buckled and she sank to the ground.

Crying quietly, she gazed up through the branches of the willow at the starless sky—until the hound began licking her face. She pushed him away. When he nuzzled up again, she grabbed his ears and squeezed until he finally broke free and scampered back to the house.

Soon Maggie began to fuss, the sound drifting into the yard, adding a dissonant voice to the chorus of insects, peepers, and other night creatures that hummed and grated and rattled against the night.

"I don't even know who your father is!" Jamie yelled.

The crying on the porch grew louder and more demanding, drowning out the night sounds.

Epilogue

Lillian was worried about her daughter long before Abby called her for the second time that night. "You actually saw Will?" she said. "Tonight?"

"I did. He was right here in my room. I'd just figured out the real reason Jamie Lang killed him, and he agreed with me. He even put his hand on my shoulder."

In a rambling, disjointed way, Abby had gone on to explain exactly why Will was murdered.

"When do you plan to come home, Abby?" Lillian asked in an anxious voice.

"Tomorrow morning, right after I meet Luke for breakfast."

"Your friend at the FBI?"

"Yep. Special Agent Lucas Benjamin Dawson. After we compare notes and say our goodbyes, I'll hit the road."

In as gentle a tone as she could muster, Lillian told Abby she was not in her right mind and, therefore, not in any condition to drive. "I want you to stay where you are, honey, and I'll come get you. After you get your meds adjusted, you can rest up here for a few days, and then I'll drive you back to Wisteria so you can pick up your car."

"I'm not manic, Mom. I'm just depressed. Who wouldn't be after witnessing Jamie Lang commit suicide and knowing she had no reason whatsoever to kill Will.

I'll get some sleep and eat breakfast and then I'll be fine. I'm going to hang up now. I'm turning off my cell phone and my room phone, so don't bother trying to call me back."

Lillian did try calling Abby back—twice. There was no answer either time, and she began to panic. *How the hell can I get someone to do something about this?* she wondered. She thought of calling the motel and explaining her problem to whoever answered the phone, but she doubted Abby would pay the slightest attention to a night clerk or anyone else who might knock on her motel room's door. Then she thought of Luke Dawson. In desperation she looked up the number for the Federal Bureau of Investigation, dialed it, and told the man who answered that she had an urgent need to talk to Lucas Benjamin Dawson, an agent assigned to the Wisteria, Virginia area.

It took Lillian a while to convince the man that this was not a crank call. Finally, she was transferred to someone in the FBI's Charlottesville office. The agent she talked to there seemed sympathetic, but he told her that regulations prohibited his giving out information about any FBI personnel.

"This is a life-and-death situation for my daughter," Lillian insisted. "Luke is supposed to meet her in the morning for breakfast, and he's the only person I know that she might listen to."

Eventually, the agent said he would try to contact Luke himself. "If I'm successful, I'll tell him your situation and ask him to call you. If I can't reach him, I'll call you back."

Twenty minutes later Lillian's phone rang, and it was Luke.

She explained that Abby was in the throes of a severe mixed episode. "She's not only manic and depressed, she's also delusional. She's in no condition to drive a car, Luke. Would you please, please, do whatever it takes to keep her in Wisteria until I can get there to drive her home."

"I'll drive her myself if she'll let me," Luke replied. "Just sit tight for now, and I'll give you an update as soon as I can."

Reluctant to leave Nelson Lang alone so soon after his wife's death, Luke asked a neighbor to stay with him.

Shortly after three a.m., Luke drove his Dodge to the Shenandoah Inn, where he found the light still on in Abby's room. When he knocked on the door, there was no response. He knocked again, louder, with the same result. He had just started toward the motel's office to get a pass key when he heard what sounded like someone out of breath laboring across the darkened parking area. Turning, he saw a haggard-looking young woman in running attire staggering toward him.

"You're about—four hours—early, Special Agent," Abby huffed and collapsed against the side of Luke's car, clutching the door handle to keep from sinking to the ground. "In case you're—wondering, my shrink said the best way to—stave off depression is to—run, run, run—until I drop."

A few minutes later, when Luke informed Abby that he intended to drive her to Scarboro, she was too out of it to object. She slept much of the way home, communicating just enough to let Luke know about Mel Taggart's plight and to make sure she and Luke had come to the same conclusion about Jamie's motive for killing Will. When Luke said he was taking her straight to the Scarboro hospital instead of to her mother's house, Abby put up only a token resistance.

In the BSU, an anti-psychotic was added to Abby's medication regimen, and after a day or two, she responded well, eventually showing no signs of psychosis. Though she was still depressed, it was nothing she couldn't handle—a low-grade depression, she called it—and the psychiatrist assigned to her case let her go home after a week. Lillian gave her an additional week to recuperate and then drove her to Wisteria to pick up her car.

Abby had let Luke know they were coming, and he had agreed to meet them for lunch at Sullivan's Diner. When Abby switched to her own car at the Shenandoah Inn, she called Luke on her cell phone to let him know of their arrival.

Ten minutes later when Abby arrived at Sullivan's Diner, Lillian had already found a booth and was talking to the waitress. The cook, the same man who had been Abby's waiter the last time she had eaten there, gave her a friendly wave as she passed the griddle, but she was too preoccupied to notice him. She sat down across the table from her mother, saw the extra menu, and told the waitress it wouldn't be needed.

"It's just the two of us," she said in a somber voice. No longer hungry, Abby ordered a plain grilled cheese sandwich, instead of the deluxe turkey club she had intended to order.

"Where's Luke?" Lillian asked after the waitress left.

"He said something unexpected came up and he couldn't get away."

"Don't let that get you down, sweetheart. I imagine that kind of thing happens a lot with FBI agents."

"When I told him I could hang around a while before heading back, he said he was going to be tied up all day." Abby looked down at her silverware and then back at her mother. "Mom, I've got a feeling this is the beginning of the end of our relationship."

"Oh, Abby. Aren't you jumping to conclusions? I'm sure Luke has a good reason for not being available today."

"Time will tell," Abby said in a forlorn voice.

Abby managed to exchange small talk with her mother while they ate, but clearly her heart wasn't in it. She still felt weighed down by all that had happened lately, and now that Luke had canceled out on her without giving a specific reason, the manageable low-grade depression she felt at the beginning of the day was now threatening to overwhelm her.

"I can't do it," she muttered as she picked at her sandwich. "And I'm not going to."

"Can't do what, Abby—finish your sandwich? Mine is delicious."

"I wasn't talking about my sandwich, Mom."

"Then what were you talking about?"

Abby hadn't intended to be talking at all. The words had just slipped out, and now she wished she could take them back. "Just some nonsense that popped in my head," she said. "It's gone now and good riddance."

What Abby had been thinking about was her job at the *Gazette* and what would be expected of her when she returned. Charlene would want at least one lengthy article about Will Ramsdell and his killer Jamie Lang, something Abby couldn't see herself providing.

There was no way she would tell her mother any of this. The woman definitely didn't need anything more to worry about.

Abby took a bite of her sandwich. "Actually, this is pretty good. I'm glad I ordered it."

As they were leaving the restaurant, Lillian told Abby to take the lead and she would follow her. "Just don't go too fast. I might not remember the way back, and I don't want to lose sight of you."

"You just want to be in a position to clean up the mess if I have an accident," Abby said in a lame attempt at humor.

"Just keep your mind on your driving. For the next two

and a half hours, you've got one job, Abby, and one job only—getting home safe."

As Abby headed east on Highway 64, her depression deepened. Like a rapidly spreading cancer, it seemed to engulf her. She felt trapped between an immediate past that made her want to burst into tears whenever she thought of it and a future that seemed bleak any way she looked at it. Under no circumstances could she see herself writing about how and why Will Ramsdell had died. And if she didn't write about it, Charlene Greer, who was just looking for a reason to fire her, would do exactly that. And then what? Still lacking a college degree, what kind of job would she be able to get?

Even if she somehow managed to keep her job at the *Gazette*, it was probably just a matter of time before Luke Dawson lost interest in her, assuming he hadn't already. Abby really liked the man and had hoped their relationship would not only continue but grow. Was it realistic to think that would happen? *Absolutely not*, she told herself. *What desirable guy would want a long-term relationship with a nut case like me?*

A blaring horn snapped Abby back to the here and now. She had drifted into the left lane and an oncoming truck was warning her. She pulled back into her own lane in plenty of time and checked her rearview mirror to make sure her mother was still behind her, hoping Lillian hadn't noticed her momentary lapse in concentration.

I should have just plowed head on into that truck, Abby thought. For the next few minutes, she toyed with the idea of unbuckling her seatbelt and waiting for another eighteen wheeler to come along. She could use it the same way Jamie Lang had used her husband's pistol—as a means of escaping grief—past, present, and future. *Too much of a gamble*, she told herself. *I might live and be a cripple or the trucker might die, or wish he had.*

Wasn't there another reason too—one even more important? Of course, there was.

Kevin would miss her, Abby decided, but he would probably be okay. She wasn't the greatest mother in the world. Far from it. Abby would be the first to admit that Kevin was a well-adjusted, level-headed boy in spite of, not because of, her. In the long run, he would be fine. Not so her mother, however. On numerous occasions, Lillian, who had already lost her husband and only son, had made it abundantly clear to Abby that she simply couldn't stand losing her too.

As Abby passed through the small town of Emmitt's Corners, she found herself thinking about the little switch engine she had bought Kevin for Christmas. It was a bittersweet thought, sad because it was Will's favorite engine and he would never again experience the pleasure of running it or even seeing it. And yet Will probably would have been glad to know that engine was being passed on to Kevin. Abby hoped so anyway.

Suddenly, it occurred to her that Kevin would need a lot more than that engine if he was going to take much pleasure in the gift. He would need track, a transformer, some freight cars to push and pull, and at least a couple of switches. She thought of the Whistle Shop in Charlottesville. Everything needed for an interesting layout was right there. It would take some serious money that she really couldn't afford, though, especially if she lost her job at the *Gazette*. Plus she and her mother weren't planning to stop so soon. They had decided to wait until they were closer to Richmond before taking a break.

Abby glanced again in the rearview mirror, saw her mother's car following at its usual safe distance.

"Fuck it," she said. "I'm going to give that boy one hell of a Christmas."

About the Author

John W. Daniel grew up in North Carolina and sets most of his fiction there. He has a BA from North Carolina State University and an MA from Wake Forest University. He has taught English at Fishburne Military School in Waynesboro, Virginia (where he also coached the baseball team); the College of the Albemarle in Elizabeth City, North Carolina; and the State University of New York Agricultural and Technical College at Alfred, New York. He also has worked as a contract specialist and an industrial specialist at the US Army Tank, Automotive, and Armaments Command (TACOM) in Warren, Michigan. Now retired, at least from gainful employment, he lives with his wife Sharon and their cat Fonzie in the hills north of Elmira, New York. He especially enjoys O-scale model railroading; reading; gardening; and, on days when the course isn't getting the better of him, golfing.